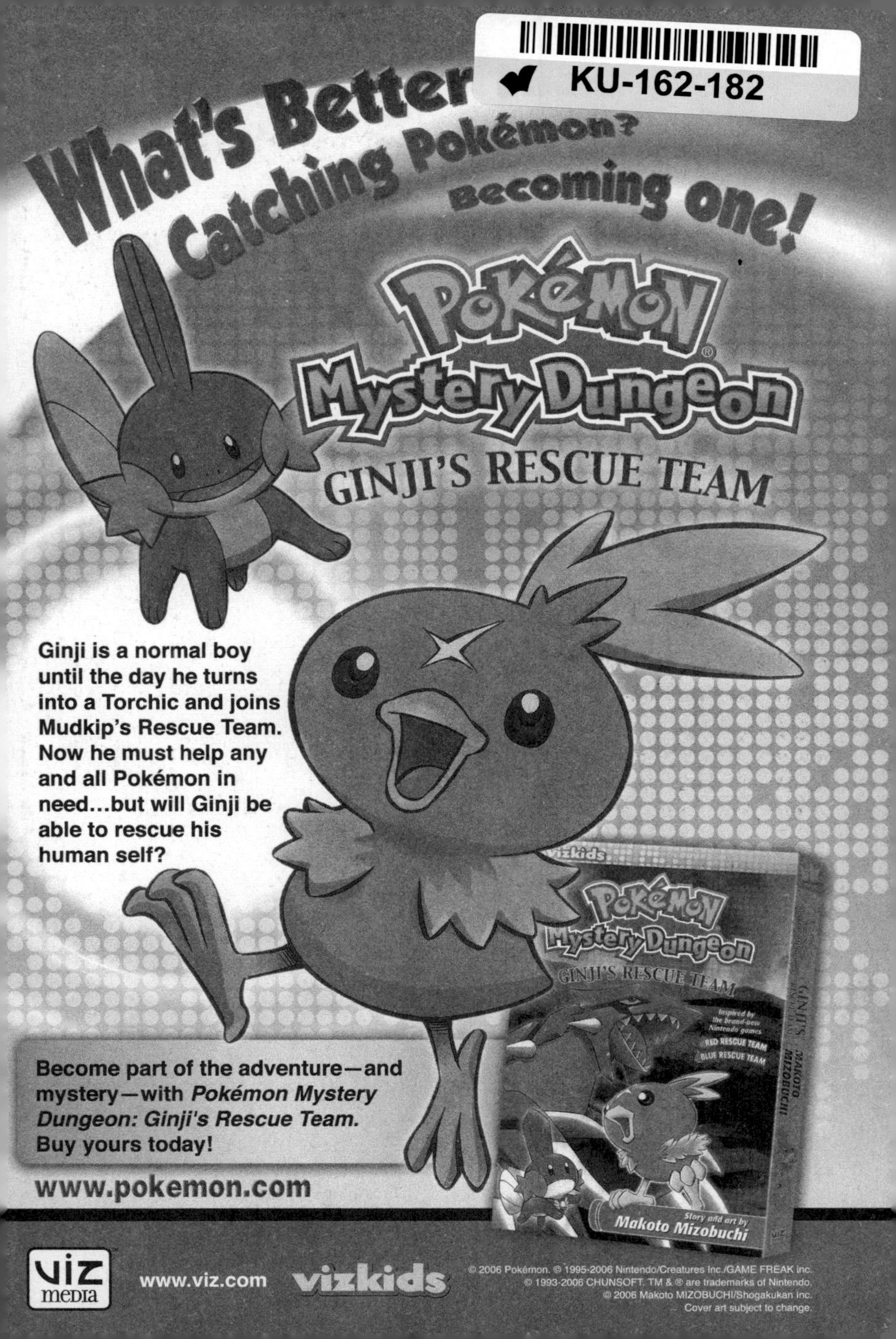
What's Better Than Catching Pokémon?
Becoming one!
Pokémon Mystery Dungeon
GINJI'S RESCUE TEAM
Ginji is a normal boy until the day he turns into a Torchic and joins Mudkip's Rescue Team. Now he must help any and all Pokémon in need...but will Ginji be able to rescue his human self?
vizkids
Pokémon Mystery Dungeon
GINJI'S RESCUE TEAM
Inspired by the brand-new Nintendo games
RED RESCUE TEAM
BLUE RESCUE TEAM
Story and art by Makoto Mizobuchi
Become part of the adventure—and mystery—with Pokémon Mystery Dungeon: Ginji's Rescue Team. Buy yours today!
www.pokemon.com
viz media
www.viz.com
vizkids
© 2006 Pokémon. © 1995-2006 Nintendo/Creatures Inc./GAME FREAK inc.
© 1993-2006 CHUNSOFT. TM & ® are trademarks of Nintendo.
© 2006 Makoto MIZOBUCHI/Shogakukan Inc.
Cover art subject to change.

**Pokémon® ADVENTURES
BLACK AND WHITE**
Volume 1
VIZ Kids Edition

Story by HIDENORI KUSAKA
Art by SATOSHI YAMAMOTO

© 2013 Pokémon.
© 1995–2013 Nintendo/Creatures Inc./GAME FREAK inc.
TM and ® and character names are trademarks of Nintendo.
POCKET MONSTER SPECIAL Vol. 43
by Hidenori KUSAKA, Satoshi YAMAMOTO
© 1997 Hidenori KUSAKA, Satoshi YAMAMOTO
All rights reserved.
Original Japanese edition published by SHOGAKUKAN
English translation rights in the United States of America, Canada,
the United Kingdom and Ireland arranged with SHOGAKUKAN.

Translation/Tetsuichiro Miyaki
English Adaptation/Annette Roman
Touch-up & Lettering/Susan Daigle-Leach
Design/Shawn Carrico
Editor/Annette Roman

Printed in the U.S.A.

Published by VIZ Media, LLC
P.O. Box 77010
San Francisco, CA 94107

10 9 8 7 6 5 4 3 2 1
First printing, July 2013

www.vizkids.com

www.viz.com

POKÉMON ADVENTURES BLACK & WHITE

1 VOLUME ONE

CONTENTS

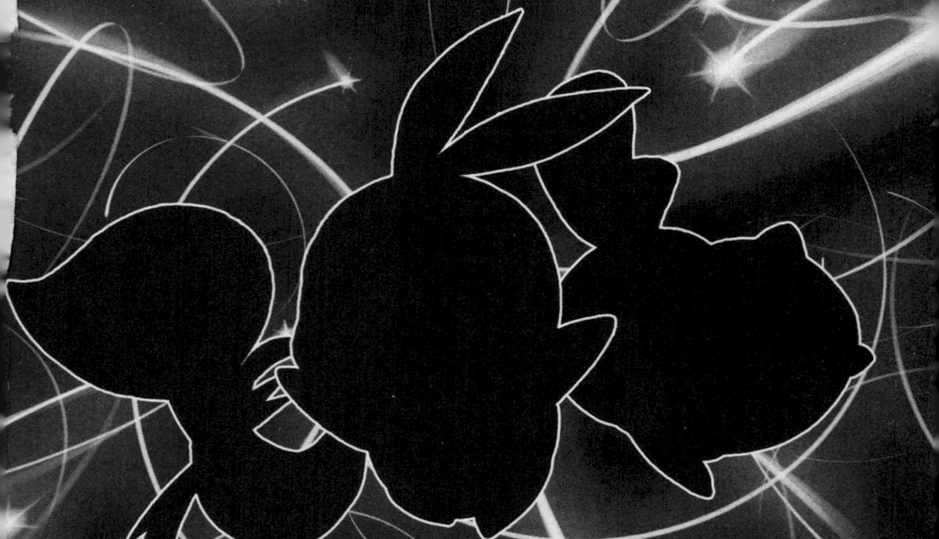

Pokémon Adventures Black & White

The Tenth Chapter 10

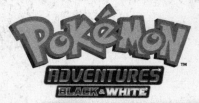

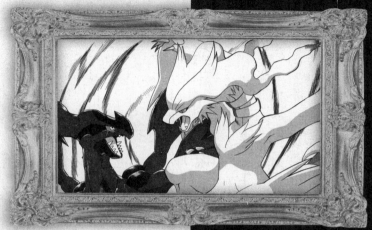

UNOVA

—IDEALS—

Black Dragon type

UNOVA

—TRUTH—

White Dragon type

BLACK & WHITE

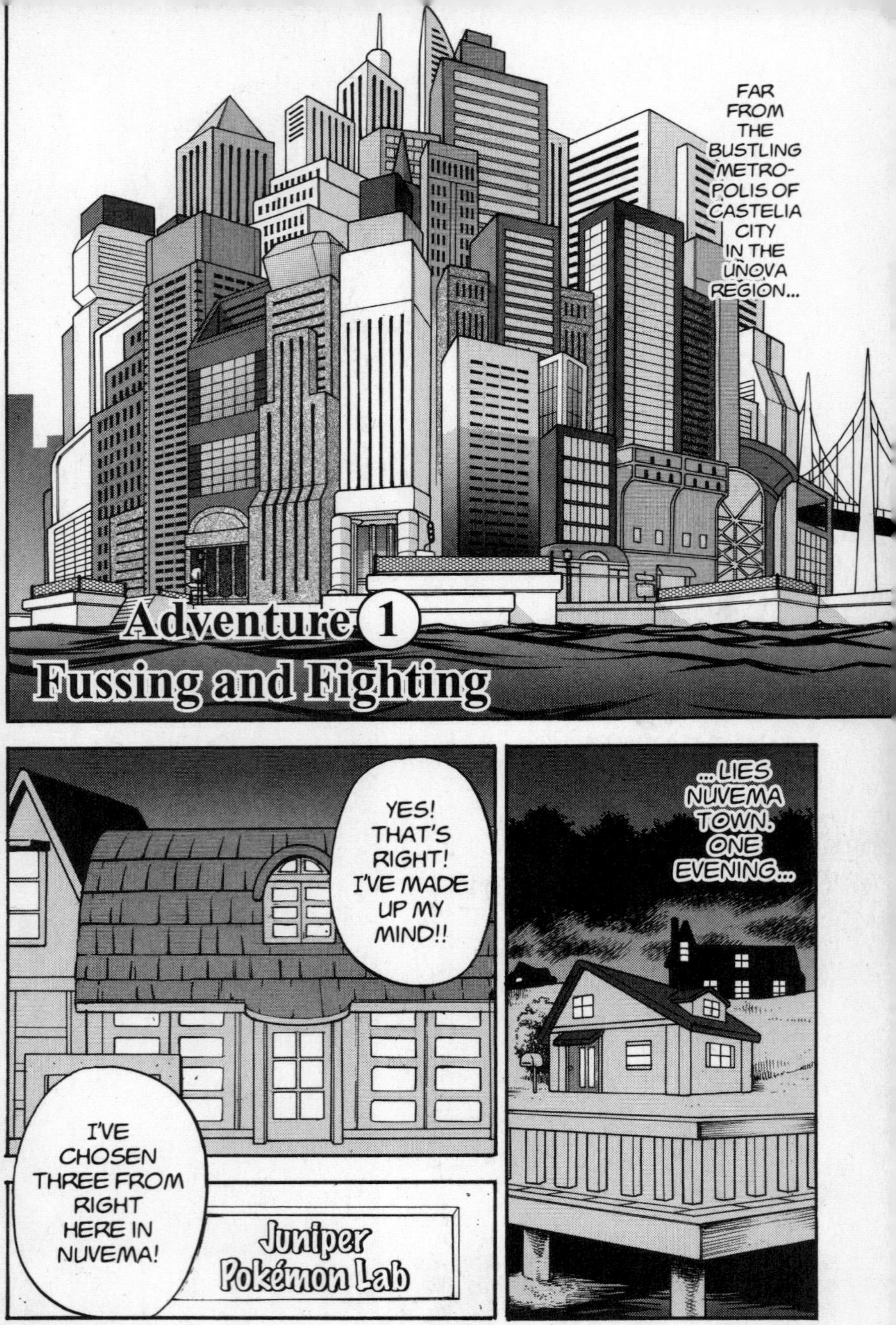
FAR FROM THE BUSTLING METRO-POLIS OF CASTELIA CITY IN THE UNOVA REGION...
Adventure 1
Fussing and Fighting
...LIES NUVEMA TOWN. ONE EVENING...
YES! THAT'S RIGHT! I'VE MADE UP MY MIND!!
I'VE CHOSEN THREE FROM RIGHT HERE IN NUVEMA!
Juniper Pokémon Lab

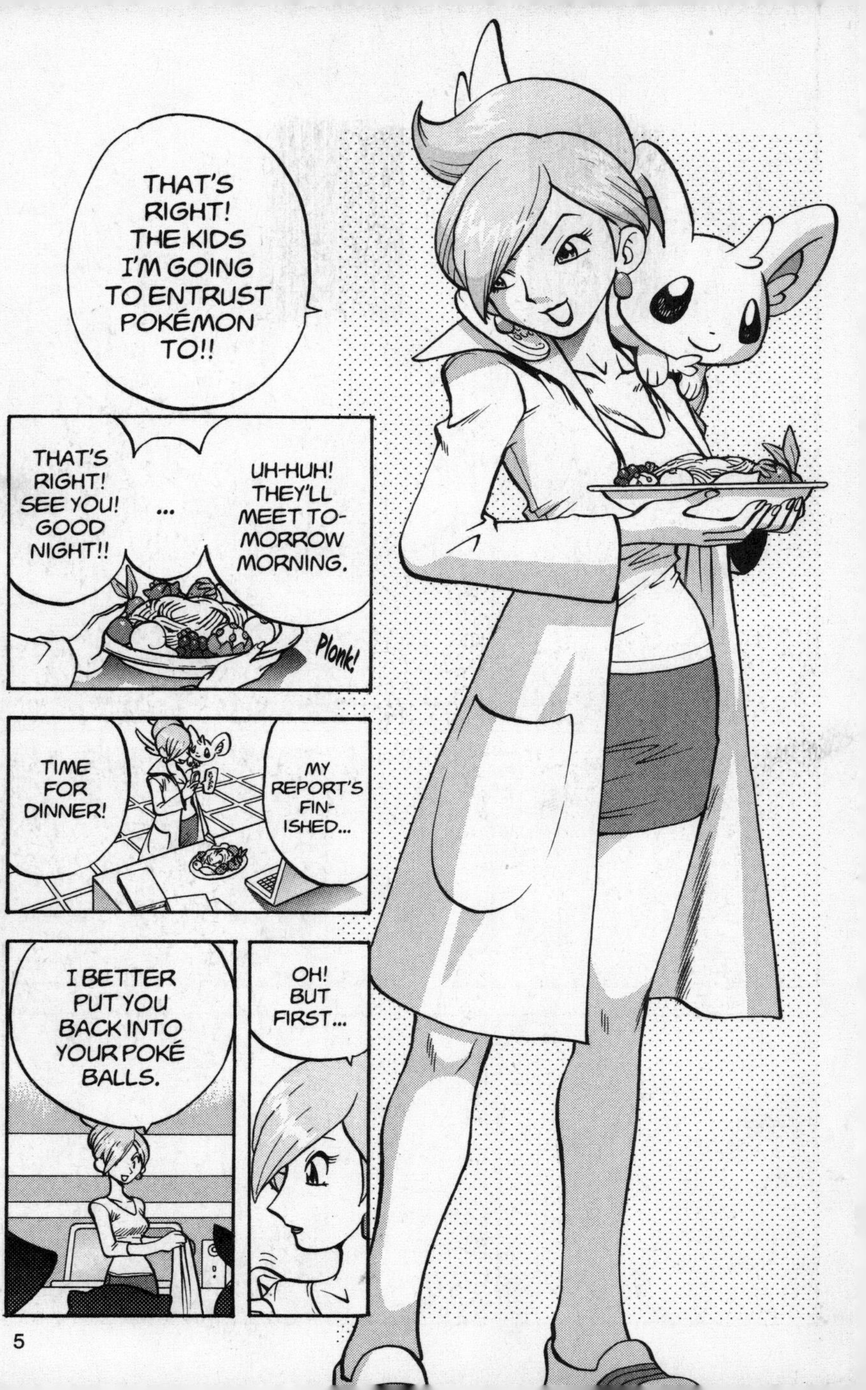
THAT'S RIGHT! THE KIDS I'M GOING TO ENTRUST POKÉMON TO!!
UH-HUH! THEY'LL MEET TO-MORROW MORNING.
...
THAT'S RIGHT! SEE YOU! GOOD NIGHT!!
Plonk!
MY REPORT'S FIN-ISHED...
TIME FOR DINNER!
OH! BUT FIRST...
I BETTER PUT YOU BACK INTO YOUR POKÉ BALLS.

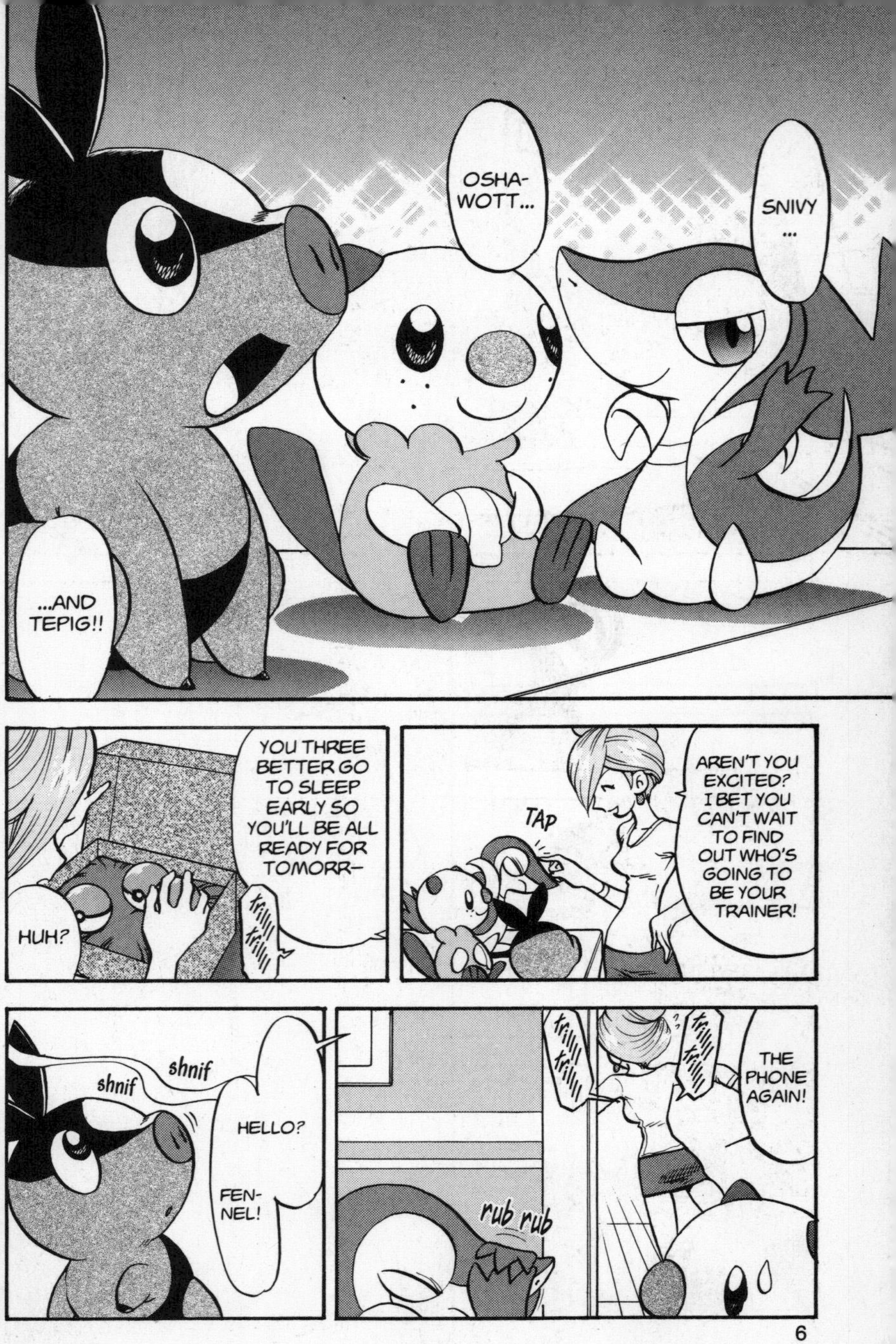
SNIVY ...
OSHA-WOTT...
...AND TEPIG!!
AREN'T YOU EXCITED? I BET YOU CAN'T WAIT TO FIND OUT WHO'S GOING TO BE YOUR TRAINER!
TAP
YOU THREE BETTER GO TO SLEEP EARLY SO YOU'LL BE ALL READY FOR TOMORR–
trill trill
HUH?
trill trill
trill trill
THE PHONE AGAIN!
rub rub
HELLO?
FEN-NEL!
shnif
shnif

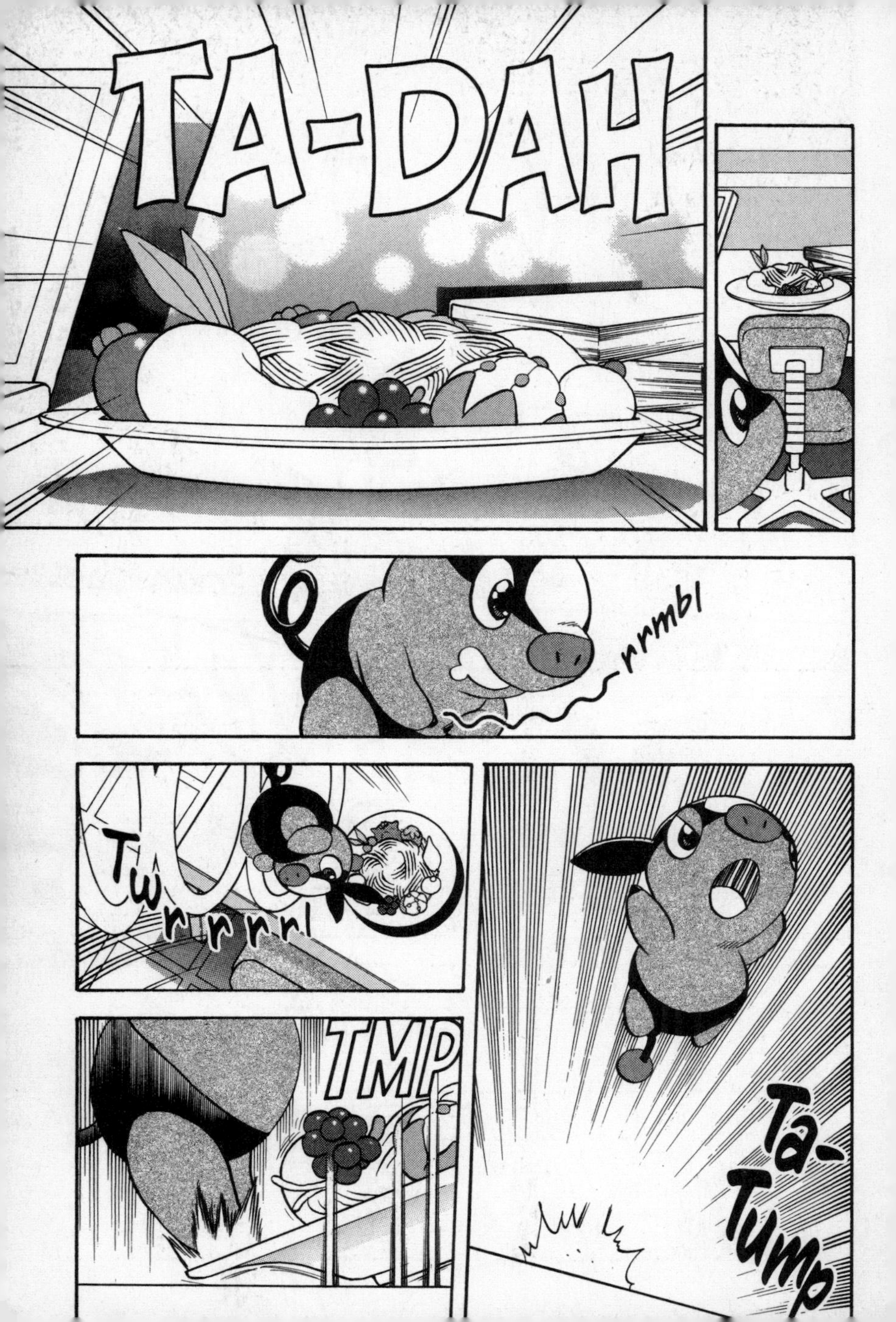
TA-DAH
rrmbl
Ta-Tump
Twrrrrrl
TMP

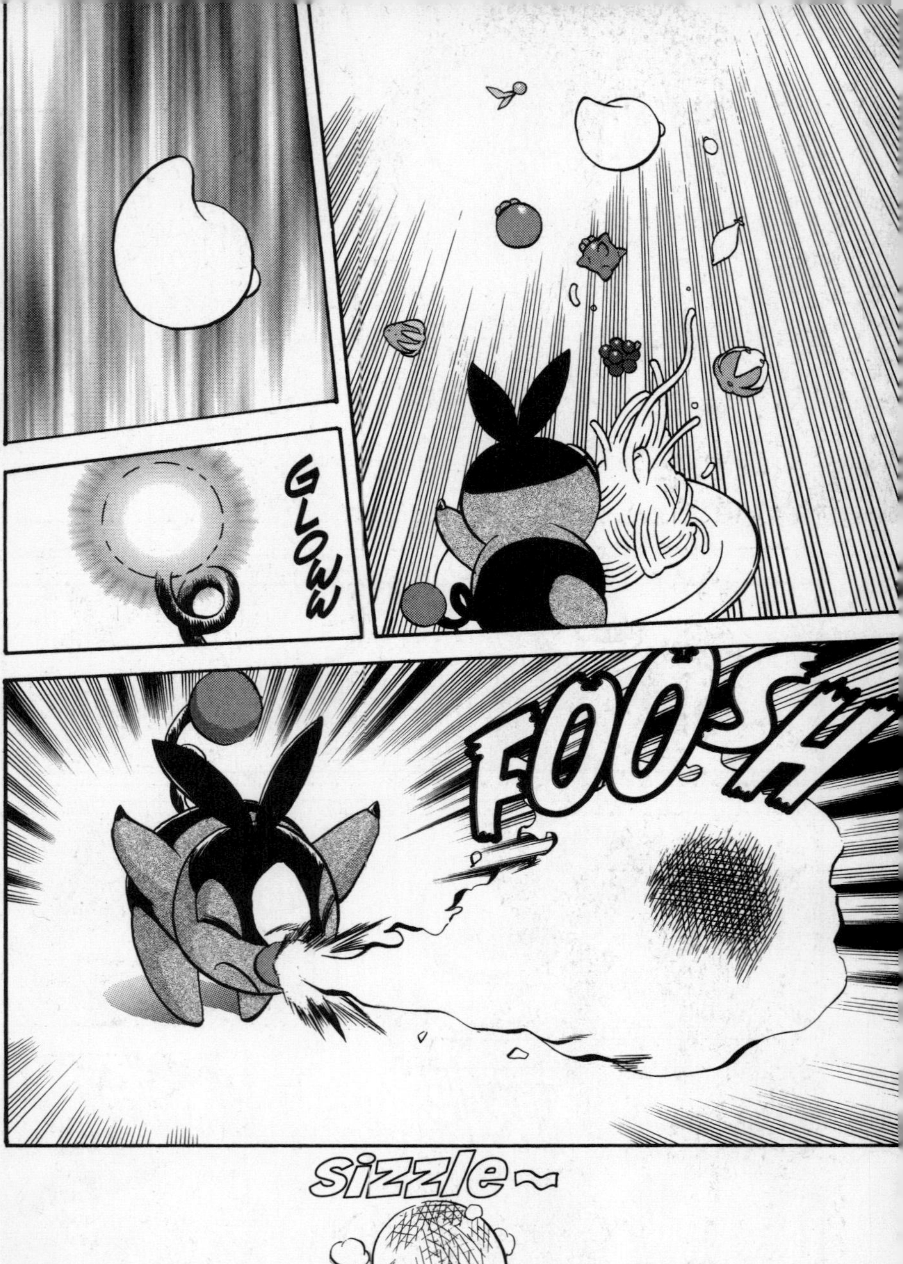
GLOWW
FOOSH
sizzle~

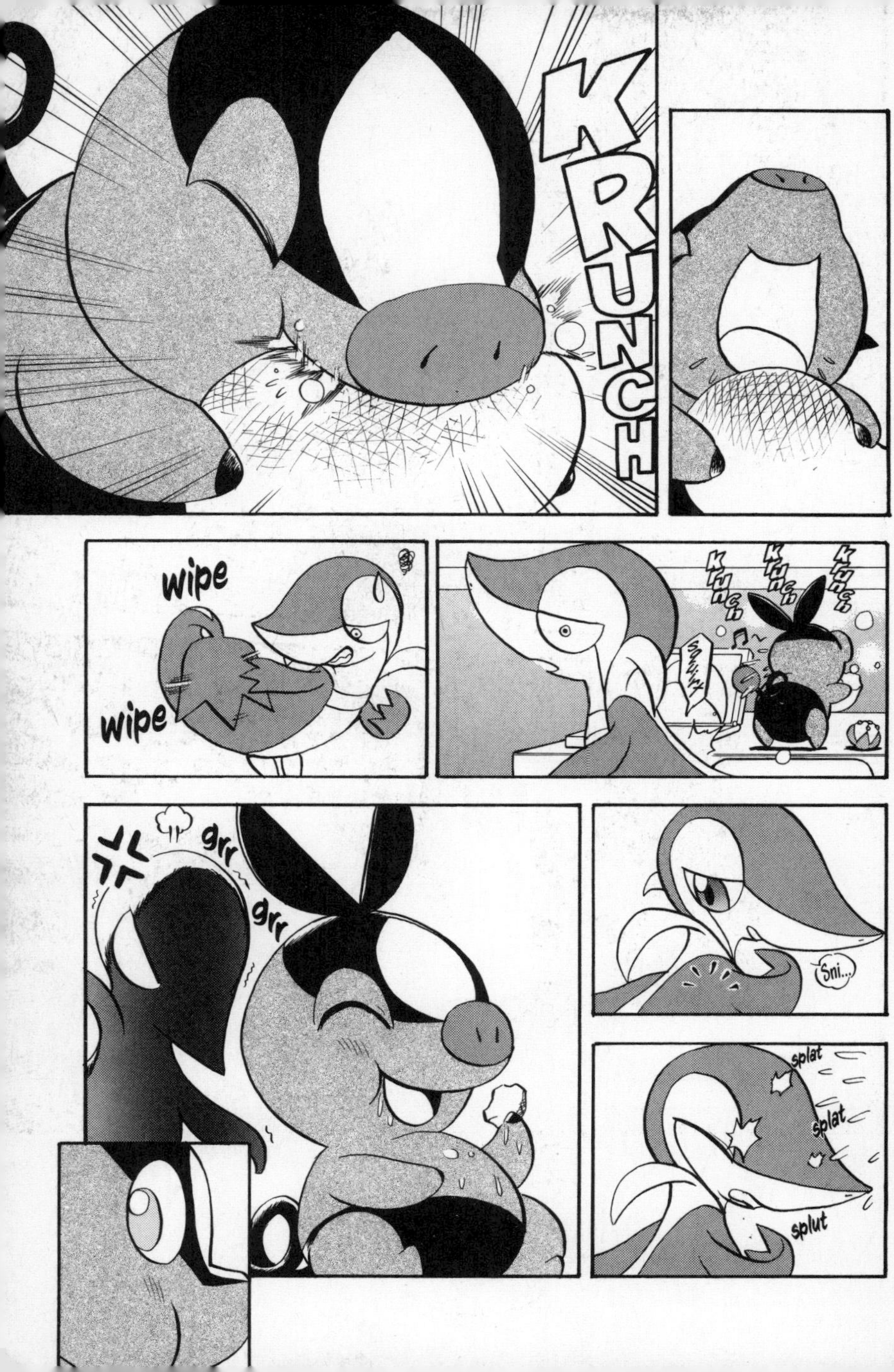
KRUNCH
krunch
krunch
krunch
SQUIRT
wipe
wipe
Sni...
splat
splat
splut
grr
grr

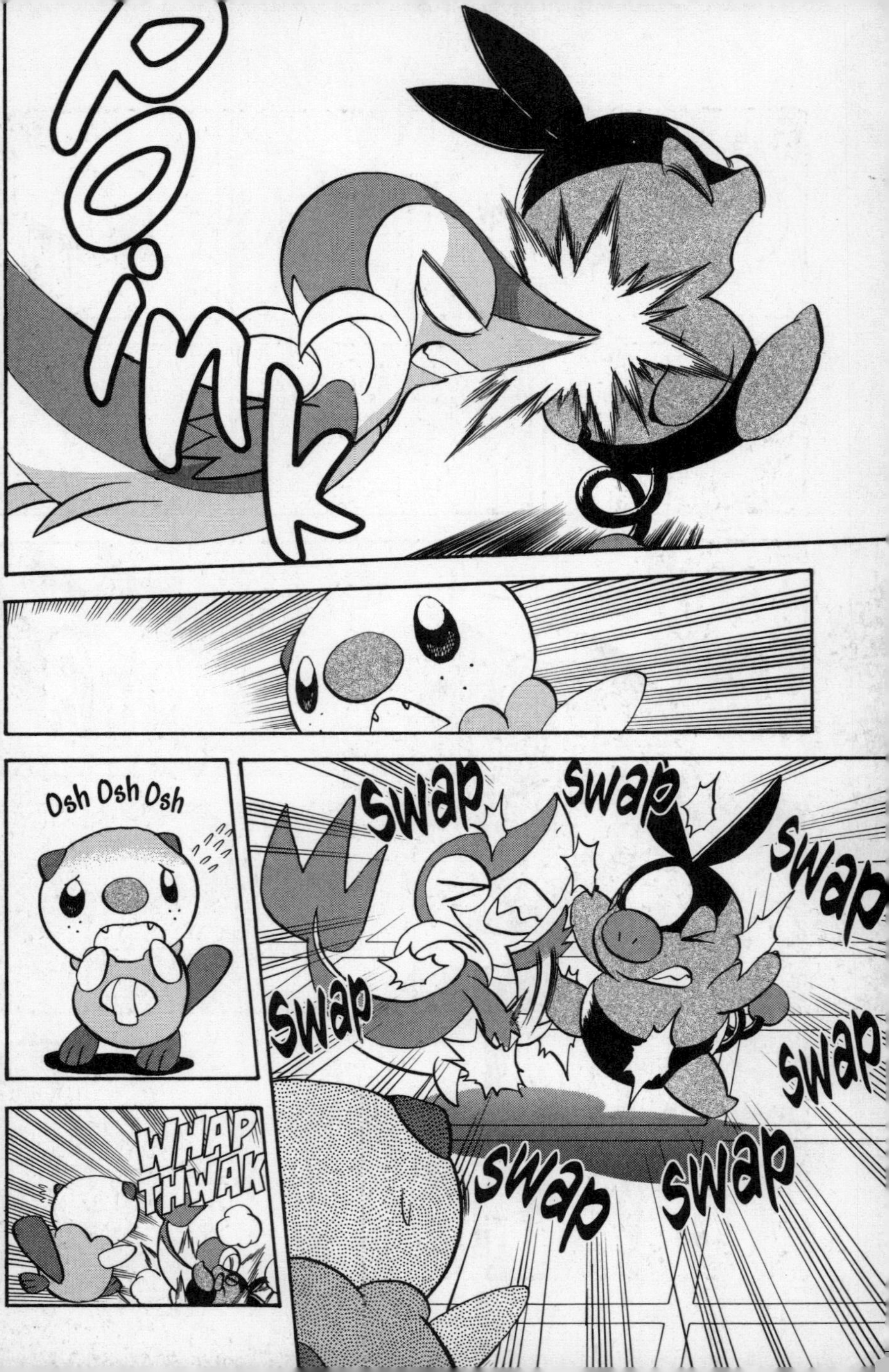
Poink
swap
swap
swap
swap
swap
swap
swap
Osh Osh Osh
WHAP
THWAK

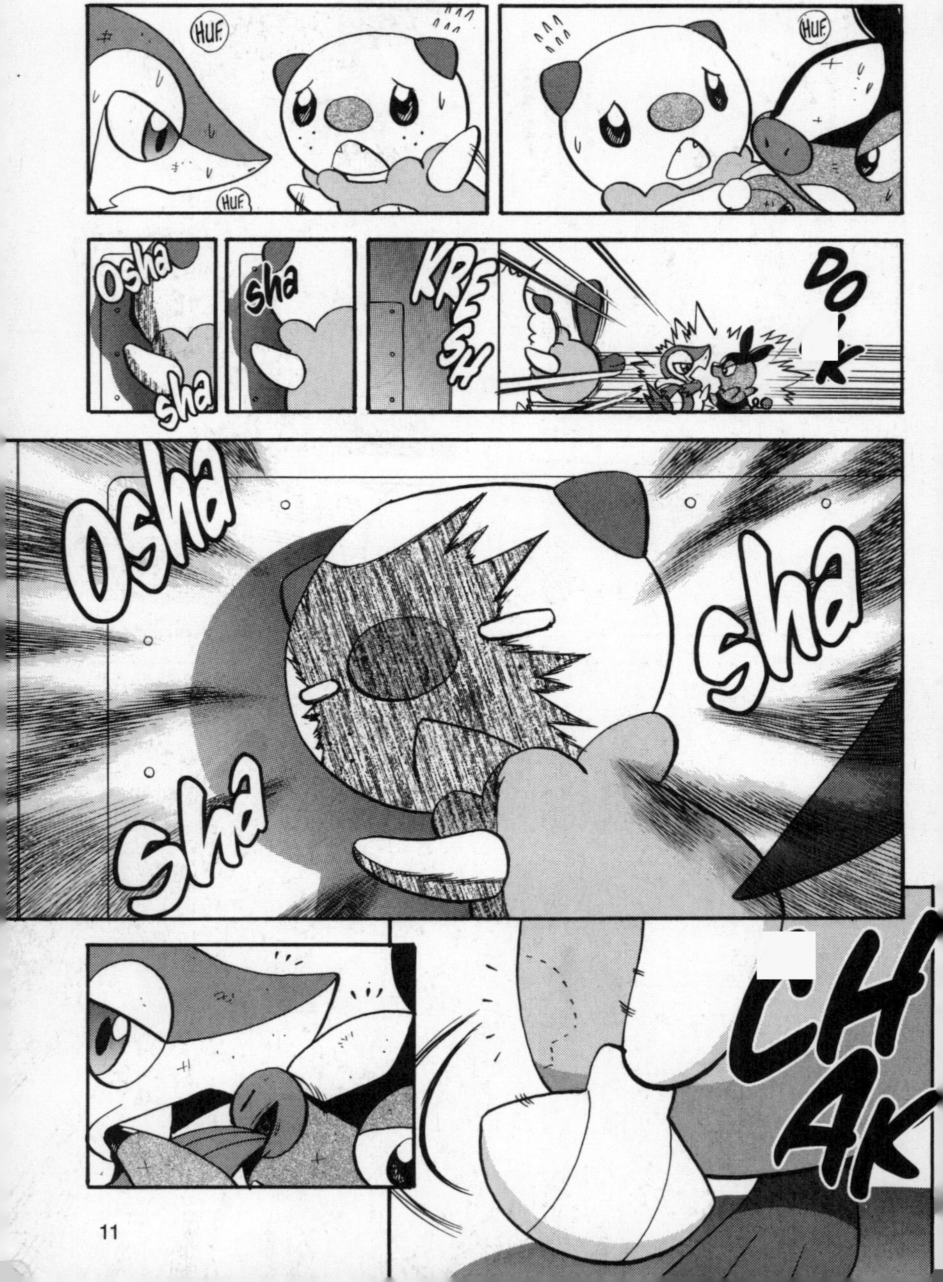
HUF.
HUF.
HUF.
DO
K
KRESH
sha
Osha
sha
Osha
sha
sha
CH
AK

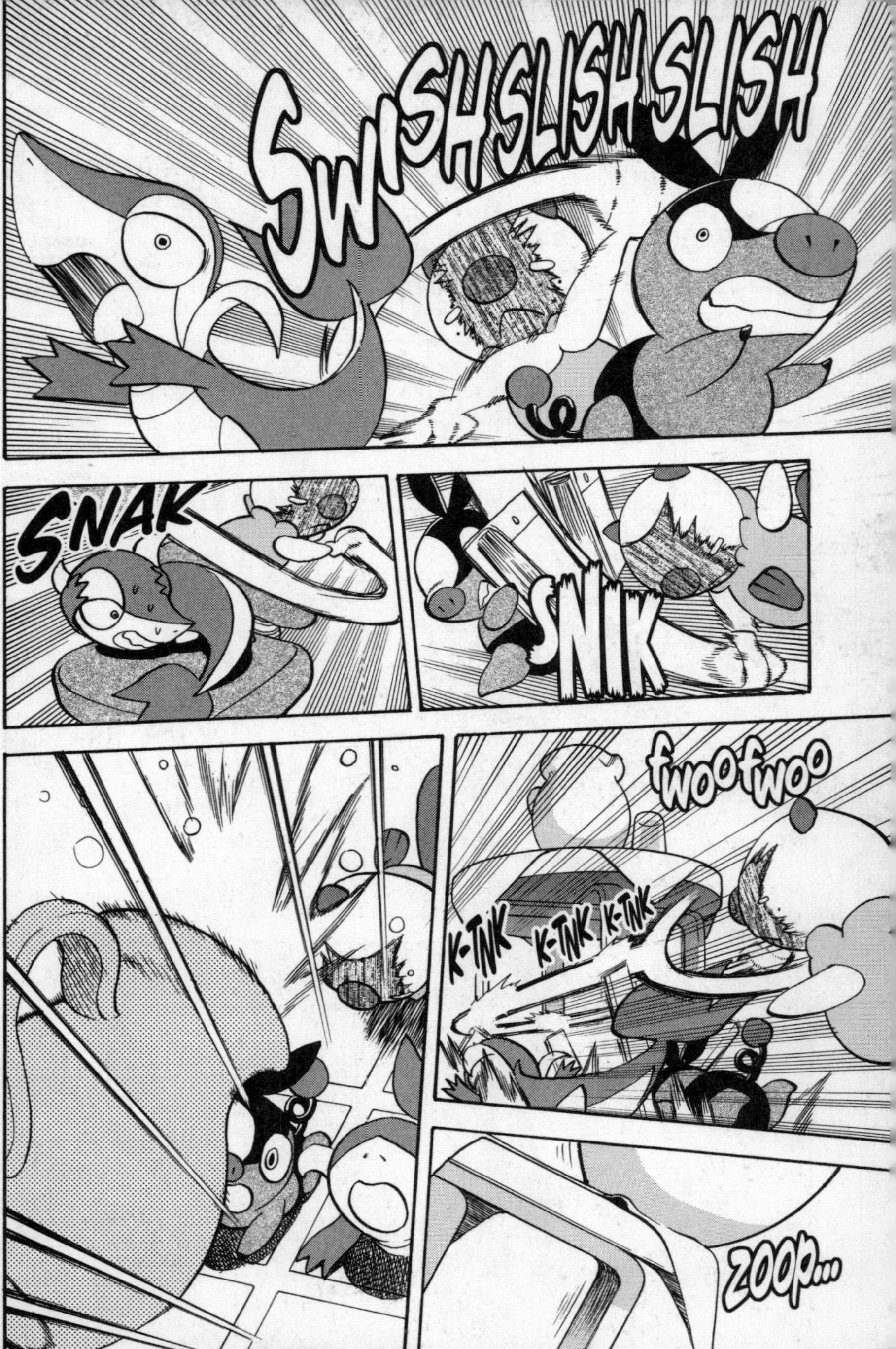
SWISH SLISH SLISH
SNIK
SNAK
fwoofwoo
K-TNK K-TNK K-TNK
zoop...

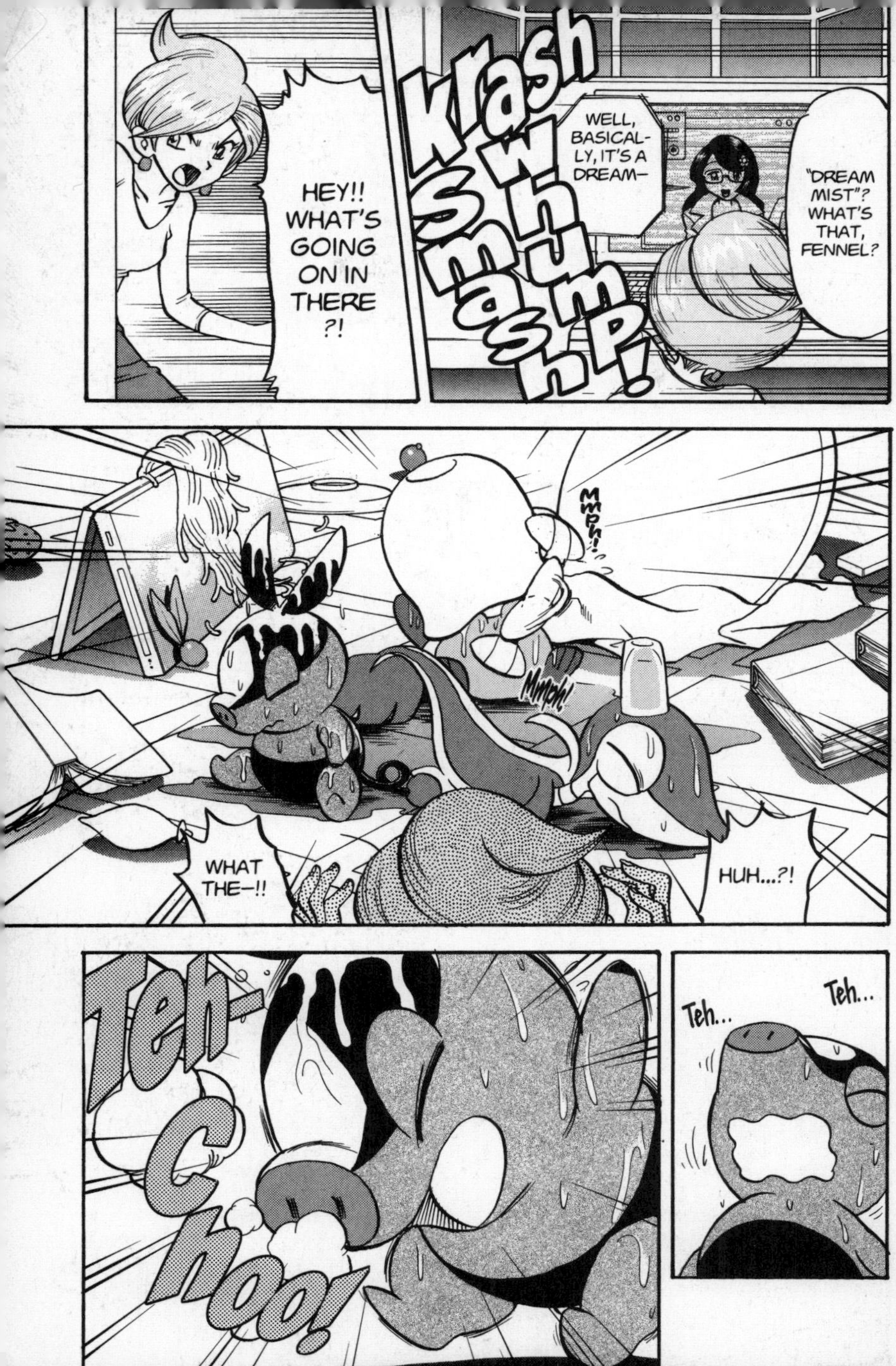
"DREAM MIST"? WHAT'S THAT, FENNEL?
WELL, BASICAL-LY, IT'S A DREAM—
Krash
Whump
Smash!
HEY!! WHAT'S GOING ON IN THERE?!
Mmph!
Mmph!
HUH...?!
WHAT THE—!!
Teh...
Teh...
Teh-Choo!

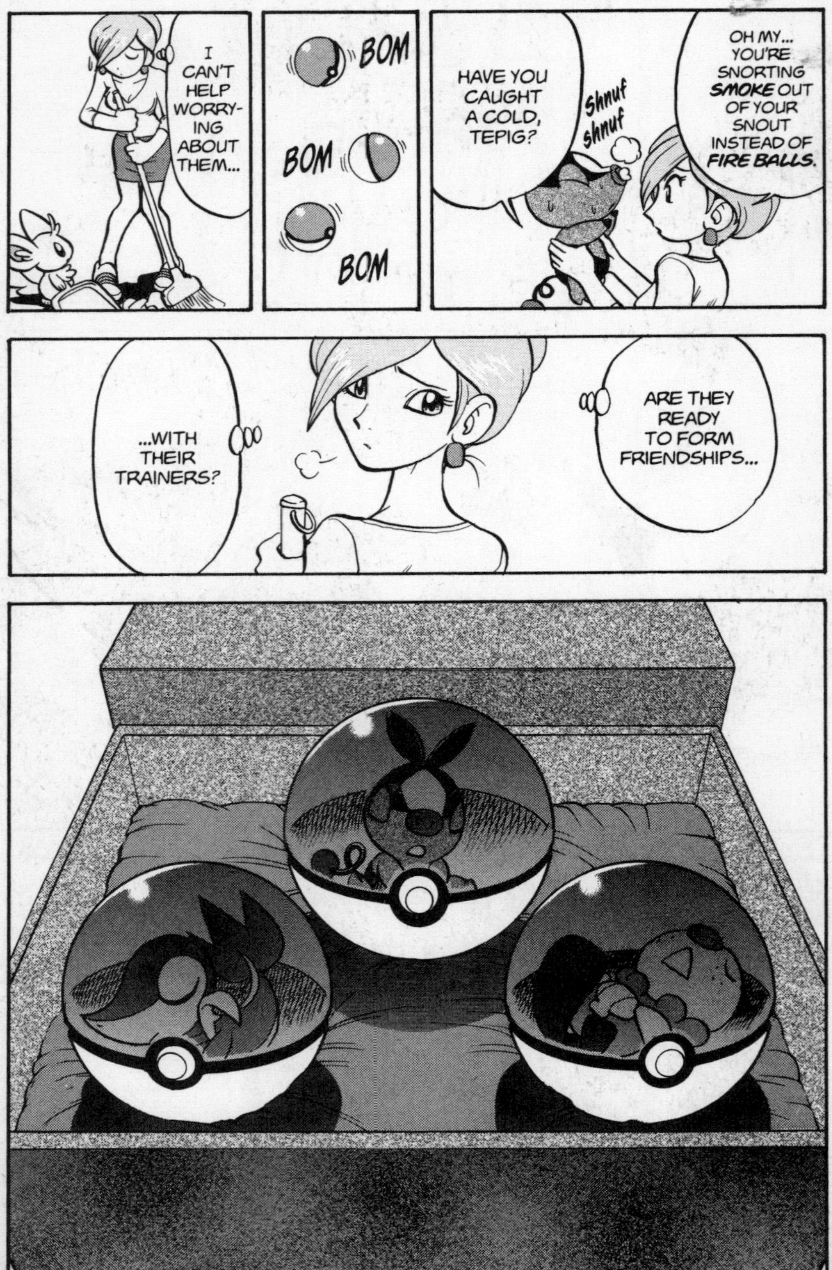
OH MY... YOU'RE SNORTING **SMOKE** OUT OF YOUR SNOUT INSTEAD OF **FIRE BALLS.**
Shnuf shnuf
HAVE YOU CAUGHT A COLD, TEPIG?
BOM
BOM
BOM
I CAN'T HELP WORRY-ING ABOUT THEM...
ARE THEY READY TO FORM FRIENDSHIPS...
...WITH THEIR TRAINERS?

Pokémon™ Adventures Black & White

Adventure 2
Choices

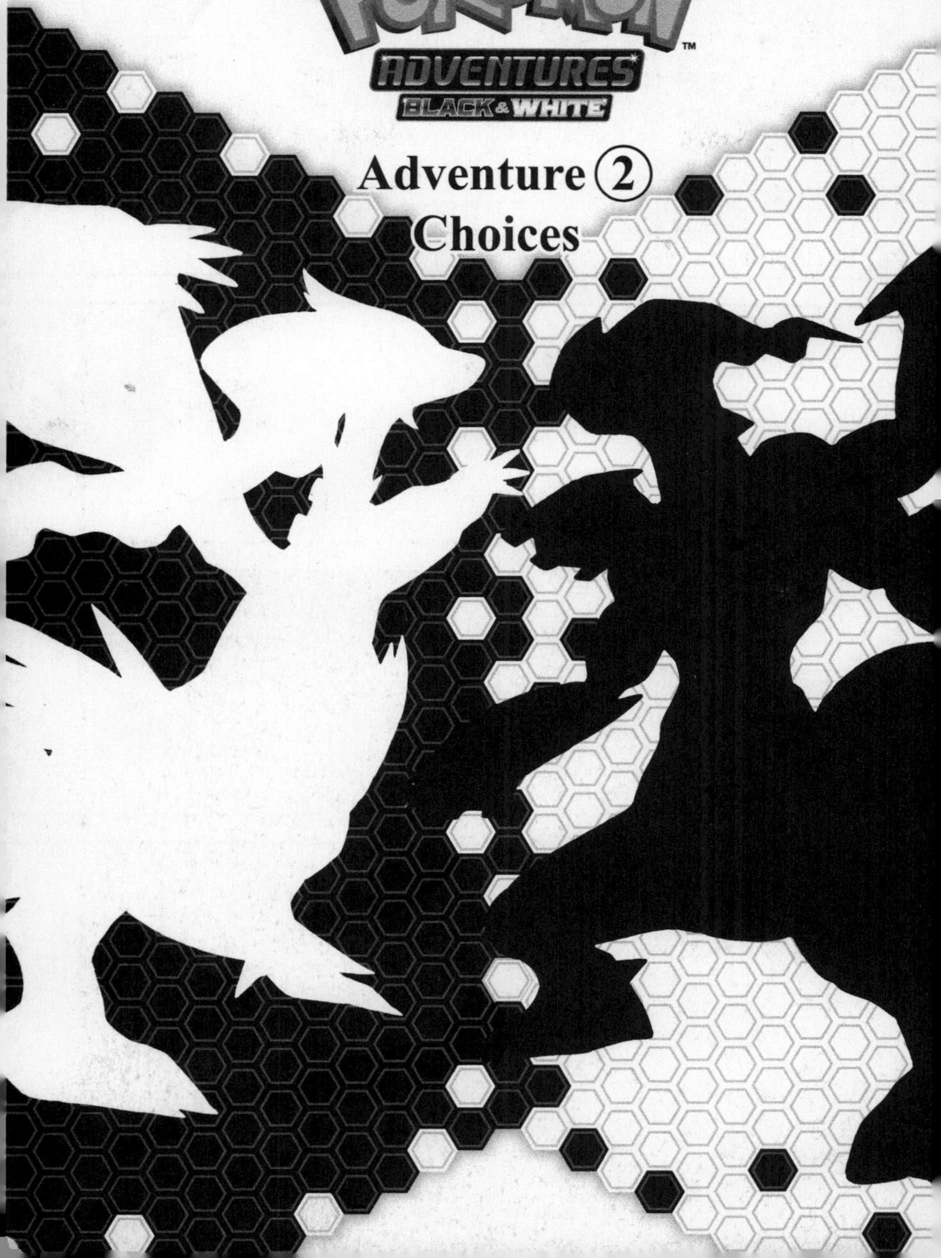

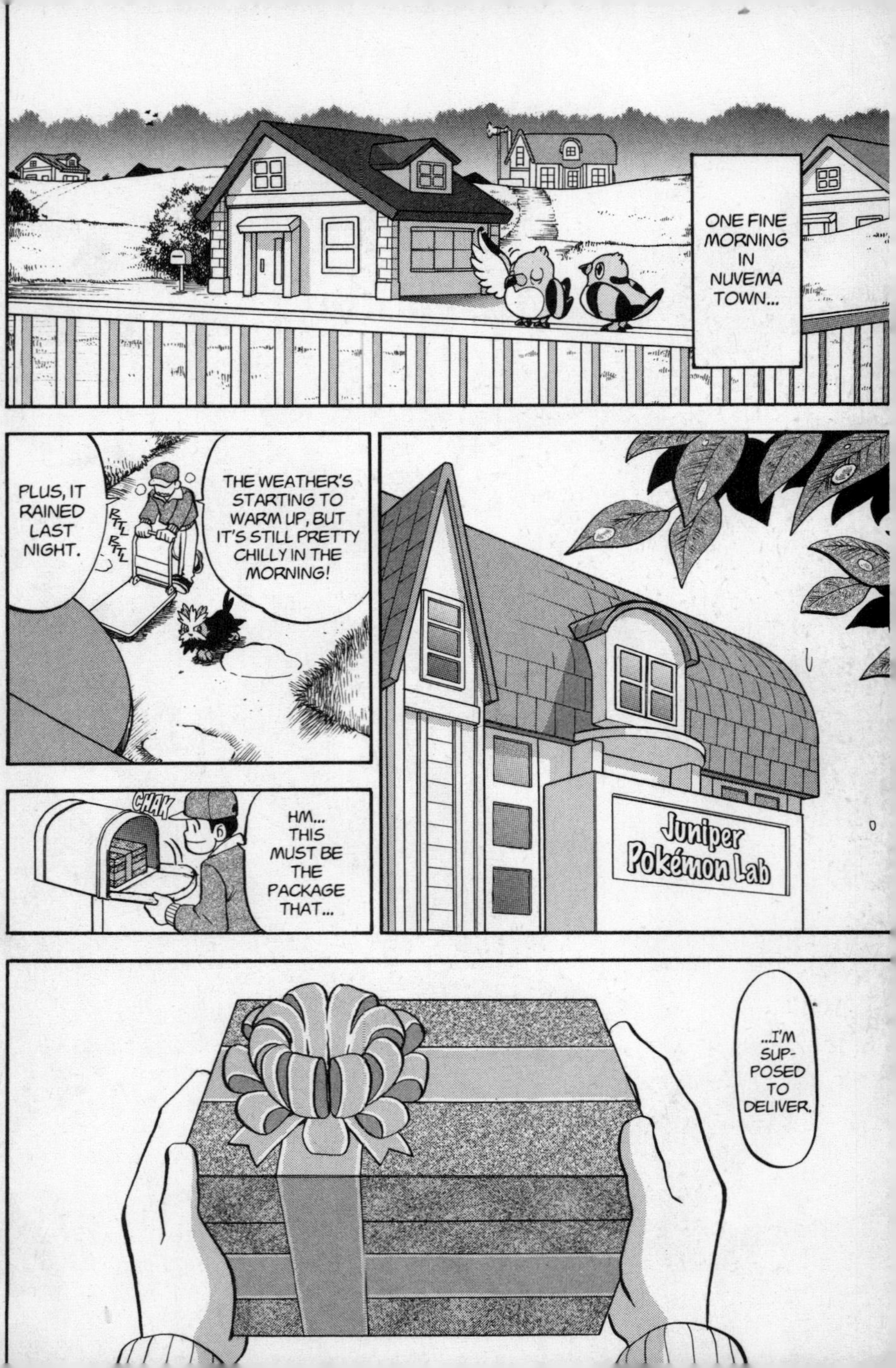
ONE FINE MORNING IN NUVEMA TOWN...
Juniper Pokémon Lab
THE WEATHER'S STARTING TO WARM UP, BUT IT'S STILL PRETTY CHILLY IN THE MORNING!
RTTL RTTL
PLUS, IT RAINED LAST NIGHT.
CHAK
HM... THIS MUST BE THE PACKAGE THAT...
...I'M SUP-POSED TO DELIVER.

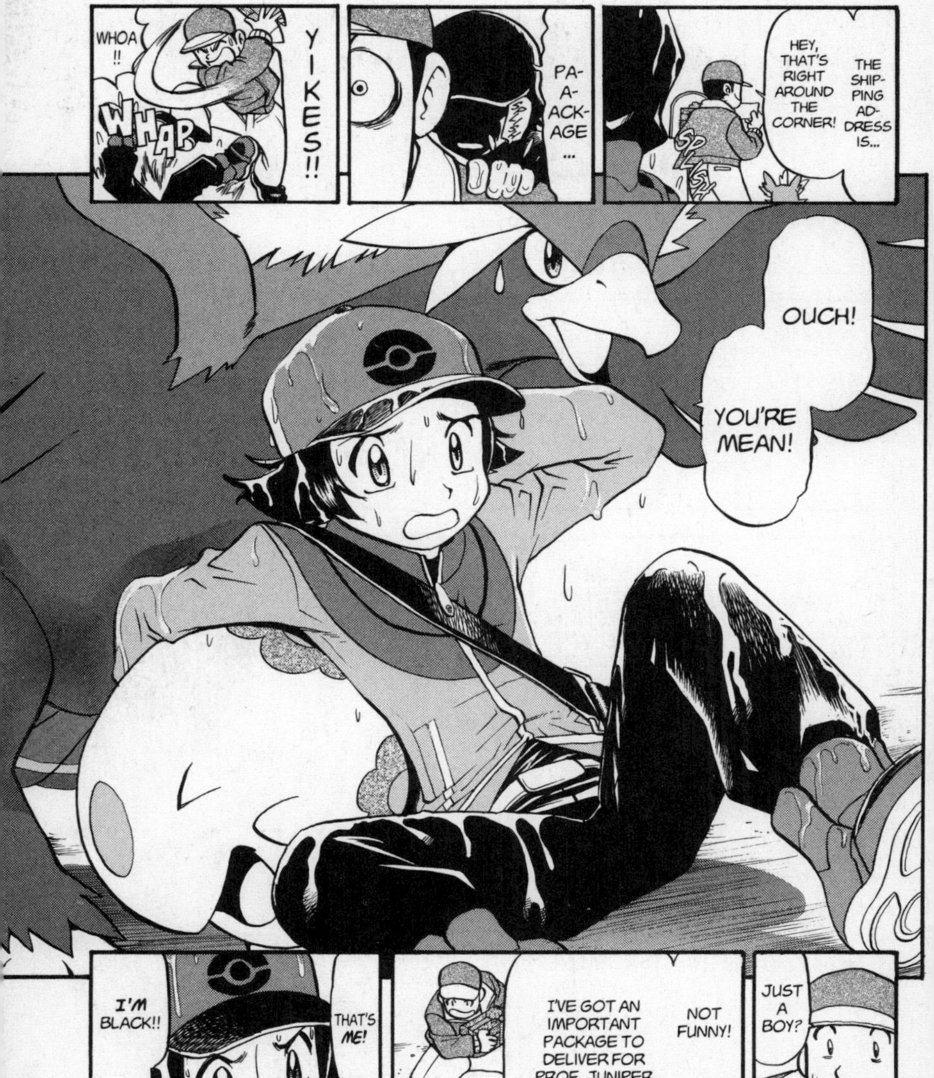
THE SHIPPING ADDRESS IS...
HEY, THAT'S RIGHT AROUND THE CORNER!
PA-A-ACK-AGE...
YIKES!!
WHOA!!
WHAP
OUCH!
YOU'RE MEAN!
JUST A BOY?
NOT FUNNY!
I'VE GOT AN IMPORTANT PACKAGE TO DELIVER FOR PROF. JUNIPER TO SOME BOY NAMED "BLACK"...
THAT'S ME!
I'M BLACK!!

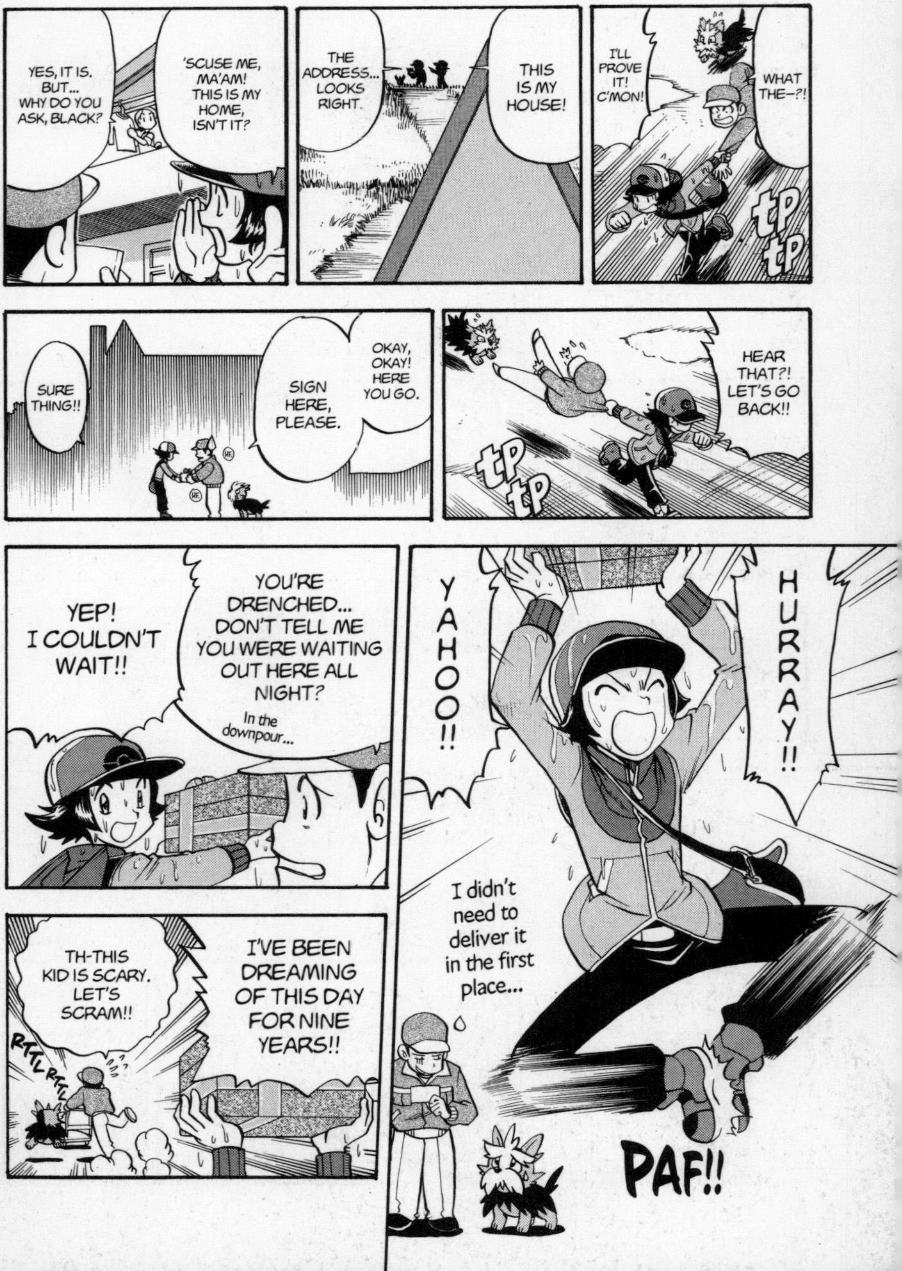
WHAT THE—?!
I'LL PROVE IT! C'MON!
tp tp
THIS IS MY HOUSE!
THE ADDRESS... LOOKS RIGHT.
'SCUSE ME, MA'AM! THIS IS MY HOME, ISN'T IT?
YES, IT IS. BUT... WHY DO YOU ASK, BLACK?
HEAR THAT?! LET'S GO BACK!!
tp tp
OKAY, OKAY! HERE YOU GO.
SIGN HERE, PLEASE.
SURE THING!!
HURRAY!!
YAHOO!!
I didn't need to deliver it in the first place...
PAF!!
YOU'RE DRENCHED... DON'T TELL ME YOU WERE WAITING OUT HERE ALL NIGHT?
In the downpour...
YEP! I COULDN'T WAIT!!
I'VE BEEN DREAMING OF THIS DAY FOR NINE YEARS!!
TH-THIS KID IS SCARY. LET'S SCRAM!!
RTTL RTTL

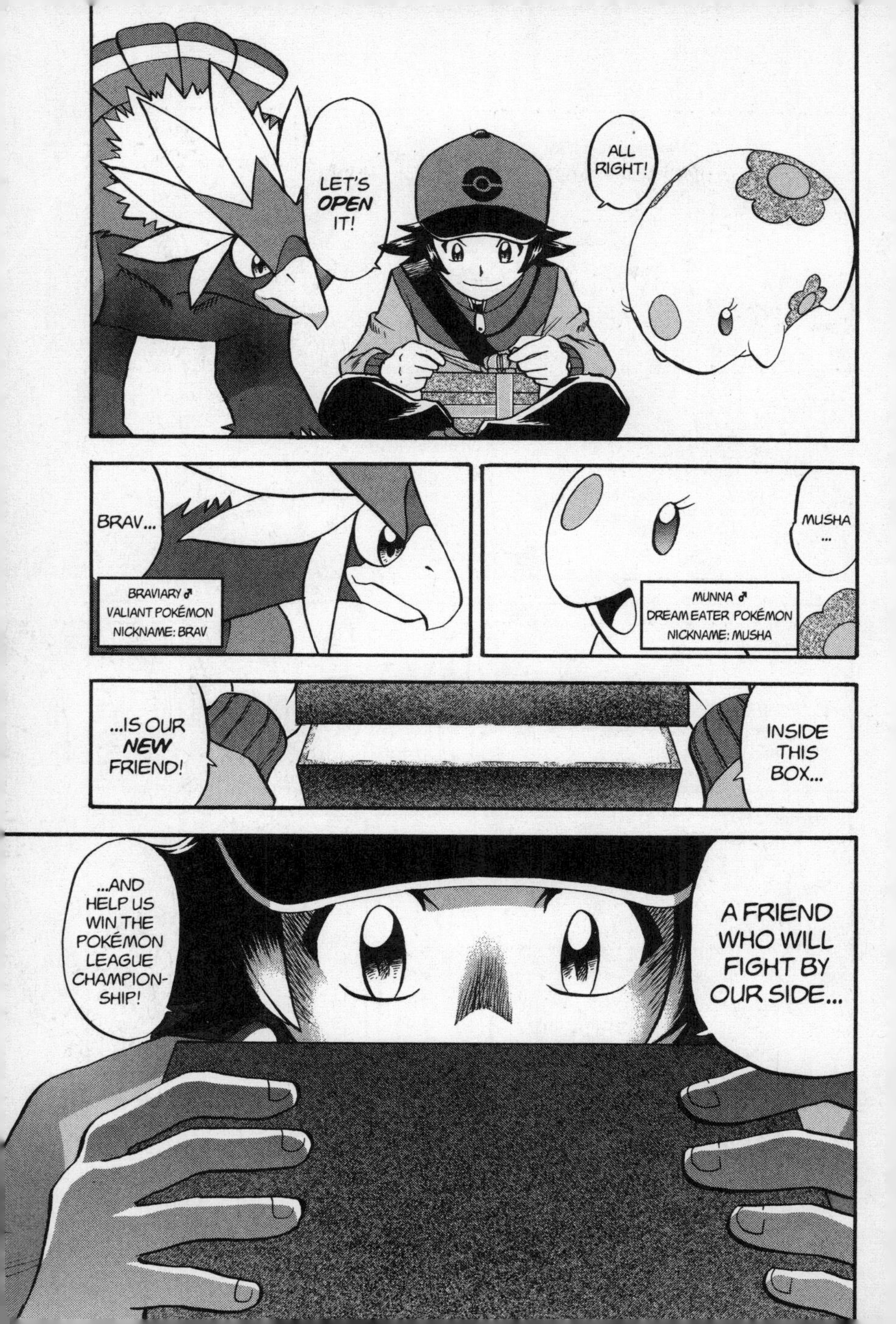
ALL RIGHT!
LET'S OPEN IT!
MUSHA...
MUNNA ♂ DREAM EATER POKÉMON NICKNAME: MUSHA
BRAV...
BRAVIARY ♂ VALIANT POKÉMON NICKNAME: BRAV
INSIDE THIS BOX...
...IS OUR NEW FRIEND!
A FRIEND WHO WILL FIGHT BY OUR SIDE...
...AND HELP US WIN THE POKÉMON LEAGUE CHAMPIONSHIP!

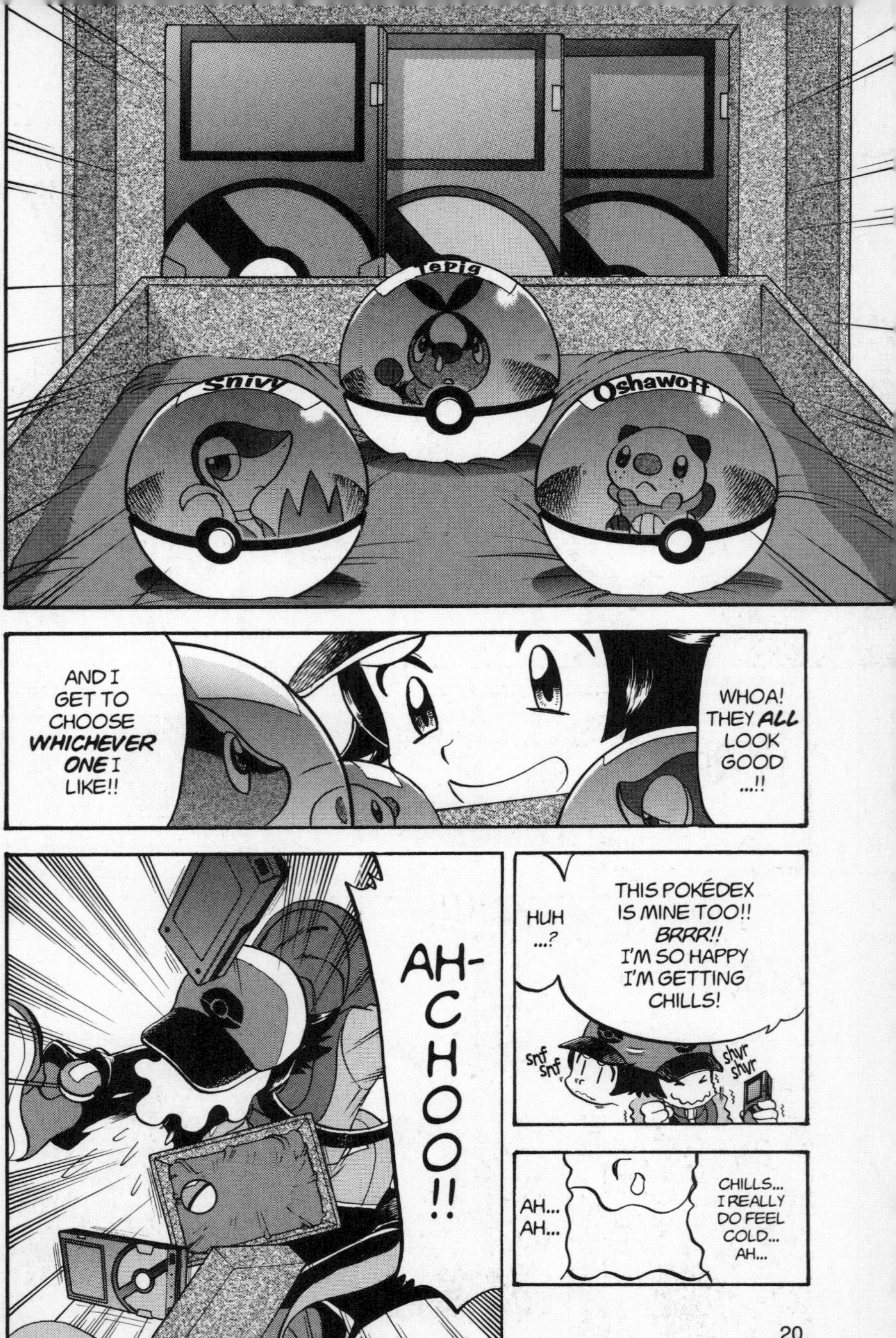
Tepig
Oshawott
Snivy
WHOA! THEY ALL LOOK GOOD ...!!
AND I GET TO CHOOSE WHICHEVER ONE I LIKE!!
THIS POKÉDEX IS MINE TOO!! BRRR!! I'M SO HAPPY I'M GETTING CHILLS!
HUH ...?
shvr shvr
snf snf
CHILLS... I REALLY DO FEEL COLD... AH...
AH... AH...
AH-CHOOO!!

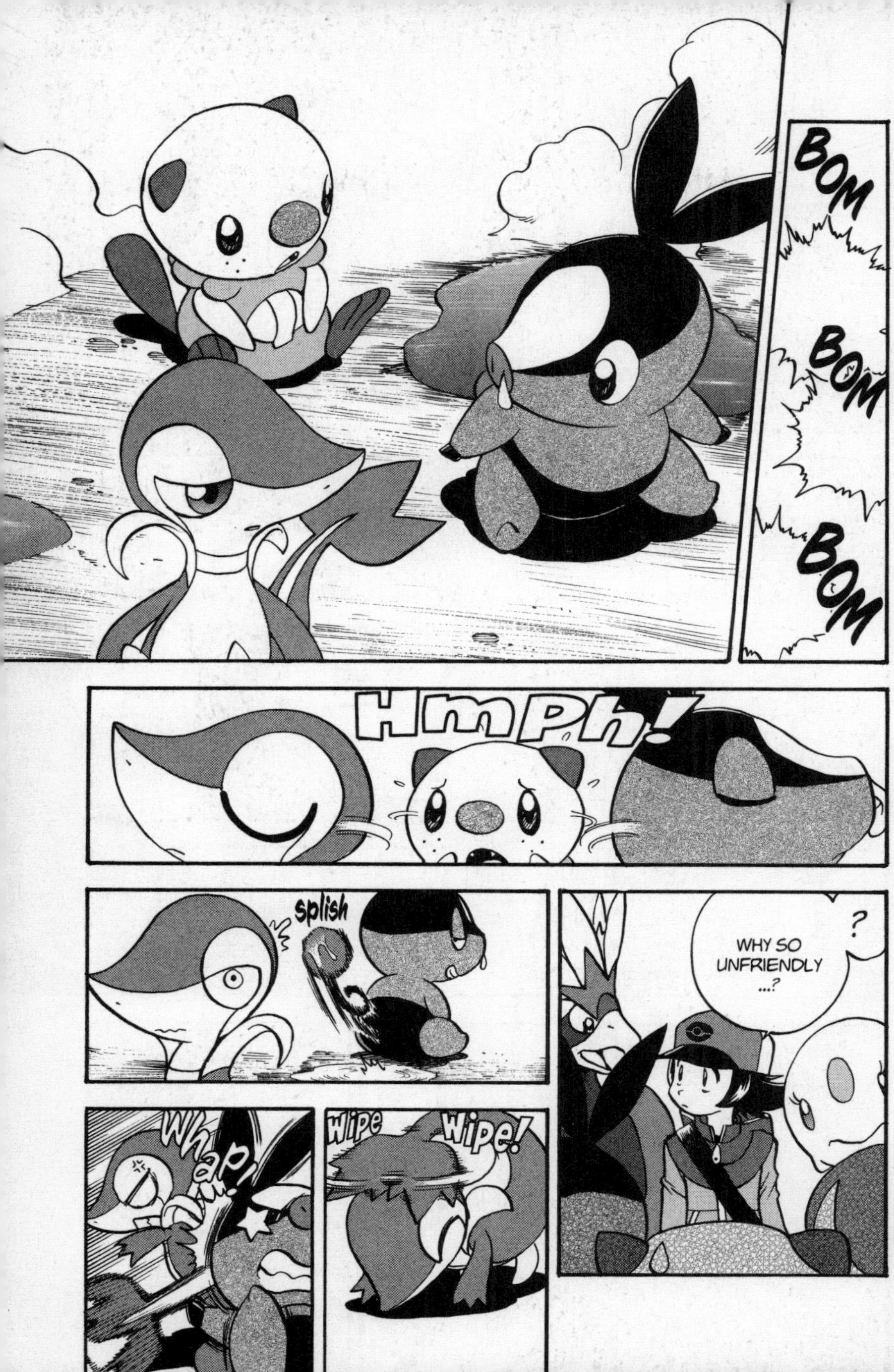
BOM
BOM
BOM
Hmph!
?
WHY SO UNFRIENDLY ...?
splish
Wipe
Wipe!
Whap!

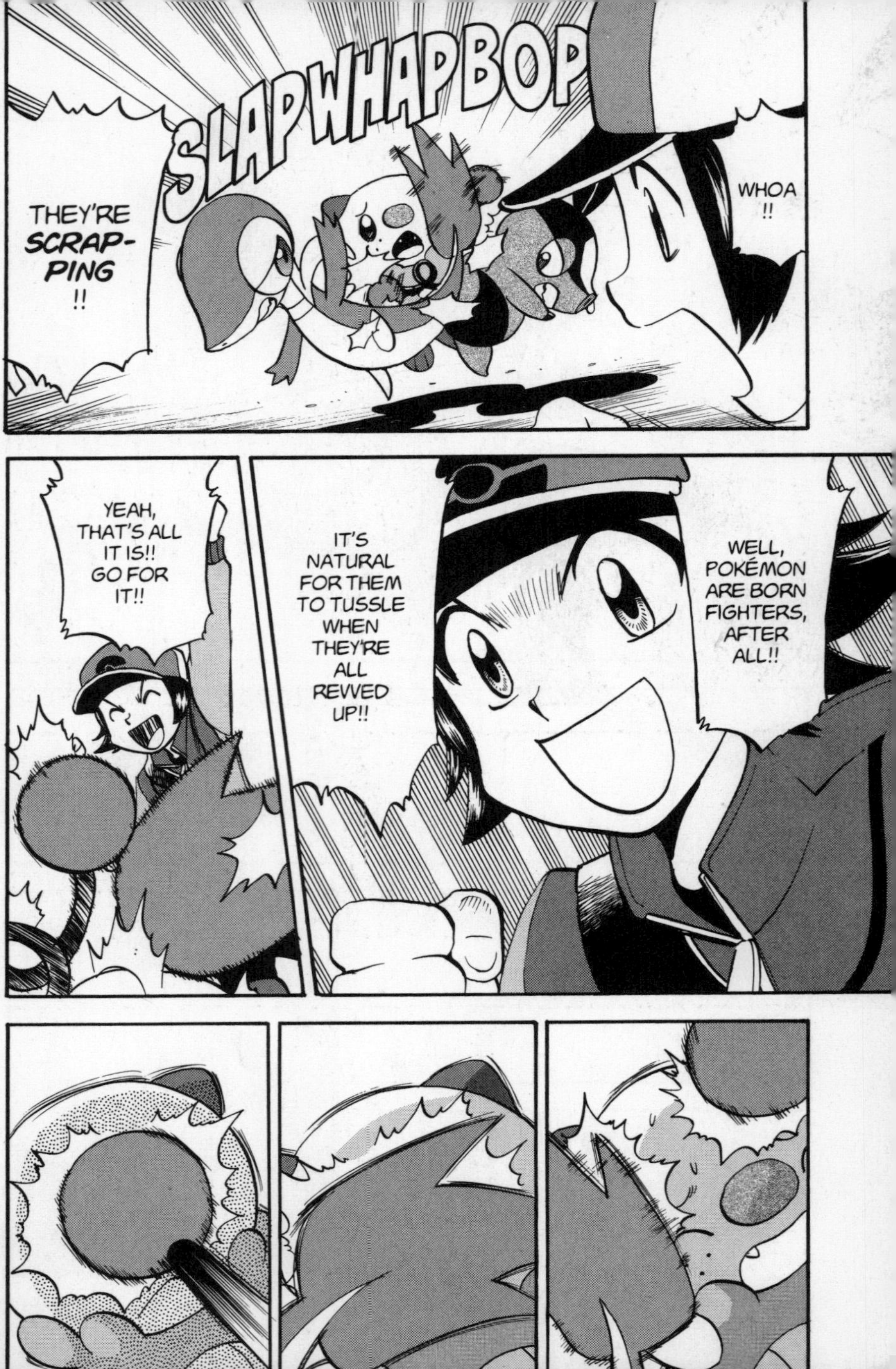
SLAPWHAPBOP
WHOA!!
THEY'RE SCRAPPING!!
WELL, POKÉMON ARE BORN FIGHTERS, AFTER ALL!!
IT'S NATURAL FOR THEM TO TUSSLE WHEN THEY'RE ALL REVVED UP!!
YEAH, THAT'S ALL IT IS!! GO FOR IT!!

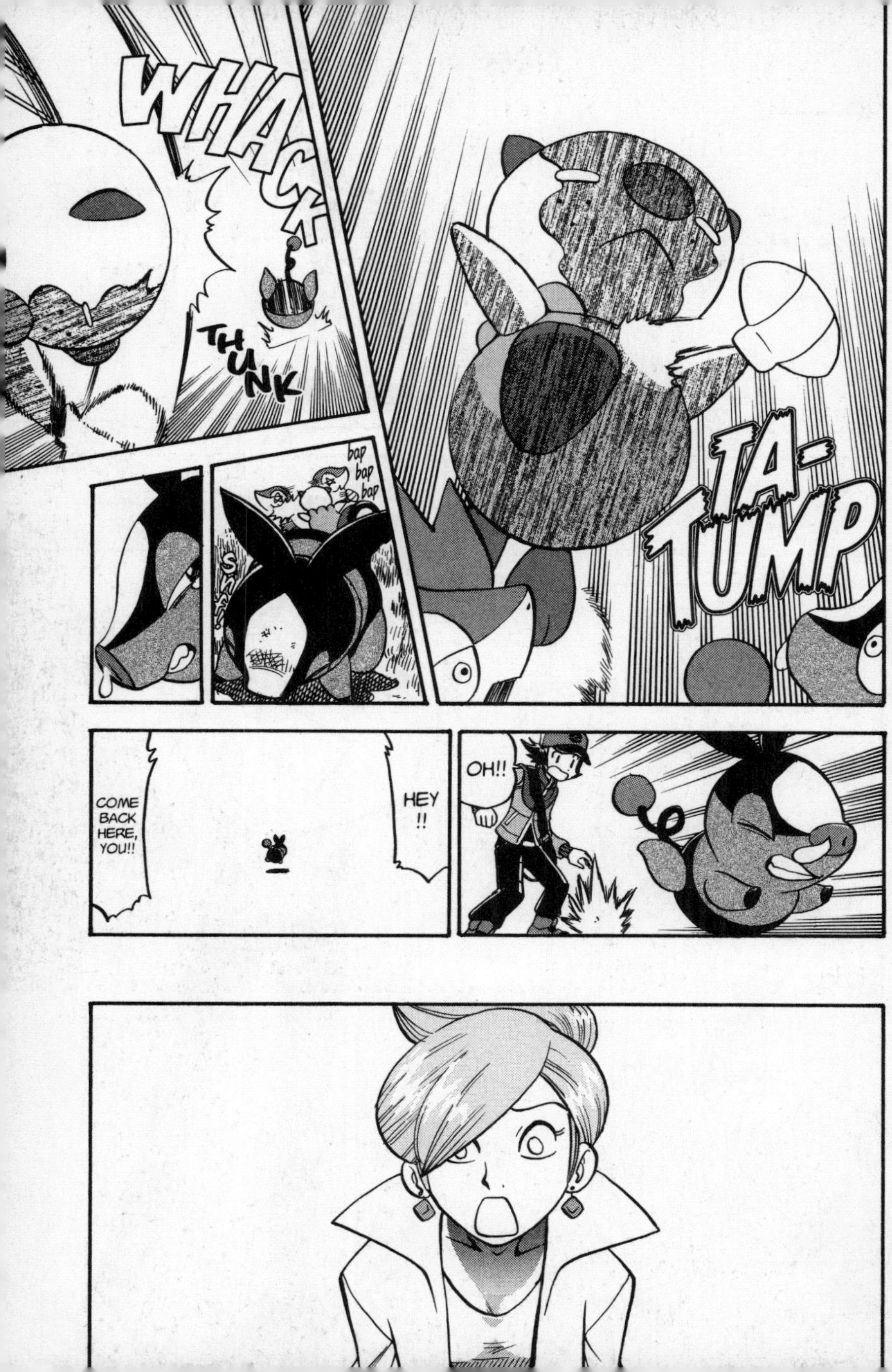
TA-TUMP
WHACK
THUNK
bap bap bap
OH!!
HEY !!
COME BACK HERE, YOU!!

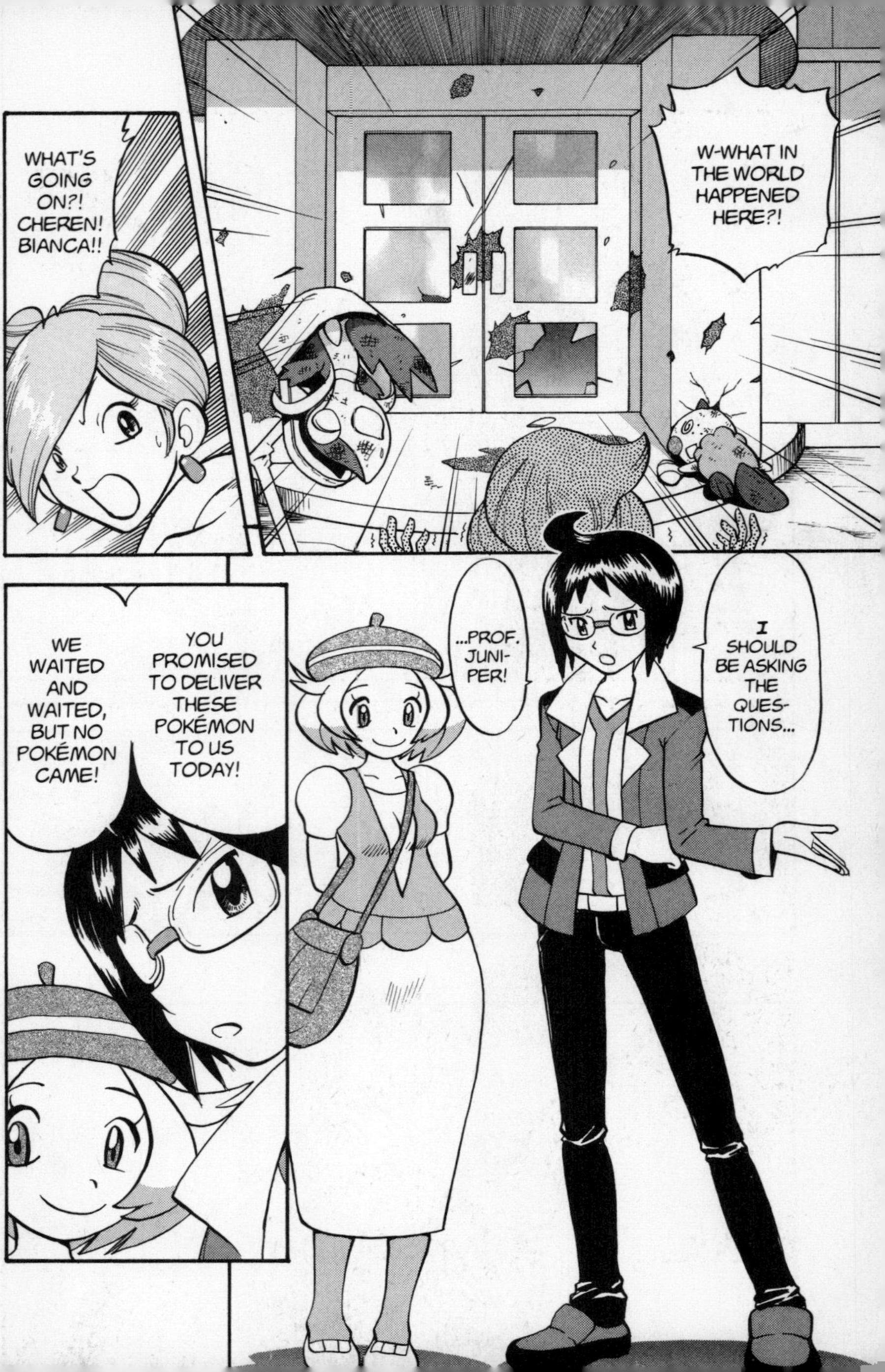
W-WHAT IN THE WORLD HAPPENED HERE?!
WHAT'S GOING ON?! CHEREN! BIANCA!!
I SHOULD BE ASKING THE QUES-TIONS...
...PROF. JUNI-PER!
YOU PROMISED TO DELIVER THESE POKÉMON TO US TODAY!
WE WAITED AND WAITED, BUT NO POKÉMON CAME!

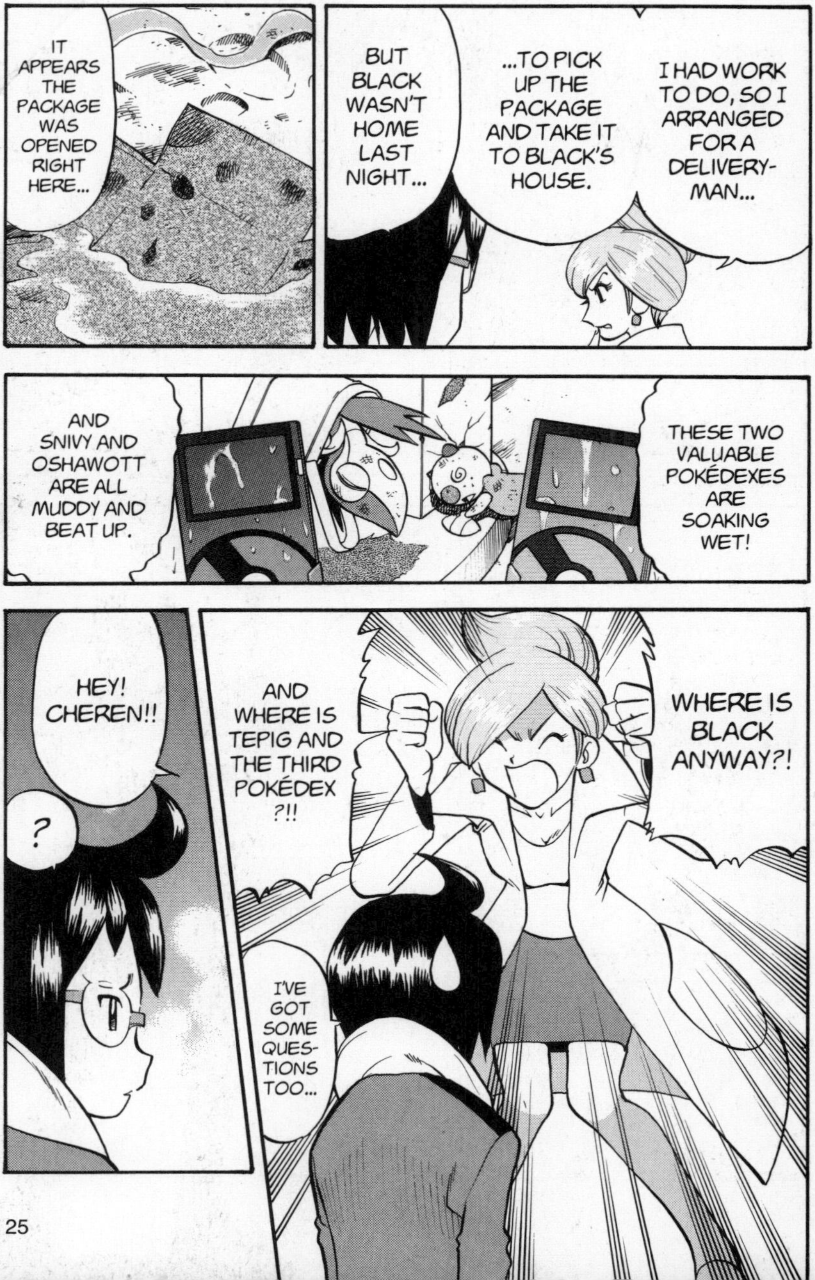
I HAD WORK TO DO, SO I ARRANGED FOR A DELIVERYMAN...
...TO PICK UP THE PACKAGE AND TAKE IT TO BLACK'S HOUSE.
BUT BLACK WASN'T HOME LAST NIGHT...
IT APPEARS THE PACKAGE WAS OPENED RIGHT HERE...
THESE TWO VALUABLE POKÉDEXES ARE SOAKING WET!
AND SNIVY AND OSHAWOTT ARE ALL MUDDY AND BEAT UP.
WHERE IS BLACK ANYWAY?!
AND WHERE IS TEPIG AND THE THIRD POKÉDEX ?!!
I'VE GOT SOME QUESTIONS TOO...
HEY! CHEREN!!
?

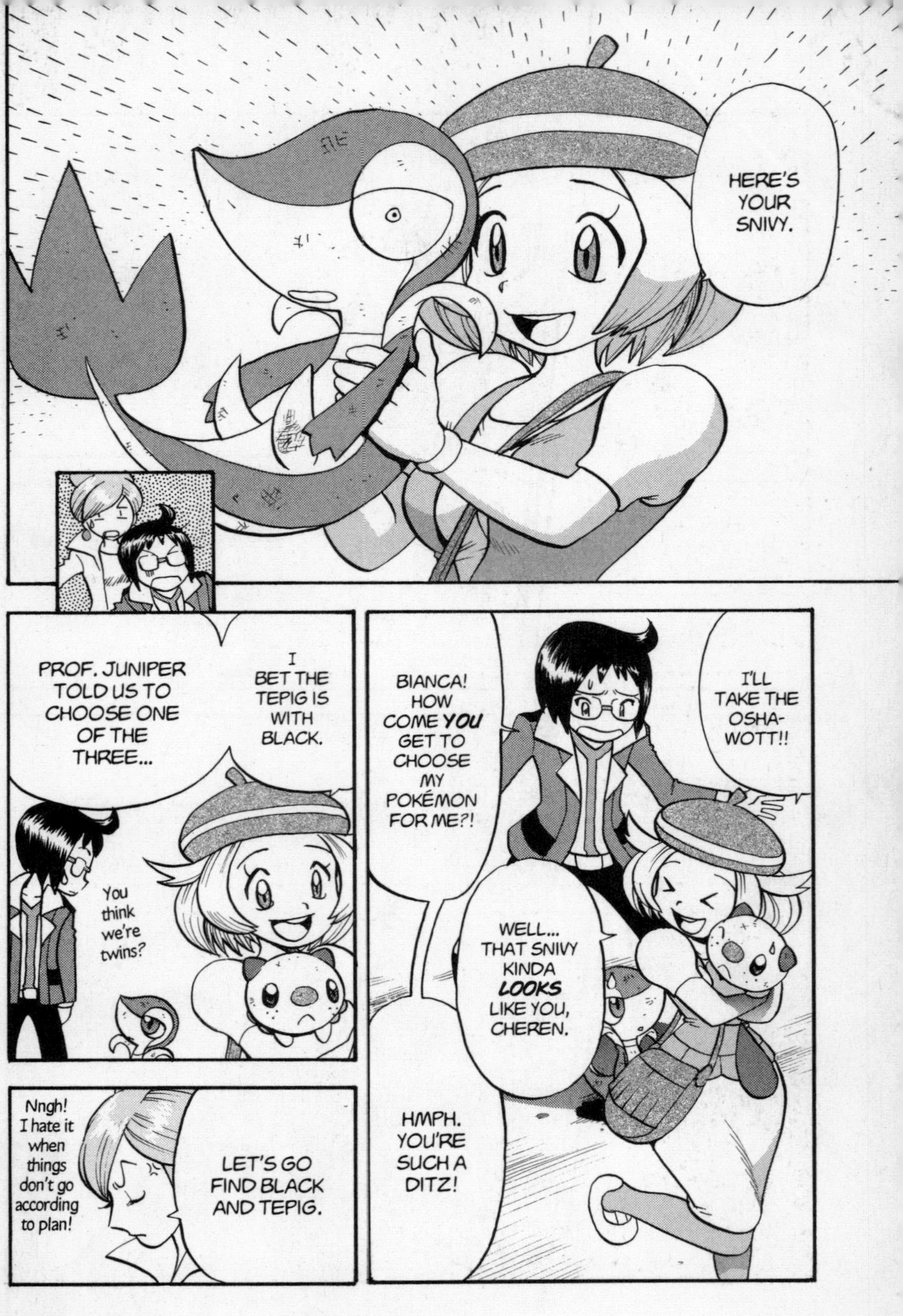
HERE'S YOUR SNIVY.
I'LL TAKE THE OSHA-WOTT!!
BIANCA! HOW COME **YOU** GET TO CHOOSE MY POKÉMON FOR ME?!
WELL... THAT SNIVY KINDA **LOOKS** LIKE YOU, CHEREN.
HMPH. YOU'RE SUCH A DITZ!
I BET THE TEPIG IS WITH BLACK.
PROF. JUNIPER TOLD US TO CHOOSE ONE OF THE THREE...
You think we're twins?
LET'S GO FIND BLACK AND TEPIG.
Nngh! I hate it when things don't go according to plan!

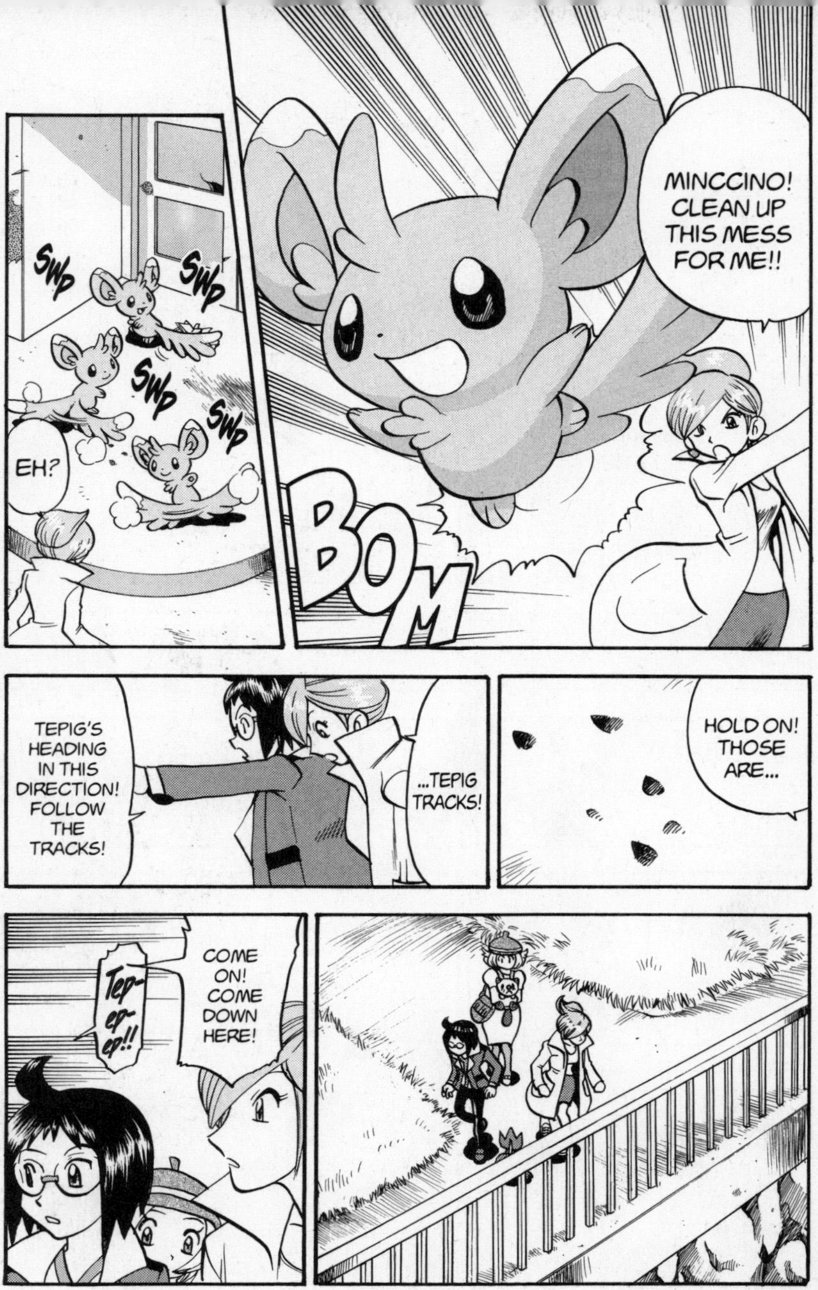
MINCCINO! CLEAN UP THIS MESS FOR ME!!
BOM
SWP
SWP
SWP
SWP
EH?
HOLD ON! THOSE ARE...
...TEPIG TRACKS!
TEPIG'S HEADING IN THIS DIRECTION! FOLLOW THE TRACKS!
COME ON! COME DOWN HERE!
Tep-ep-ep!!

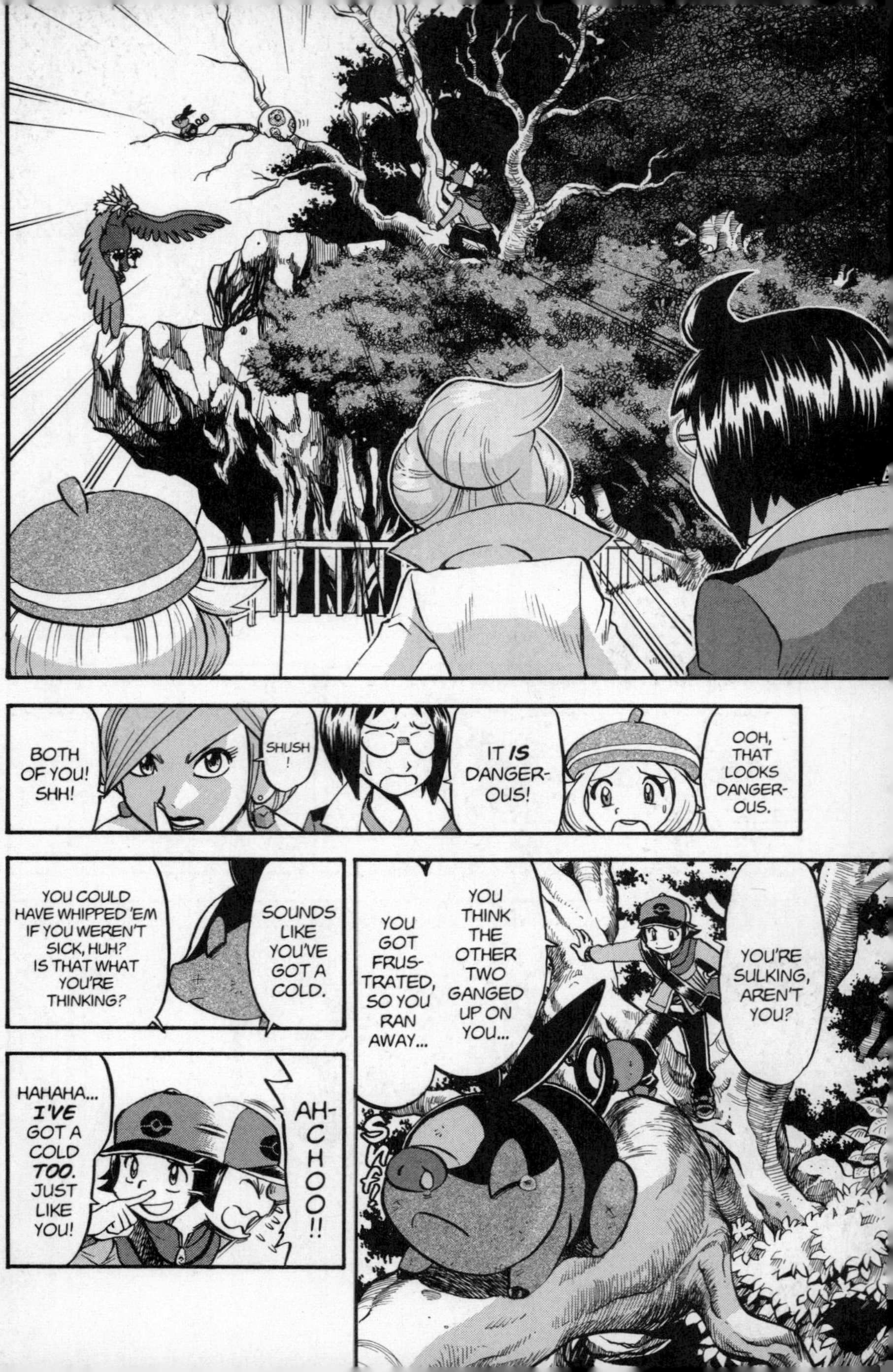
OOH, THAT LOOKS DANGEROUS.
IT *IS* DANGEROUS!
SHUSH!
BOTH OF YOU! SHH!
YOU'RE SULKING, AREN'T YOU?
YOU THINK THE OTHER TWO GANGED UP ON YOU...
YOU GOT FRUSTRATED, SO YOU RAN AWAY...
Snf!
SOUNDS LIKE YOU'VE GOT A COLD.
YOU COULD HAVE WHIPPED 'EM IF YOU WEREN'T SICK, HUH? IS THAT WHAT YOU'RE THINKING?
AH-CHOO!!
HAHAHA... *I'VE* GOT A COLD *TOO*. JUST LIKE YOU!

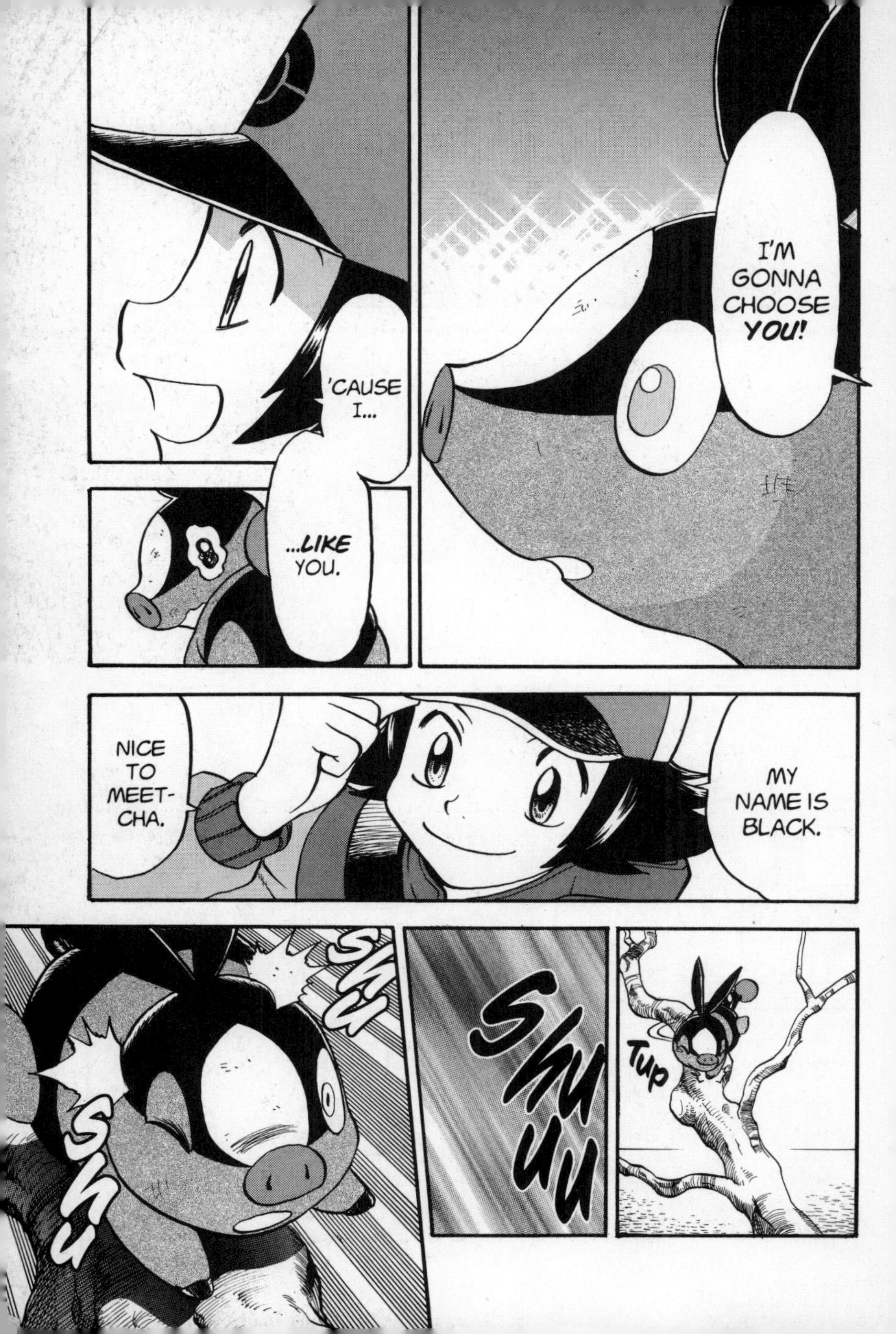
I'M GONNA CHOOSE YOU!
'CAUSE I...
...LIKE YOU.
MY NAME IS BLACK.
NICE TO MEET-CHA.
Tup
SHUUU
SHU
SHU

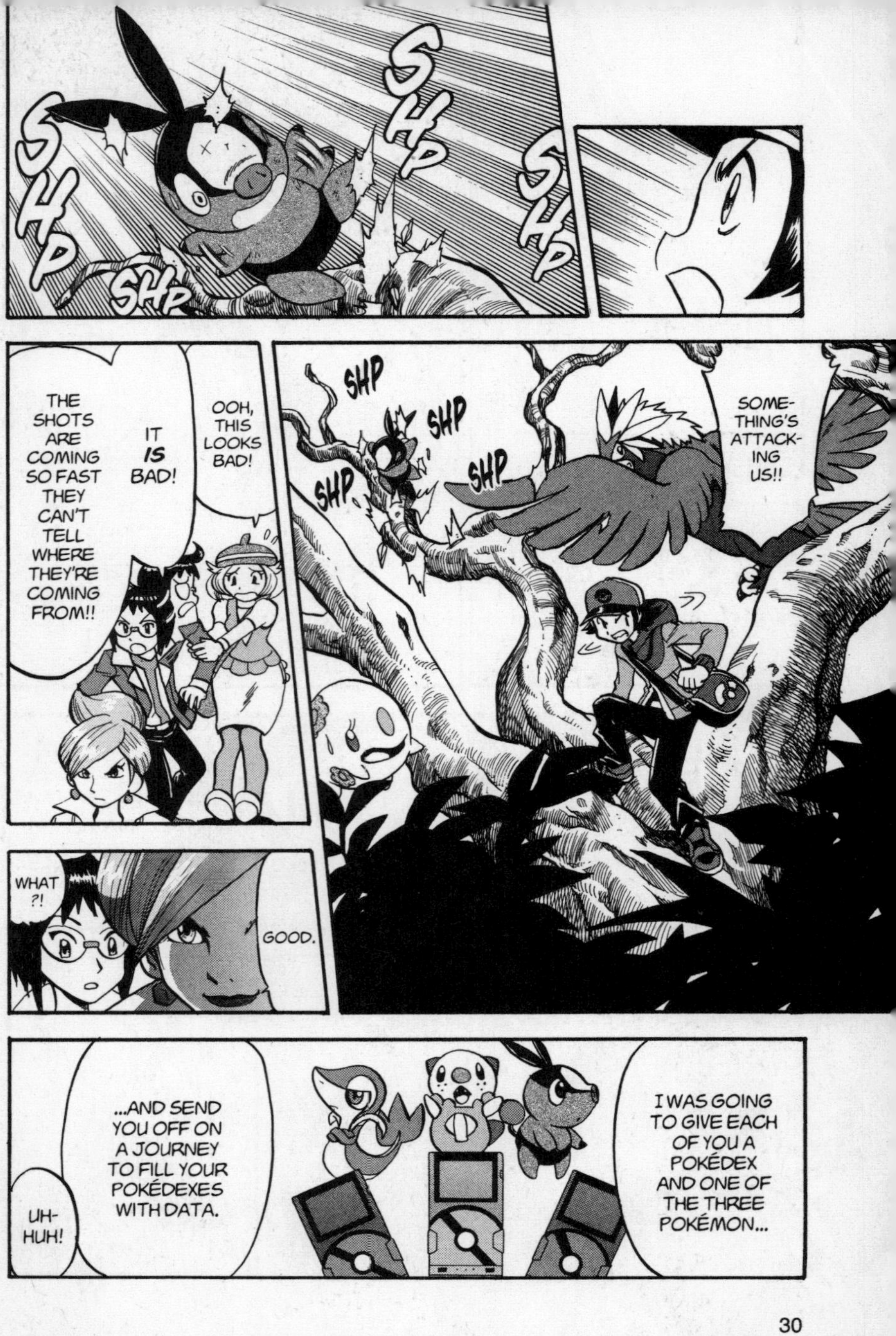
SHP
SHP
SHP
SHP
SOME-THING'S ATTACK-ING US!!
SHP
SHP
SHP
SHP
OOH, THIS LOOKS BAD!
IT IS BAD!
THE SHOTS ARE COMING SO FAST THEY CAN'T TELL WHERE THEY'RE COMING FROM!!
GOOD.
WHAT ?!
I WAS GOING TO GIVE EACH OF YOU A POKÉDEX AND ONE OF THE THREE POKÉMON...
...AND SEND YOU OFF ON A JOURNEY TO FILL YOUR POKÉDEXES WITH DATA.
UH-HUH!

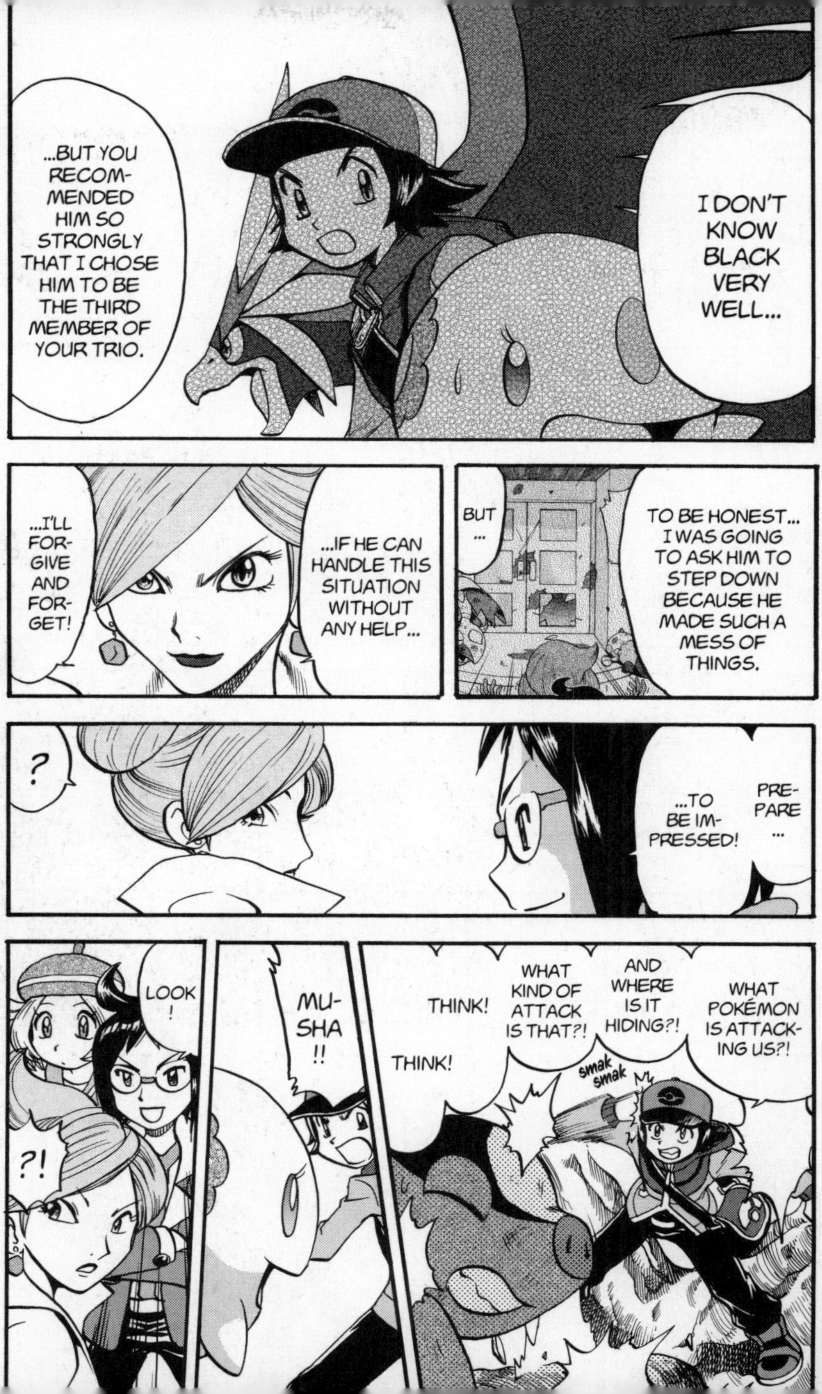
I DON'T KNOW BLACK VERY WELL...
...BUT YOU RECOMMENDED HIM SO STRONGLY THAT I CHOSE HIM TO BE THE THIRD MEMBER OF YOUR TRIO.
TO BE HONEST... I WAS GOING TO ASK HIM TO STEP DOWN BECAUSE HE MADE SUCH A MESS OF THINGS.
BUT ...
...IF HE CAN HANDLE THIS SITUATION WITHOUT ANY HELP...
...I'LL FORGIVE AND FORGET!
PREPARE ...
...TO BE IMPRESSED!
?
WHAT POKÉMON IS ATTACKING US?!
AND WHERE IS IT HIDING?!
WHAT KIND OF ATTACK IS THAT?!
THINK!
THINK!
smak smak
MUSHA!!
LOOK!
?!

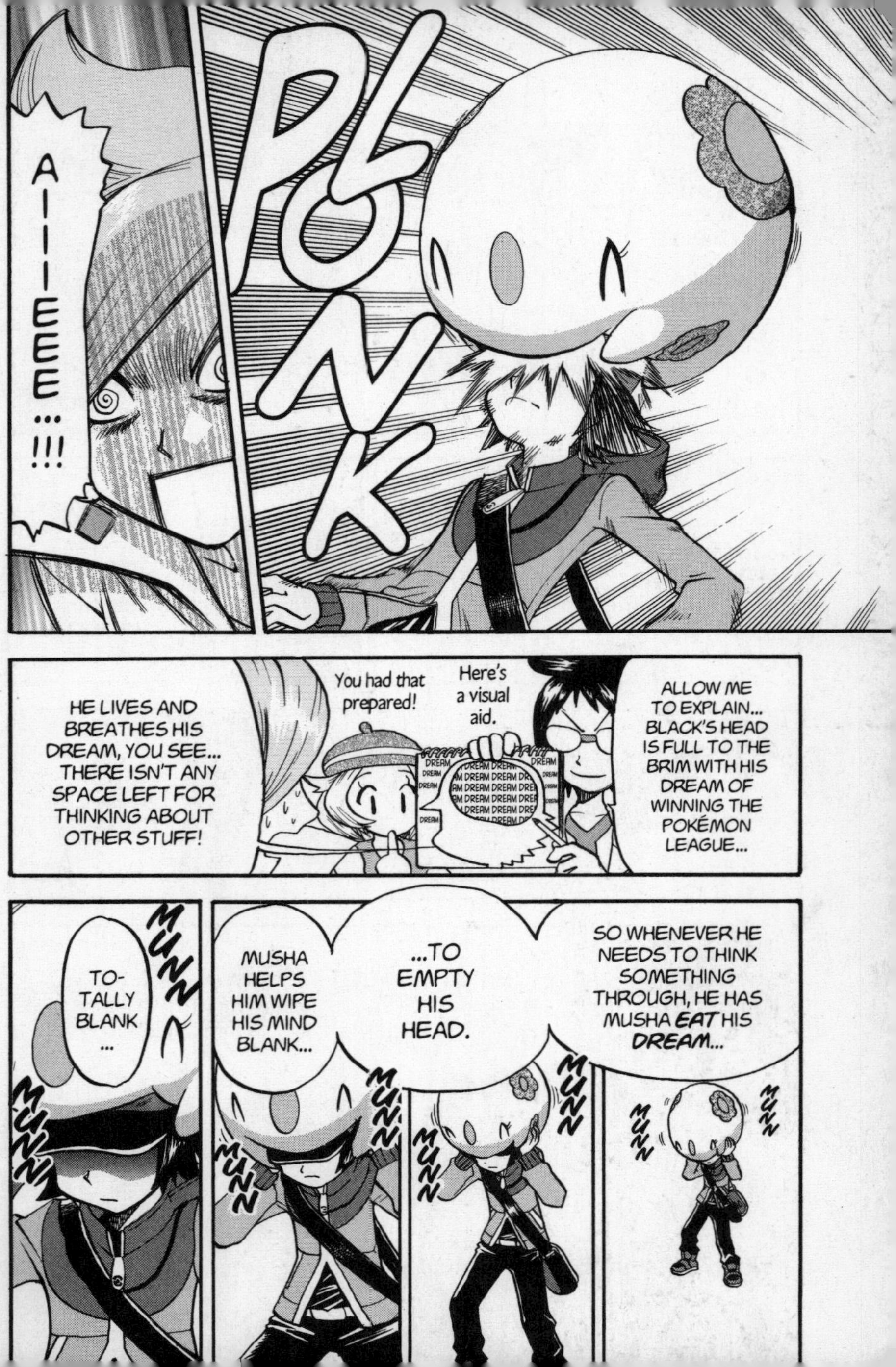
PONK
AIIIEEE...!!!
ALLOW ME TO EXPLAIN... BLACK'S HEAD IS FULL TO THE BRIM WITH HIS DREAM OF WINNING THE POKÉMON LEAGUE...
Here's a visual aid.
DREAM DREAM DREAM DREAM
You had that prepared!
HE LIVES AND BREATHES HIS DREAM, YOU SEE... THERE ISN'T ANY SPACE LEFT FOR THINKING ABOUT OTHER STUFF!
SO WHENEVER HE NEEDS TO THINK SOMETHING THROUGH, HE HAS MUSHA EAT HIS DREAM...
MUNN MUNN
...TO EMPTY HIS HEAD.
MUNN MUNN
MUSHA HELPS HIM WIPE HIS MIND BLANK...
MUNN MUNN
TO-TALLY BLANK...
MUNN MUNN

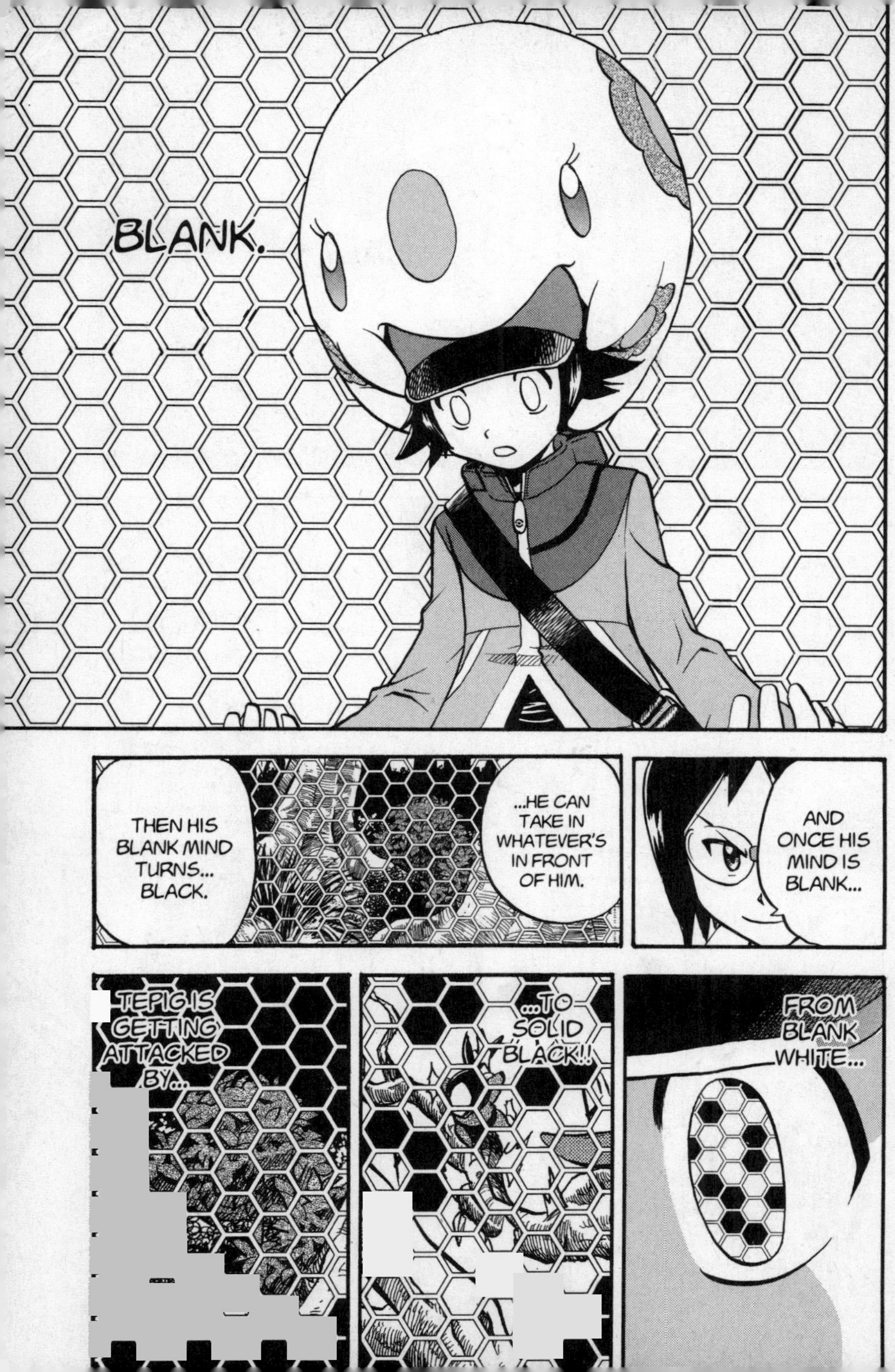
BLANK.
AND ONCE HIS MIND IS BLANK...
...HE CAN TAKE IN WHATEVER'S IN FRONT OF HIM.
THEN HIS BLANK MIND TURNS... BLACK.
FROM BLANK WHITE...
...TO SOLID BLACK!!
TEPIG IS GETTING ATTACKED BY...

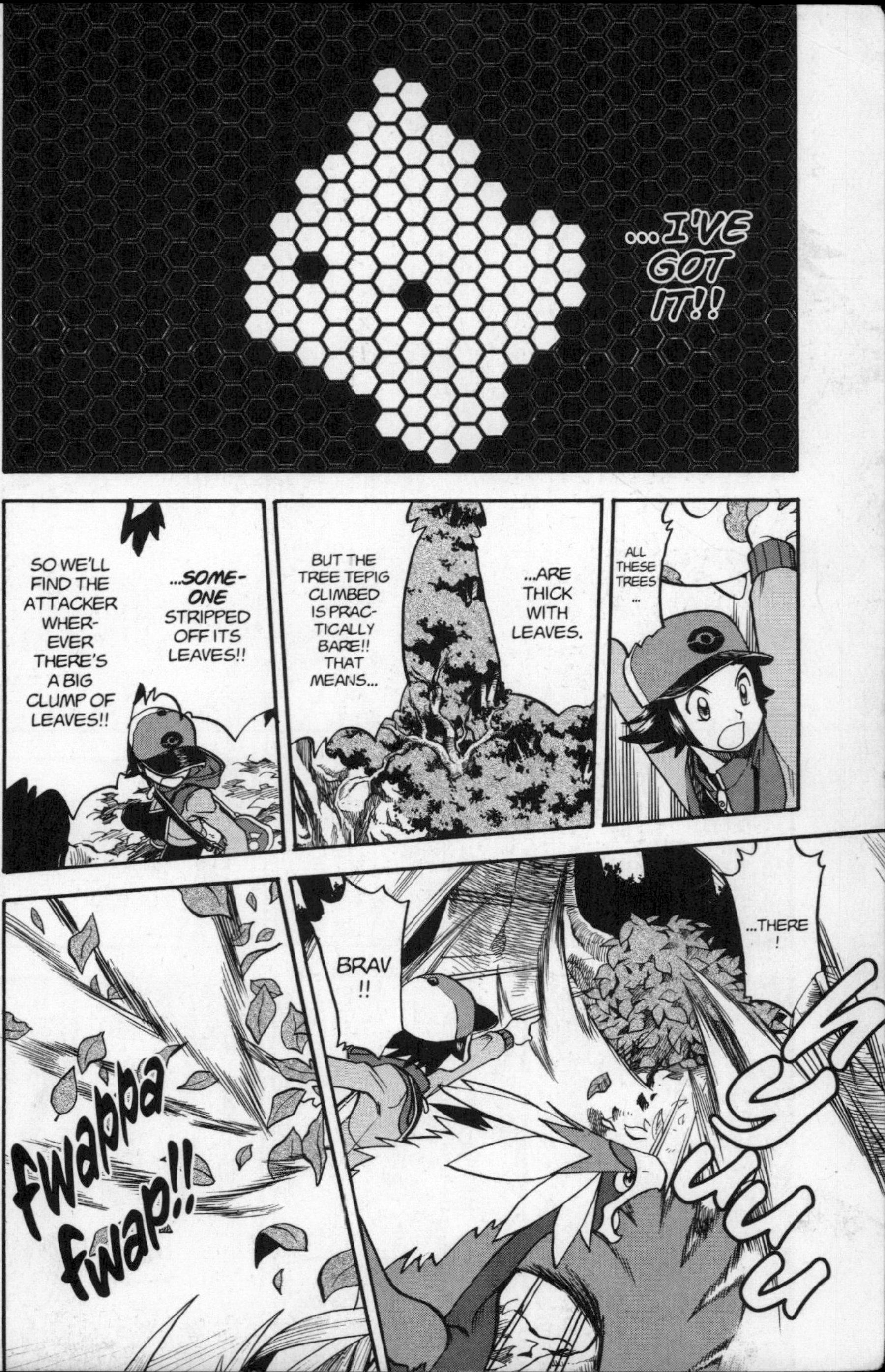
...I'VE GOT IT!!
ALL THESE TREES ...
...ARE THICK WITH LEAVES.
BUT THE TREE TEPIG CLIMBED IS PRACTICALLY BARE!! THAT MEANS...
...SOME-ONE STRIPPED OFF ITS LEAVES!!
SO WE'LL FIND THE ATTACKER WHER-EVER THERE'S A BIG CLUMP OF LEAVES!!
...THERE !
BRAV !!
fwappa fwap!!

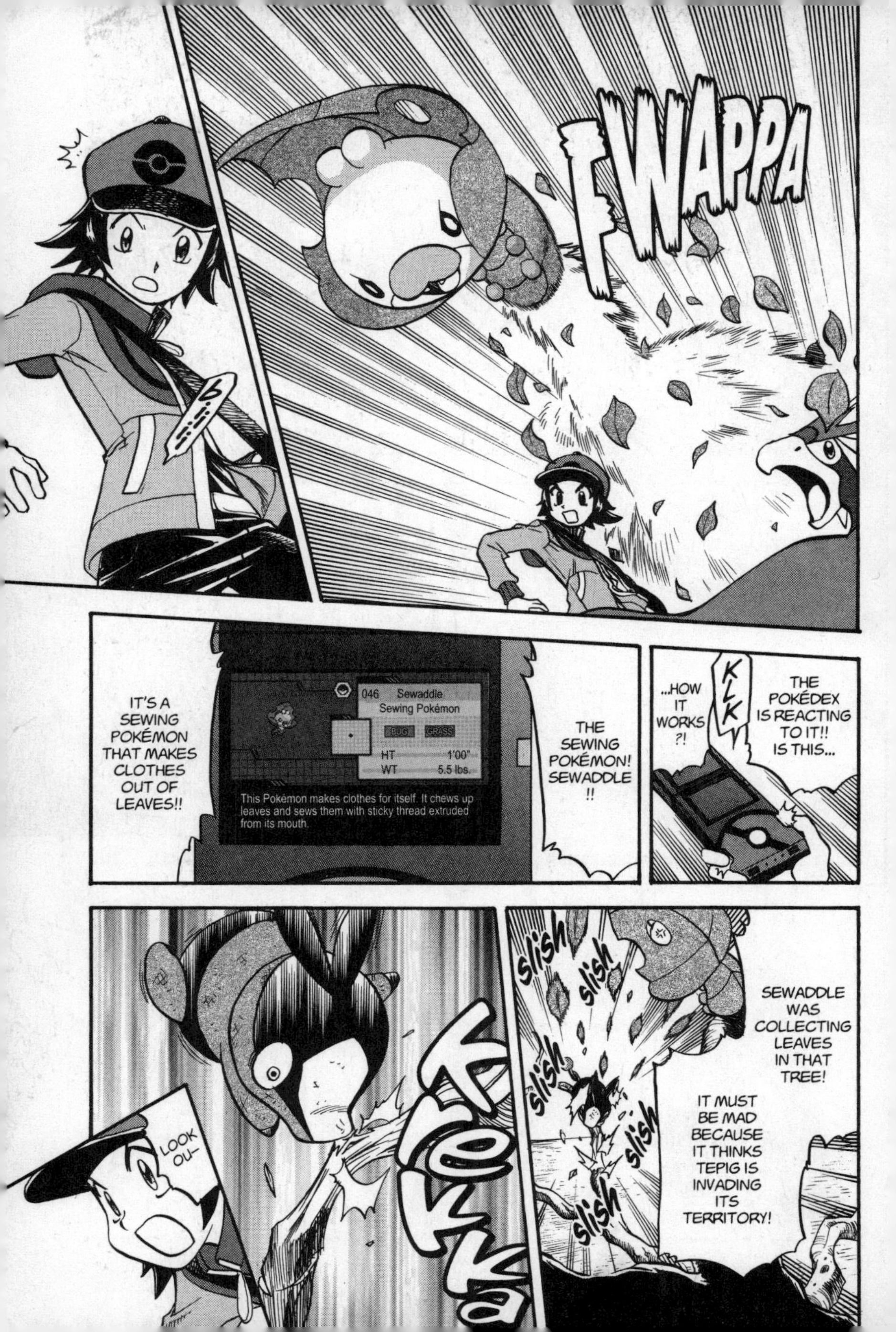
FWAPPA
THE POKÉDEX IS REACTING TO IT!! IS THIS...
KLK
...HOW IT WORKS?!
THE SEWING POKÉMON! SEWADDLE!!
046 Sewaddle
Sewing Pokémon
BUG GRASS
HT 1'00"
WT 5.5 lbs.
This Pokémon makes clothes for itself. It chews up leaves and sews them with sticky thread extruded from its mouth.
IT'S A SEWING POKÉMON THAT MAKES CLOTHES OUT OF LEAVES!!
slish slish slish slish slish slish slish
SEWADDLE WAS COLLECTING LEAVES IN THAT TREE!
IT MUST BE MAD BECAUSE IT THINKS TEPIG IS INVADING ITS TERRITORY!
LOOK OU—

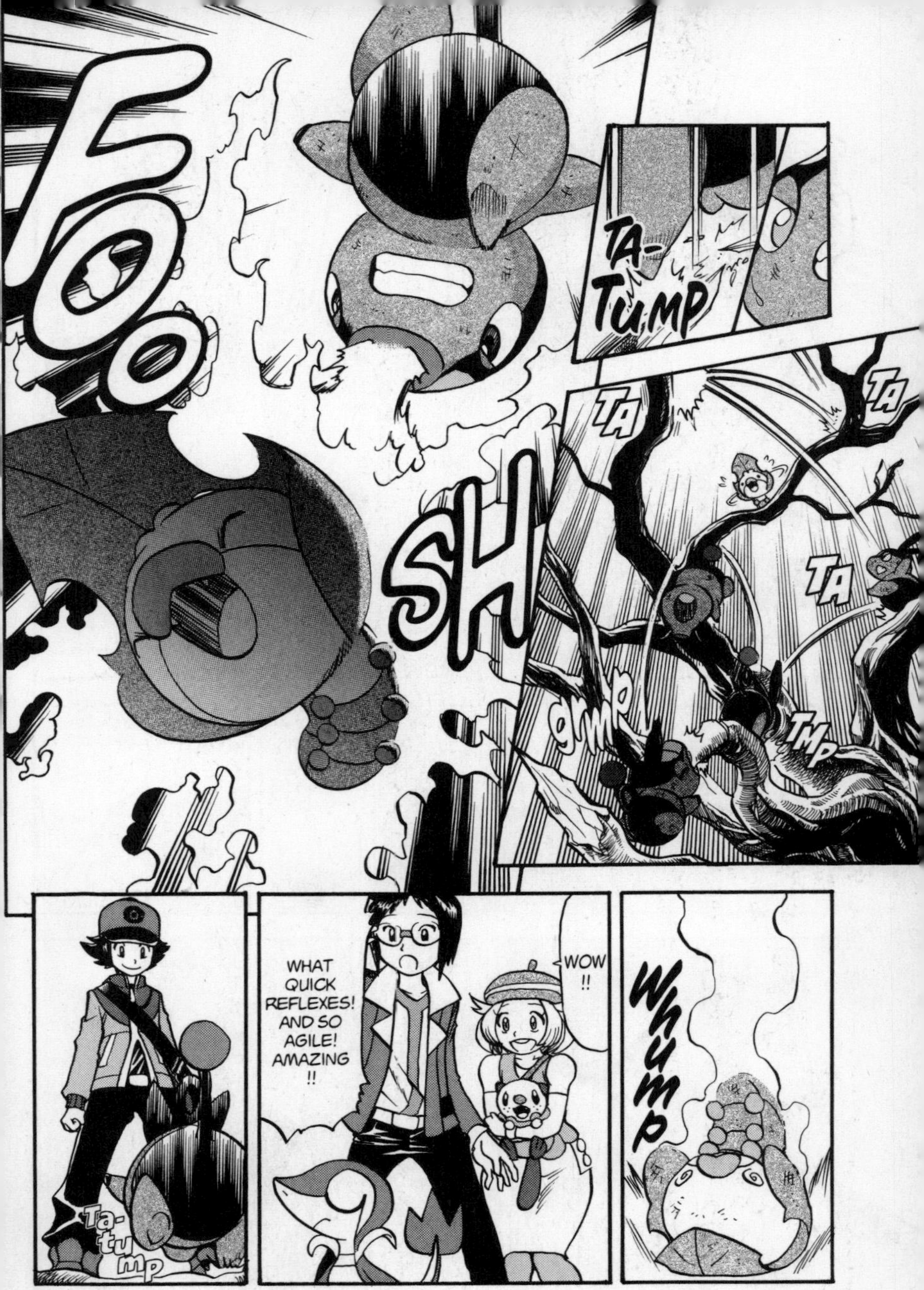
TA-TUMP
TA
TA
TA
TMP
grmp
FOO
SH
WHUMP
WOW !!
WHAT QUICK REFLEXES! AND SO AGILE! AMAZING !!
Ta-tump

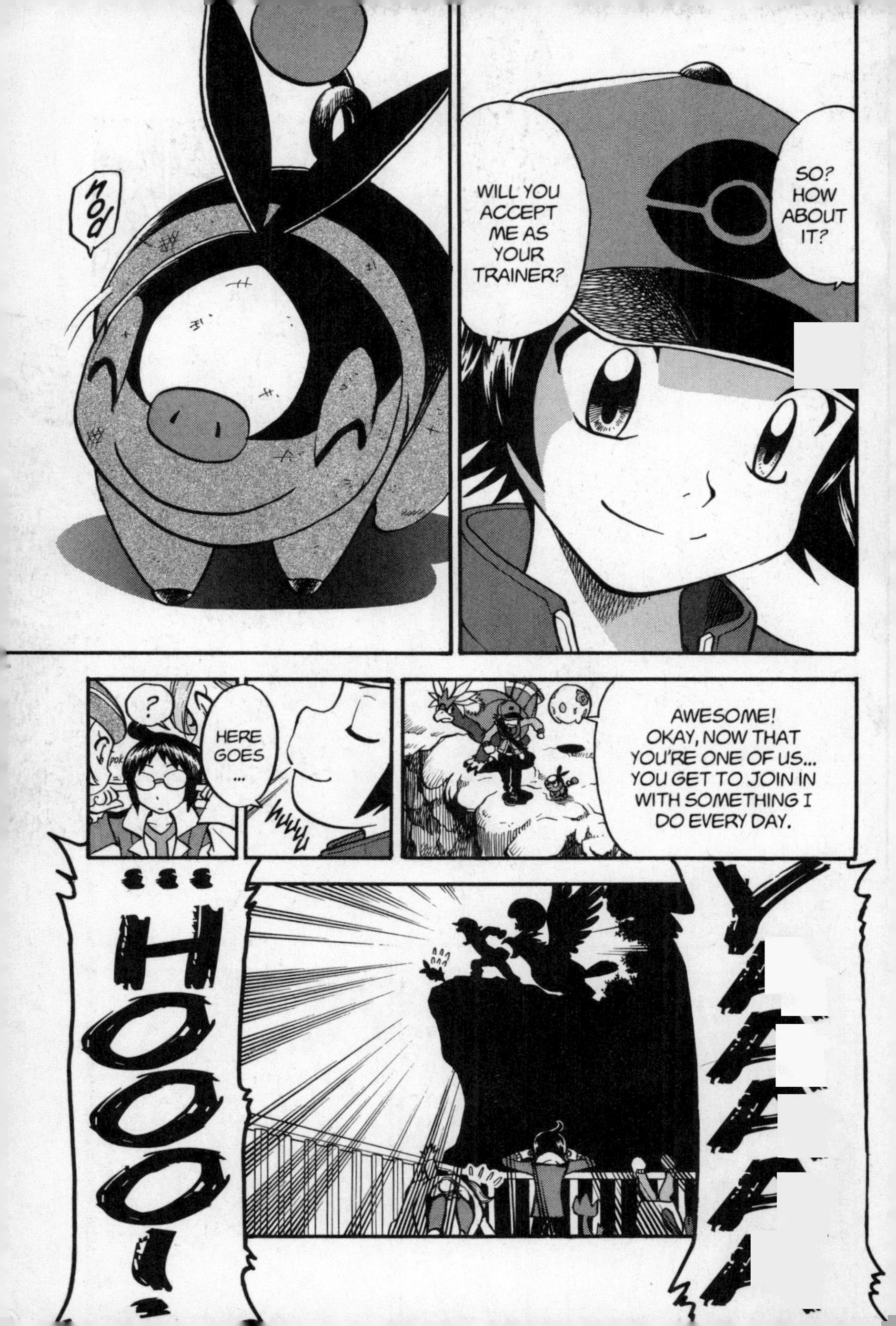
SO? HOW ABOUT IT?
WILL YOU ACCEPT ME AS YOUR TRAINER?
nod
AWESOME! OKAY, NOW THAT YOU'RE ONE OF US... YOU GET TO JOIN IN WITH SOMETHING I DO EVERY DAY.
HERE GOES ...
?
Y
...HOOO!!

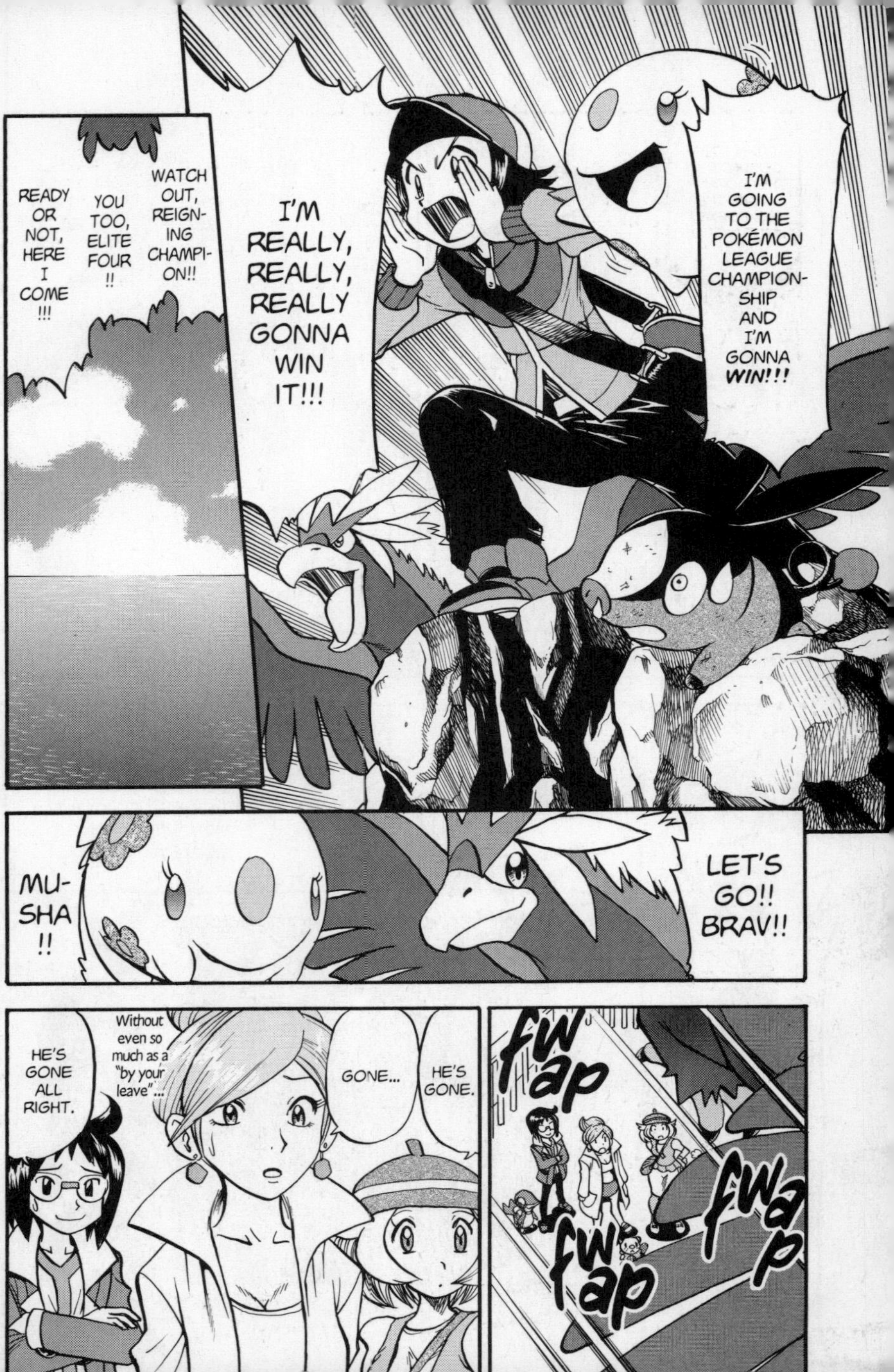
I'M GOING TO THE POKÉMON LEAGUE CHAMPIONSHIP AND I'M GONNA **WIN!!!**
I'M REALLY, REALLY, REALLY GONNA WIN IT!!!
WATCH OUT, REIGNING CHAMPION!!
YOU TOO, ELITE FOUR!!
READY OR NOT, HERE I COME!!!
LET'S GO!! BRAV!!
MU-SHA!!
fwap
fwap
fwap
HE'S GONE.
GONE...
Without even so much as a "by your leave"...
HE'S GONE ALL RIGHT.

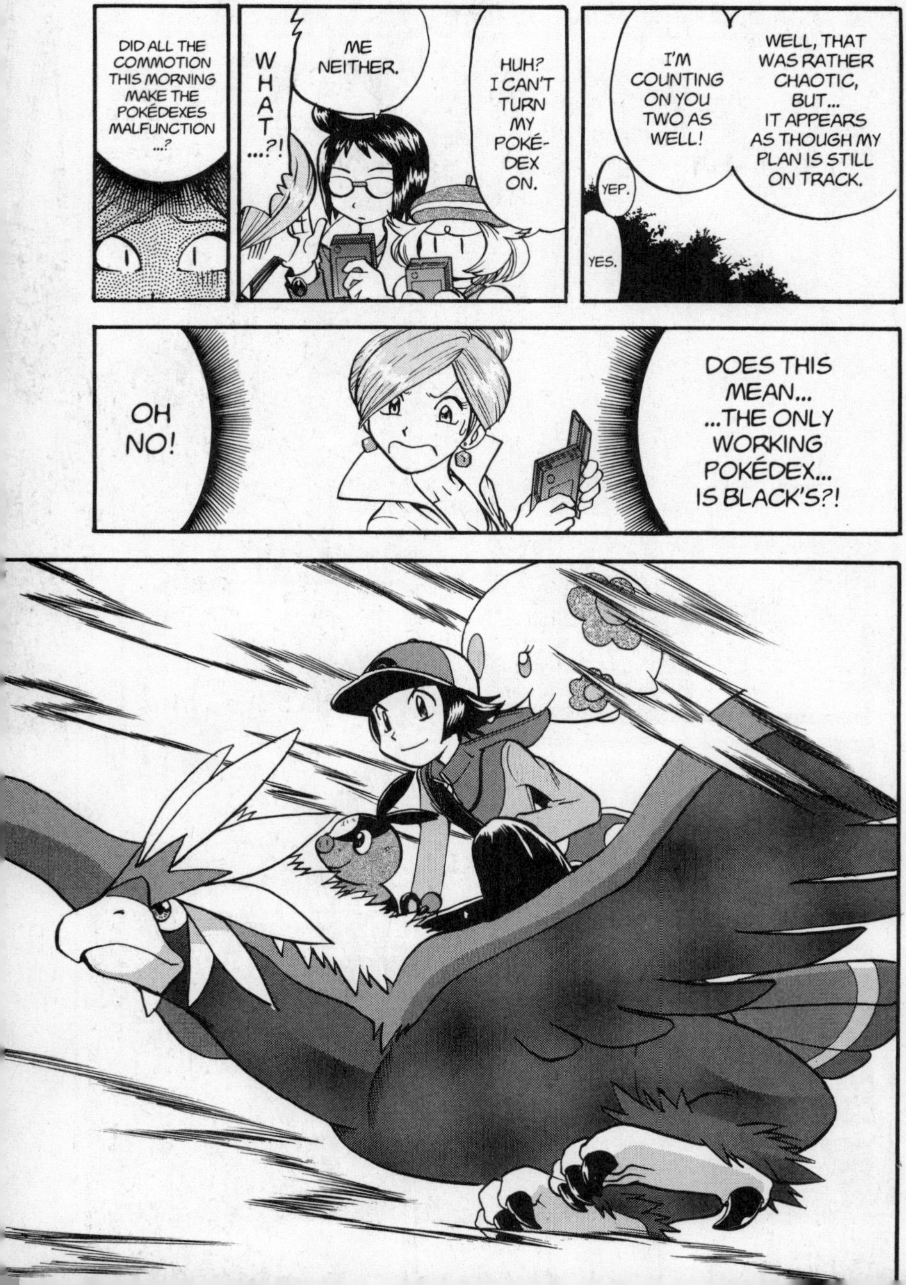
WELL, THAT WAS RATHER CHAOTIC, BUT... IT APPEARS AS THOUGH MY PLAN IS STILL ON TRACK.
I'M COUNTING ON YOU TWO AS WELL!
YEP.
YES.
HUH? I CAN'T TURN MY POKÉ-DEX ON.
ME NEITHER.
WHAT ...?!
DID ALL THE COMMOTION THIS MORNING MAKE THE POKÉDEXES MALFUNCTION ...?
DOES THIS MEAN... ...THE ONLY WORKING POKÉDEX... IS BLACK'S?!
OH NO!

ADVENTURE MAP

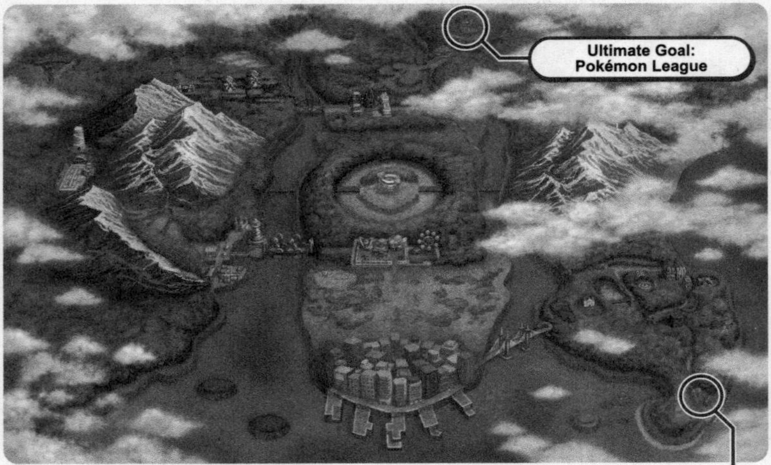
Ultimate Goal:
Pokémon League
Current Location: Nuvema Town

BLACK

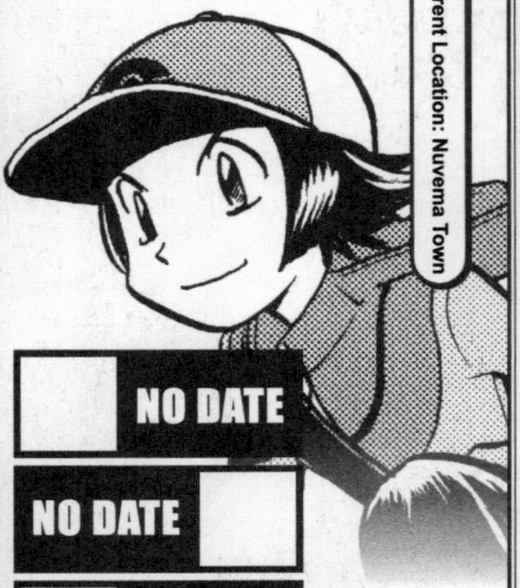

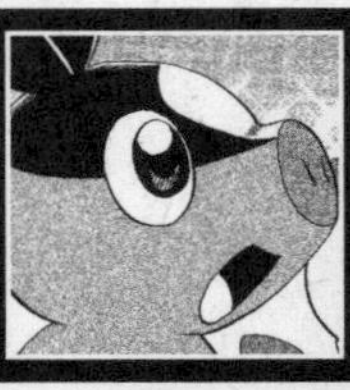

Level 8

Tepig

Tepig ♂

Fire Pig Pokémon

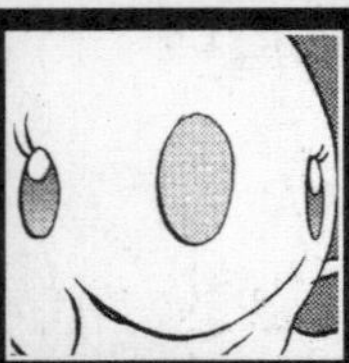

Level 30

Musha

Munna ♂

Dream Eater Pokémon

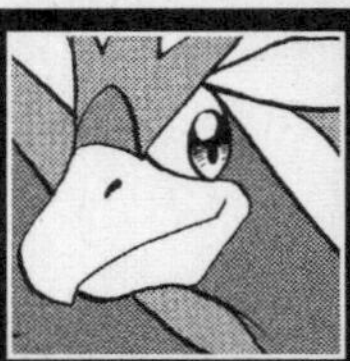

Level 54

Brav

Braviary ♂

Valiant Pokémon

NO DATE

NO DATE

NO DATE

Pokémon ADVENTURES
BLACK & WHITE

Adventure ③
A Nickname for Tepig

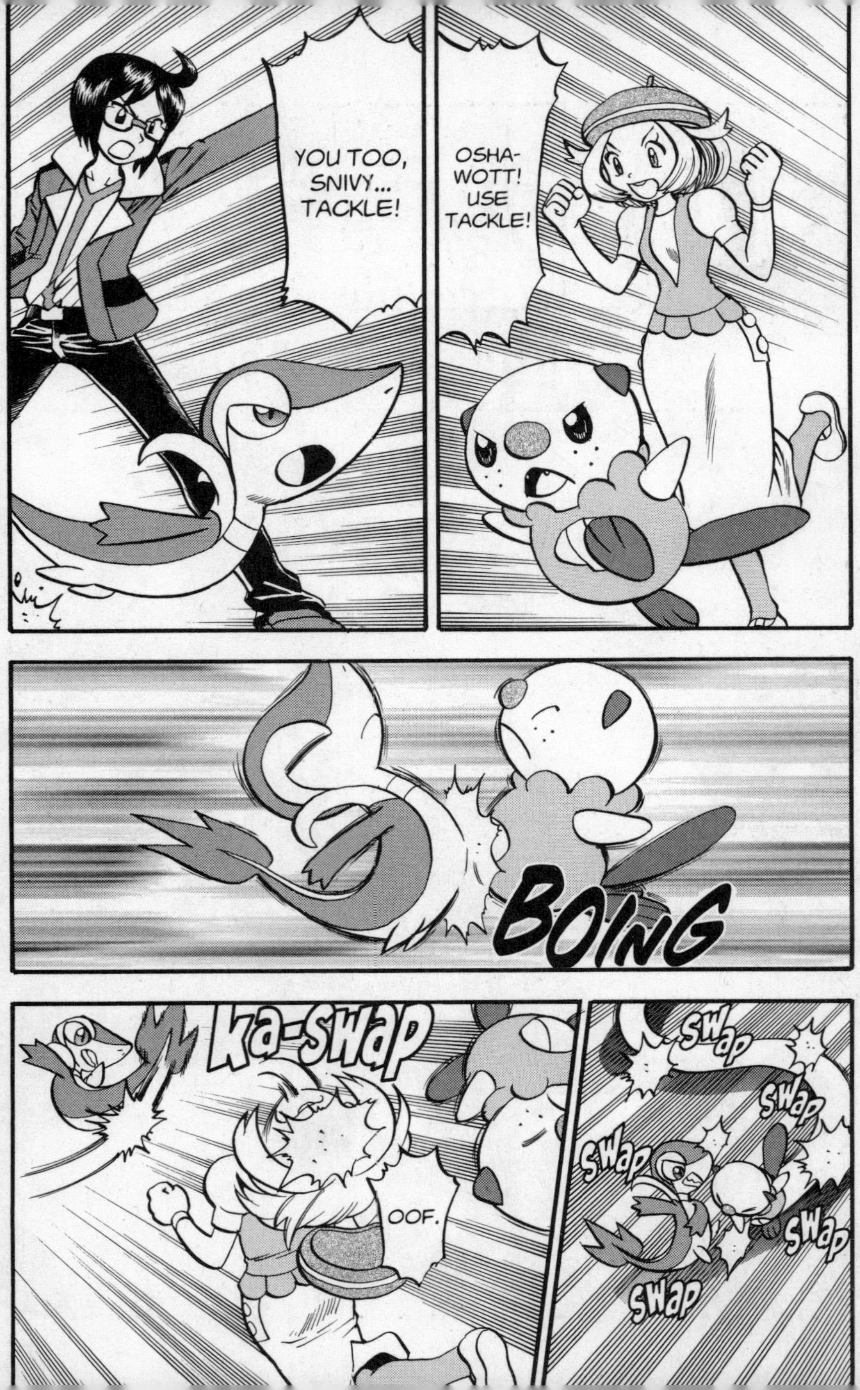
OSHA-WOTT! USE TACKLE!
YOU TOO, SNIVY... TACKLE!
BOING
SWAP
SWAP
SWAP
SWAP
SWAP
KA-SWAP
OOF.

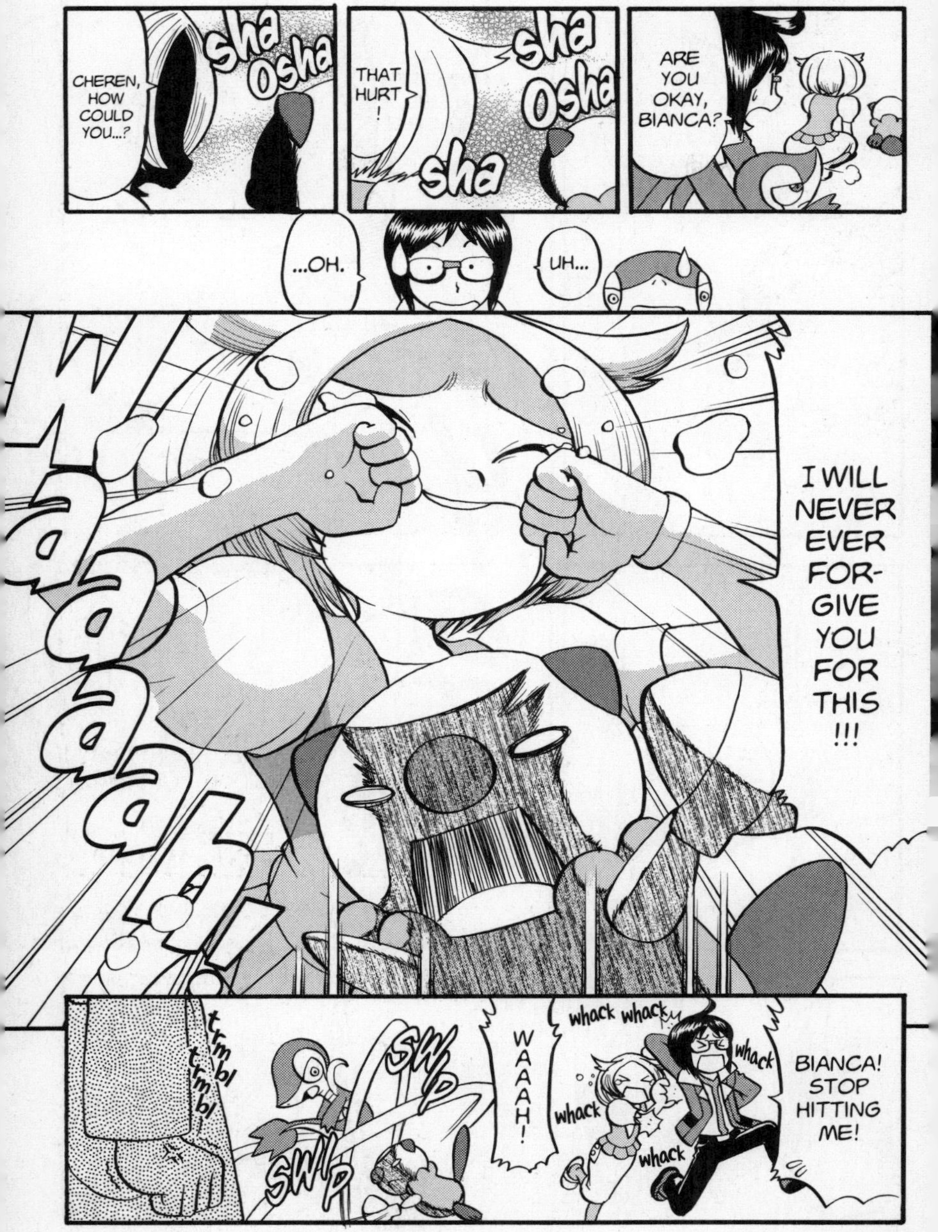
ARE YOU OKAY, BIANCA?
THAT HURT!
sha osha
sha
CHEREN, HOW COULD YOU...?
sha osha
UH...
...OH.
I WILL NEVER EVER FOR-GIVE YOU FOR THIS!!!
Waaaah!
BIANCA! STOP HITTING ME!
whack whack
whack
whack
whack
WAAAAH!
swip
swip
trmbl trmbl

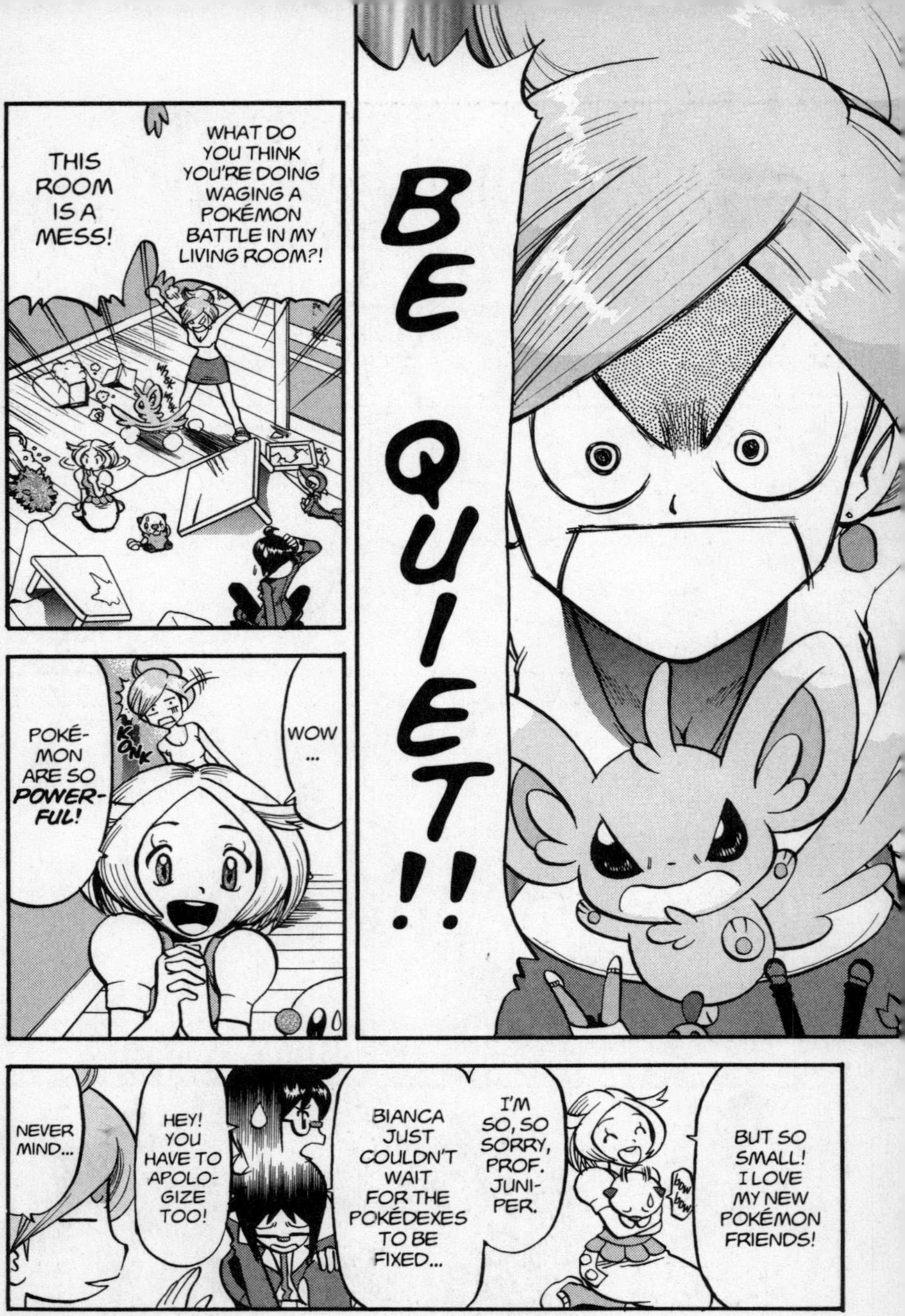
BE QUIET!!
WHAT DO YOU THINK YOU'RE DOING WAGING A POKÉMON BATTLE IN MY LIVING ROOM?!
THIS ROOM IS A MESS!
WOW...
POKÉ-MON ARE SO POWER-FUL!
KONK
BUT SO SMALL! I LOVE MY NEW POKÉMON FRIENDS!
bow bow
I'M SO, SO SORRY, PROF. JUNI-PER.
BIANCA JUST COULDN'T WAIT FOR THE POKÉDEXES TO BE FIXED...
HEY! YOU HAVE TO APOLO-GIZE TOO!
NEVER MIND...

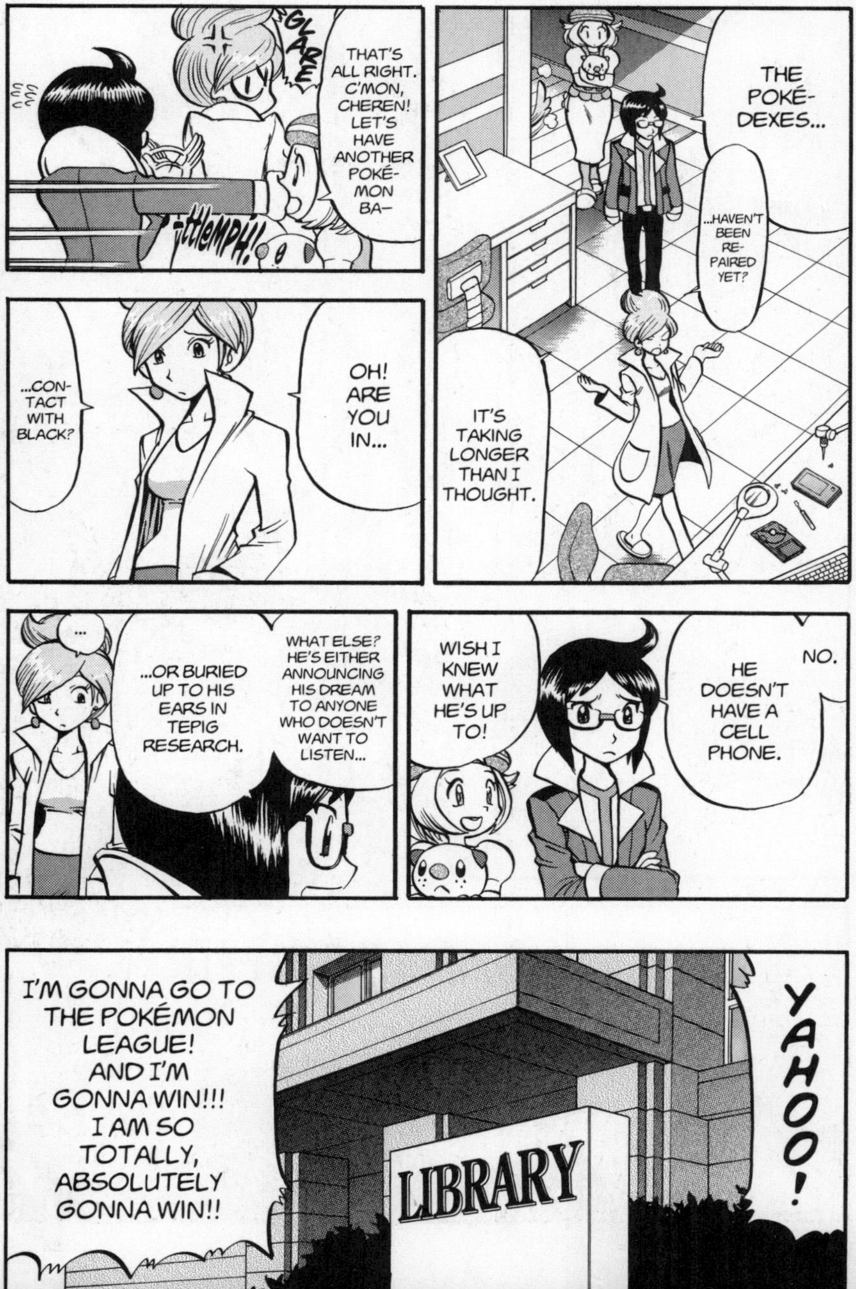
THE POKÉ-DEXES...
...HAVEN'T BEEN RE-PAIRED YET?
IT'S TAKING LONGER THAN I THOUGHT.
THAT'S ALL RIGHT. C'MON, CHEREN! LET'S HAVE ANOTHER POKÉMON BA–
GLARE
P-TTLEMPH!
OH! ARE YOU IN...
...CONTACT WITH BLACK?
NO.
HE DOESN'T HAVE A CELL PHONE.
WISH I KNEW WHAT HE'S UP TO!
WHAT ELSE? HE'S EITHER ANNOUNCING HIS DREAM TO ANYONE WHO DOESN'T WANT TO LISTEN...
...OR BURIED UP TO HIS EARS IN TEPIG RESEARCH.
...
YAHOO!
I'M GONNA GO TO THE POKÉMON LEAGUE! AND I'M GONNA WIN!!! I AM SO TOTALLY, ABSOLUTELY GONNA WIN!!
LIBRARY

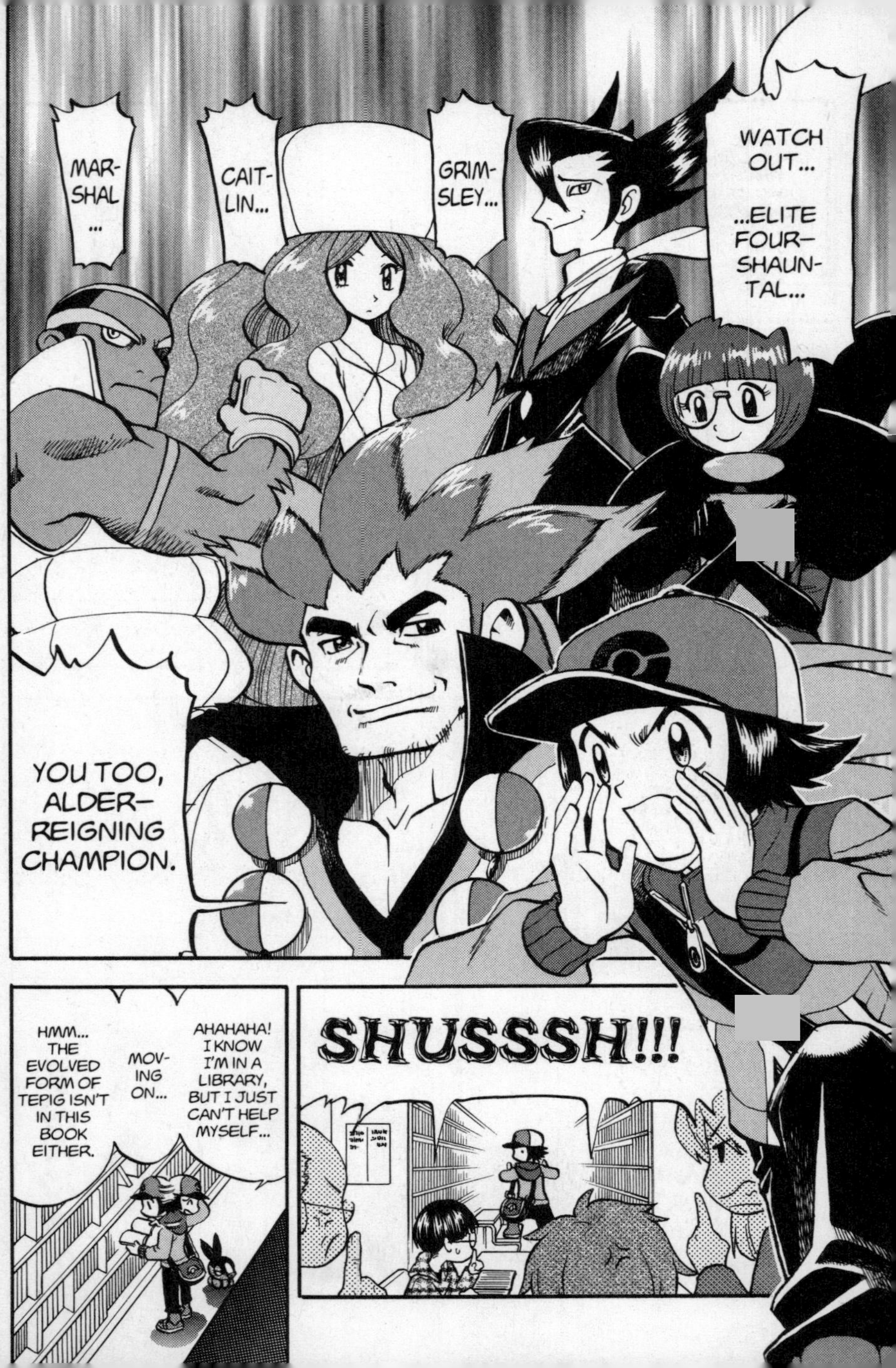
WATCH OUT... ...ELITE FOUR—SHAUNTAL...
GRIMSLEY...
CAITLIN...
MARSHAL...
YOU TOO, ALDER—REIGNING CHAMPION.
SHUSSSSH!!!
AHAHAHA! I KNOW I'M IN A LIBRARY, BUT I JUST CAN'T HELP MYSELF...
MOVING ON...
HMM... THE EVOLVED FORM OF TEPIG ISN'T IN THIS BOOK EITHER.

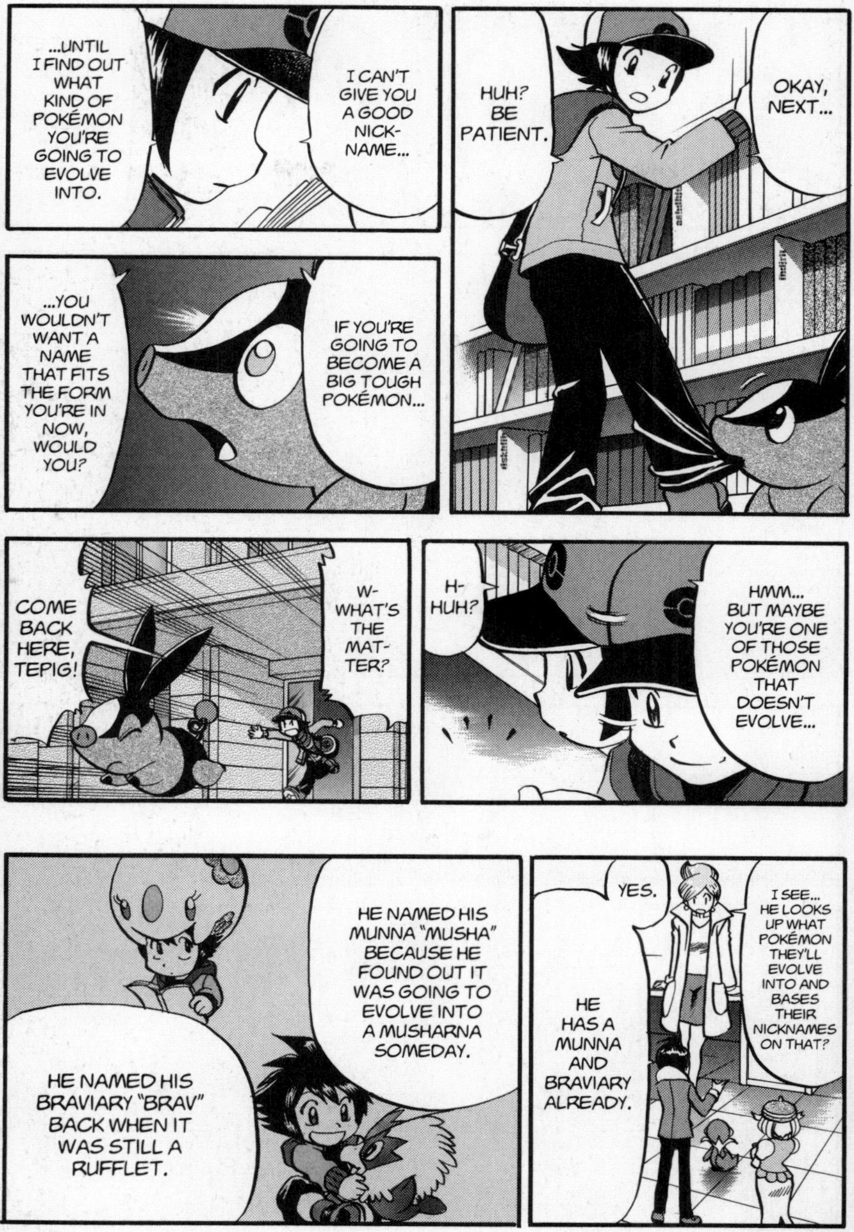
OKAY, NEXT...
HUH? BE PATIENT.
I CAN'T GIVE YOU A GOOD NICK-NAME...
...UNTIL I FIND OUT WHAT KIND OF POKÉMON YOU'RE GOING TO EVOLVE INTO.
IF YOU'RE GOING TO BECOME A BIG TOUGH POKÉMON...
...YOU WOULDN'T WANT A NAME THAT FITS THE FORM YOU'RE IN NOW, WOULD YOU?
HMM... BUT MAYBE YOU'RE ONE OF THOSE POKÉMON THAT DOESN'T EVOLVE...
H-HUH?
W-WHAT'S THE MAT-TER?
COME BACK HERE, TEPIG!
I SEE... HE LOOKS UP WHAT POKÉMON THEY'LL EVOLVE INTO AND BASES THEIR NICKNAMES ON THAT?
YES.
HE HAS A MUNNA AND BRAVIARY ALREADY.
HE NAMED HIS MUNNA "MUSHA" BECAUSE HE FOUND OUT IT WAS GOING TO EVOLVE INTO A MUSHARNA SOMEDAY.
HE NAMED HIS BRAVIARY "BRAV" BACK WHEN IT WAS STILL A RUFFLET.

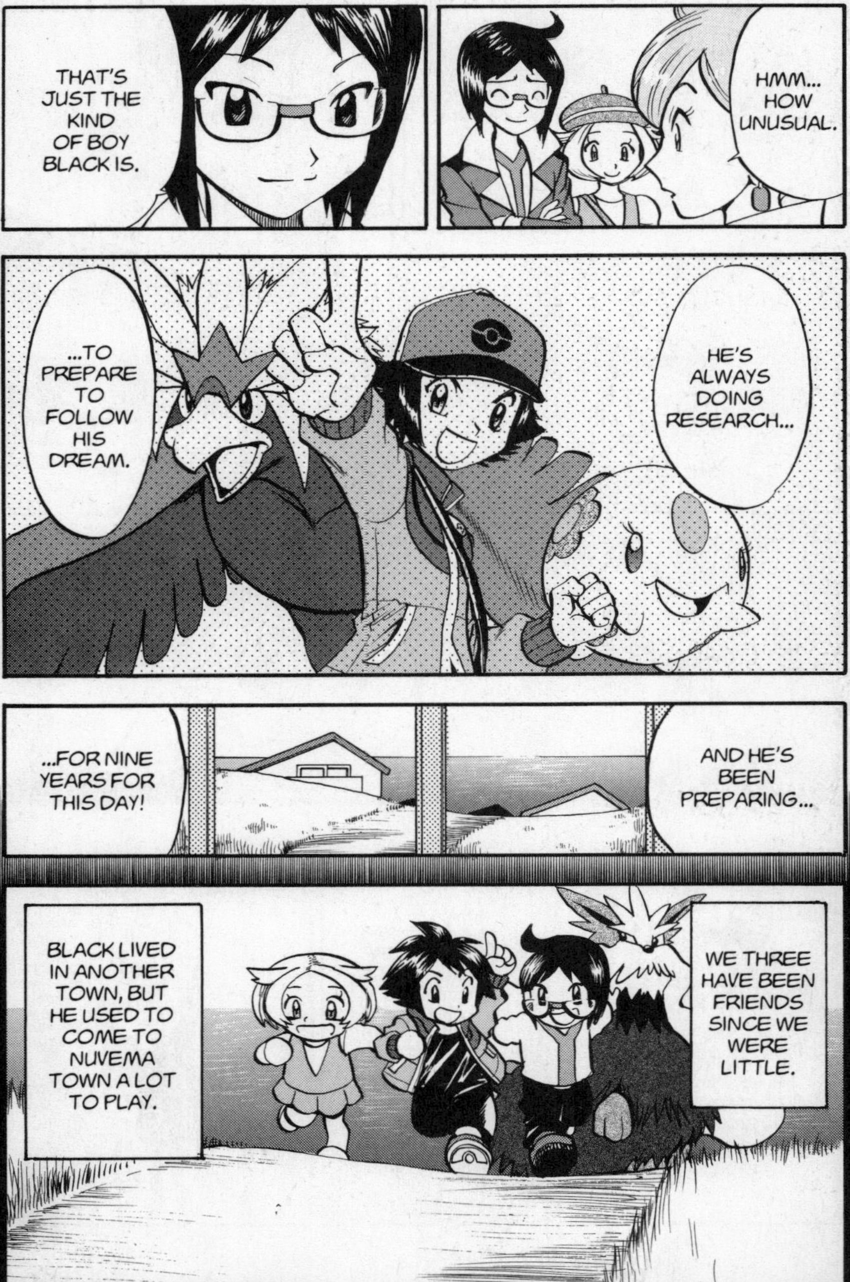
HMM... HOW UNUSUAL.
THAT'S JUST THE KIND OF BOY BLACK IS.
HE'S ALWAYS DOING RESEARCH...
...TO PREPARE TO FOLLOW HIS DREAM.
AND HE'S BEEN PREPARING...
...FOR NINE YEARS FOR THIS DAY!
WE THREE HAVE BEEN FRIENDS SINCE WE WERE LITTLE.
BLACK LIVED IN ANOTHER TOWN, BUT HE USED TO COME TO NUVEMA TOWN A LOT TO PLAY.

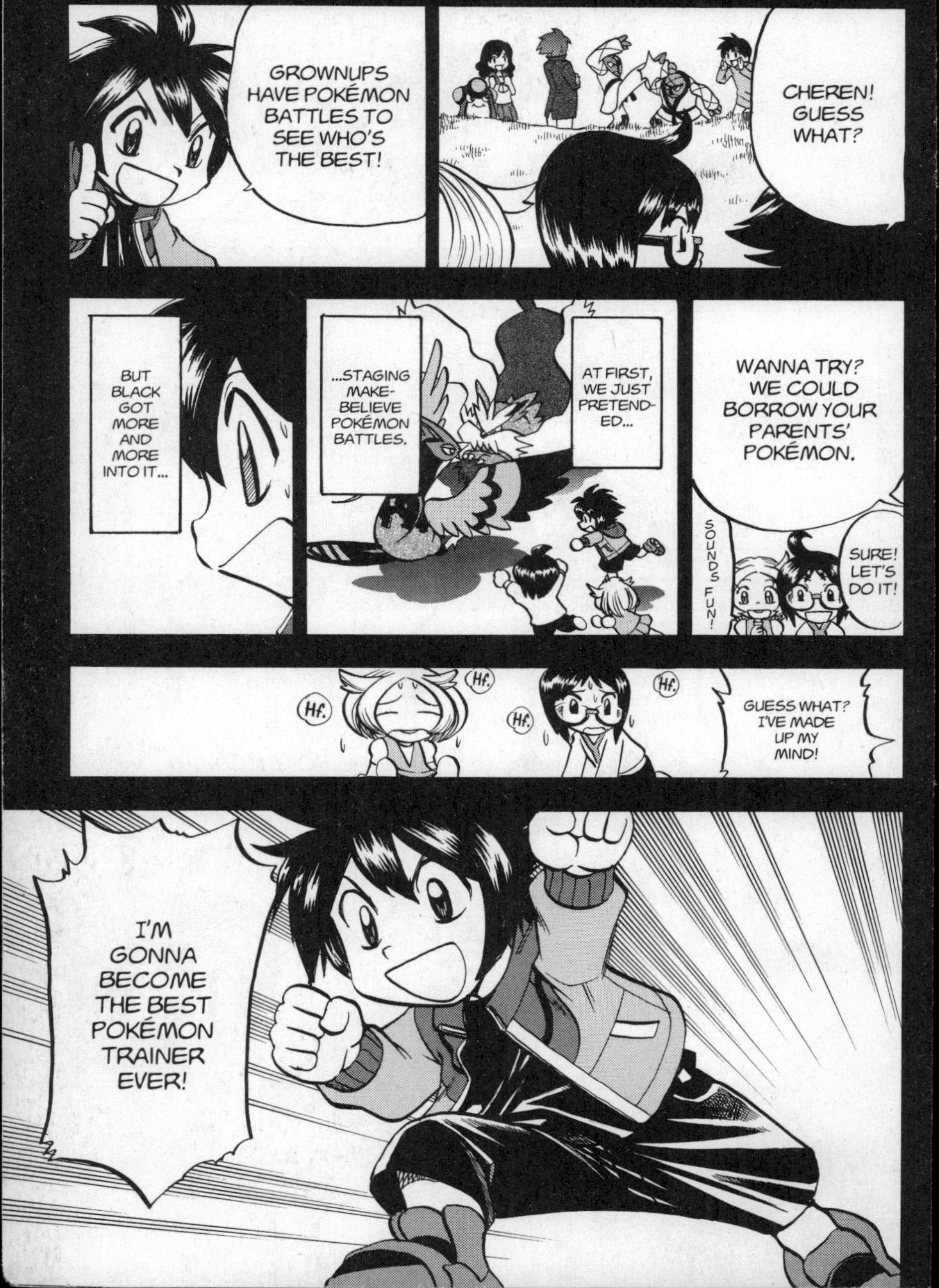
CHEREN! GUESS WHAT?
GROWNUPS HAVE POKÉMON BATTLES TO SEE WHO'S THE BEST!
WANNA TRY? WE COULD BORROW YOUR PARENTS' POKÉMON.
SURE! LET'S DO IT!
SOUNDS FUN!
AT FIRST, WE JUST PRETEND-ED...
...STAGING MAKE-BELIEVE POKÉMON BATTLES.
BUT BLACK GOT MORE AND MORE INTO IT...
GUESS WHAT? I'VE MADE UP MY MIND!
Hf.
Hf.
Hf.
Hf.
I'M GONNA BECOME THE BEST POKÉMON TRAINER EVER!

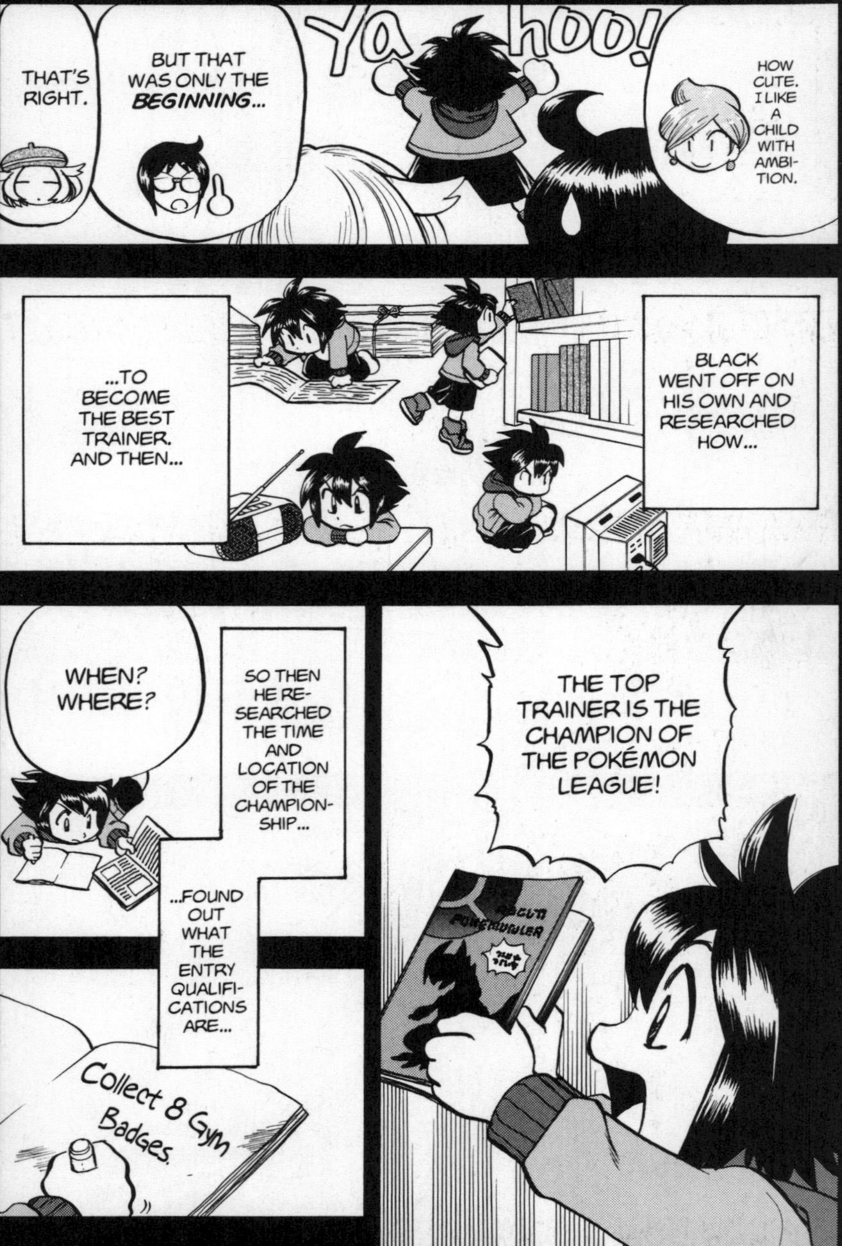
Ya hoo!
HOW CUTE. I LIKE A CHILD WITH AMBITION.
BUT THAT WAS ONLY THE ***BEGINNING***...
THAT'S RIGHT.
BLACK WENT OFF ON HIS OWN AND RESEARCHED HOW...
...TO BECOME THE BEST TRAINER. AND THEN...
THE TOP TRAINER IS THE CHAMPION OF THE POKÉMON LEAGUE!
SO THEN HE RESEARCHED THE TIME AND LOCATION OF THE CHAMPIONSHIP...
WHEN? WHERE?
...FOUND OUT WHAT THE ENTRY QUALIFICATIONS ARE...
Collect 8 Gym Badges.

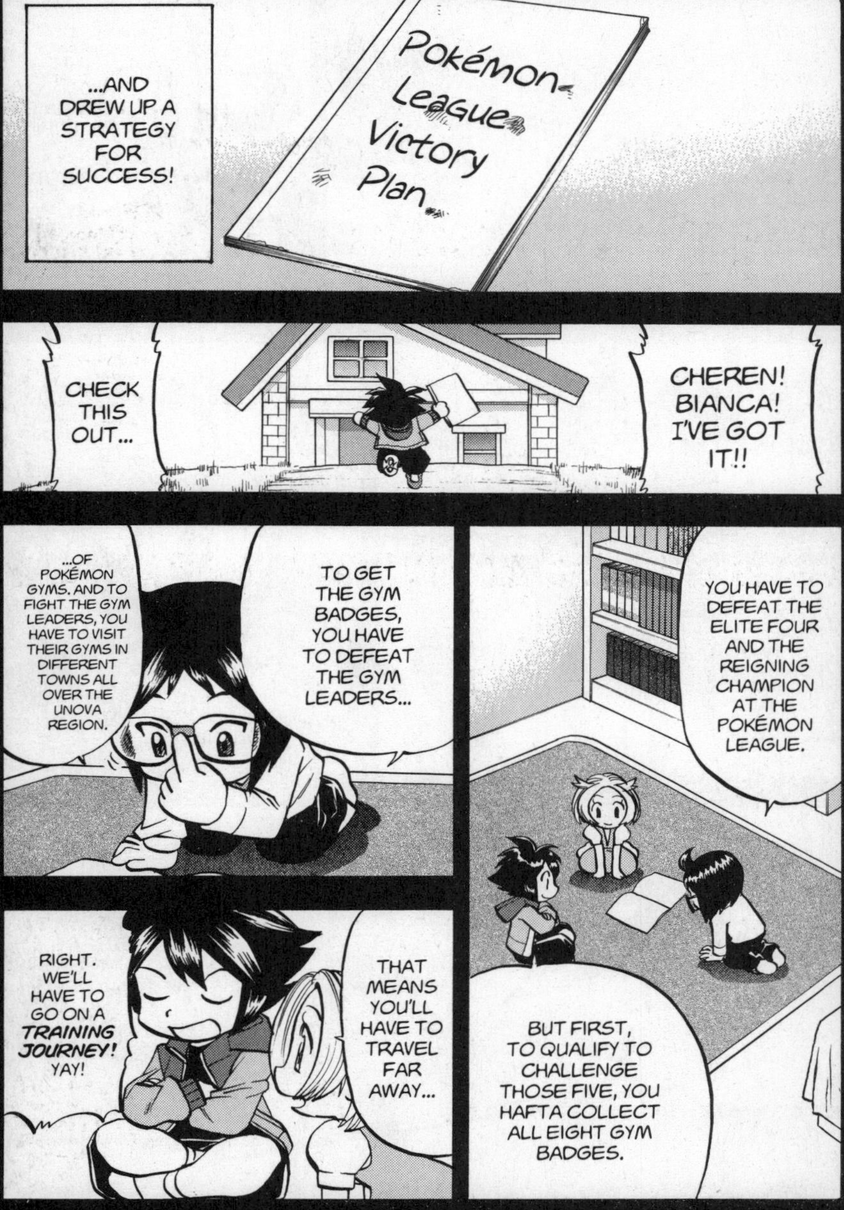
...AND DREW UP A STRATEGY FOR SUCCESS!
Pokémon League Victory Plan
CHEREN! BIANCA! I'VE GOT IT!!
CHECK THIS OUT...
YOU HAVE TO DEFEAT THE ELITE FOUR AND THE REIGNING CHAMPION AT THE POKÉMON LEAGUE.
BUT FIRST, TO QUALIFY TO CHALLENGE THOSE FIVE, YOU HAFTA COLLECT ALL EIGHT GYM BADGES.
TO GET THE GYM BADGES, YOU HAVE TO DEFEAT THE GYM LEADERS...
...OF POKÉMON GYMS. AND TO FIGHT THE GYM LEADERS, YOU HAVE TO VISIT THEIR GYMS IN DIFFERENT TOWNS ALL OVER THE UNOVA REGION.
THAT MEANS YOU'LL HAVE TO TRAVEL FAR AWAY...
RIGHT. WE'LL HAVE TO GO ON A ***TRAINING JOURNEY!*** YAY!

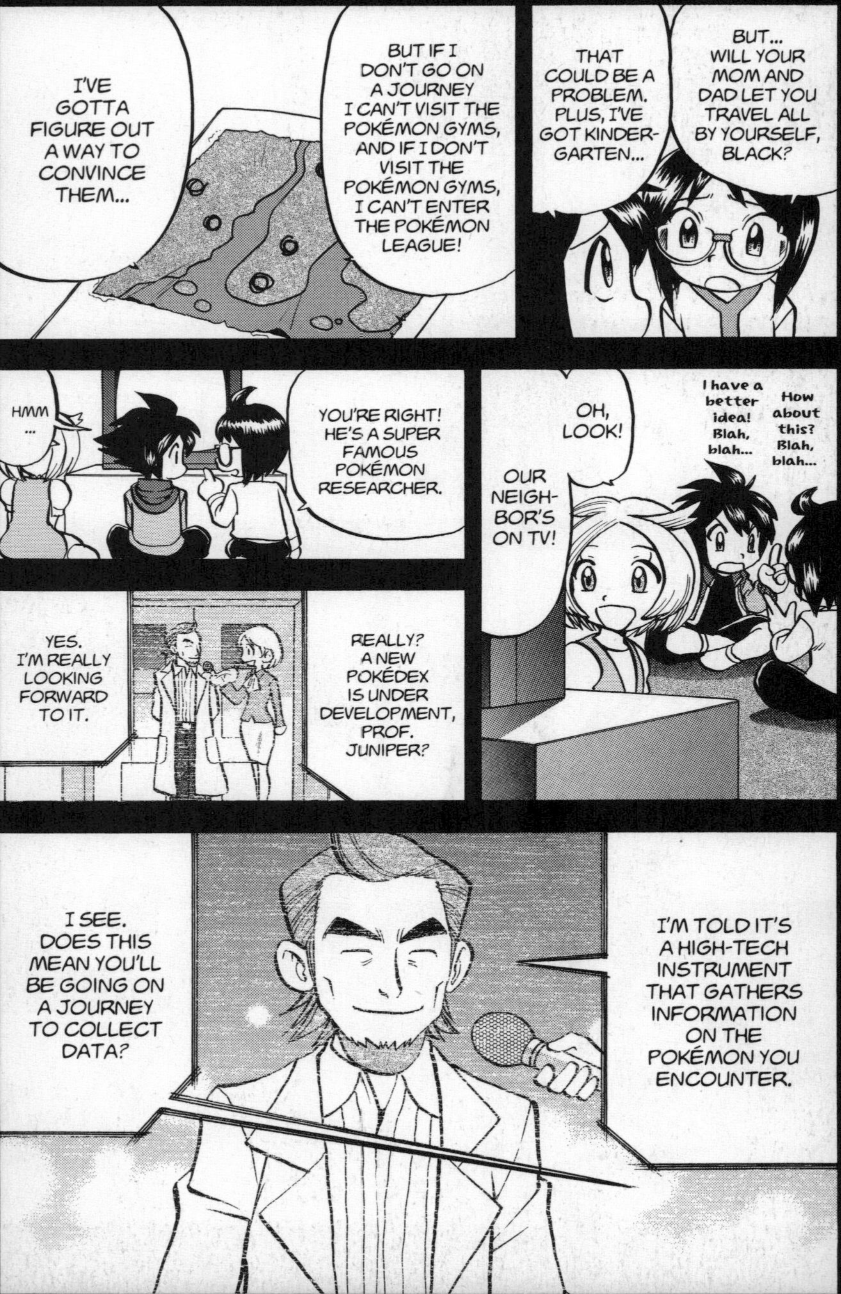
BUT... WILL YOUR MOM AND DAD LET YOU TRAVEL ALL BY YOURSELF, BLACK?
THAT COULD BE A PROBLEM. PLUS, I'VE GOT KINDER-GARTEN...
BUT IF I DON'T GO ON A JOURNEY I CAN'T VISIT THE POKÉMON GYMS, AND IF I DON'T VISIT THE POKÉMON GYMS, I CAN'T ENTER THE POKÉMON LEAGUE!
I'VE GOTTA FIGURE OUT A WAY TO CONVINCE THEM...
How about this? Blah, blah...
I have a better idea! Blah, blah...
OH, LOOK!
OUR NEIGH-BOR'S ON TV!
YOU'RE RIGHT! HE'S A SUPER FAMOUS POKÉMON RESEARCHER.
HMM ...
REALLY? A NEW POKÉDEX IS UNDER DEVELOPMENT, PROF. JUNIPER?
YES. I'M REALLY LOOKING FORWARD TO IT.
I'M TOLD IT'S A HIGH-TECH INSTRUMENT THAT GATHERS INFORMATION ON THE POKÉMON YOU ENCOUNTER.
I SEE. DOES THIS MEAN YOU'LL BE GOING ON A JOURNEY TO COLLECT DATA?

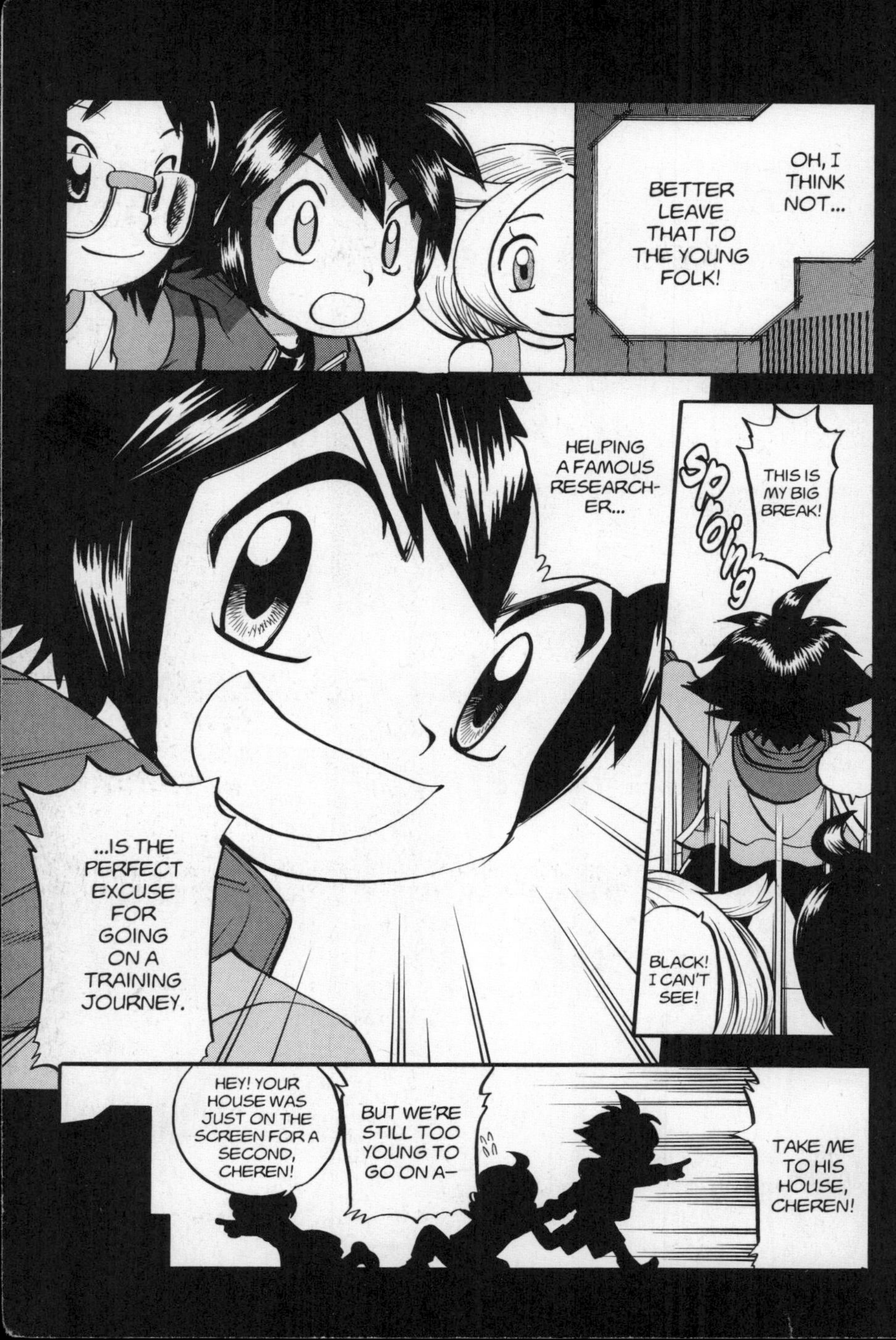
OH, I THINK NOT...
BETTER LEAVE THAT TO THE YOUNG FOLK!
THIS IS MY BIG BREAK!
Sproing
BLACK! I CAN'T SEE!
HELPING A FAMOUS RESEARCHER...
...IS THE PERFECT EXCUSE FOR GOING ON A TRAINING JOURNEY.
TAKE ME TO HIS HOUSE, CHEREN!
BUT WE'RE STILL TOO YOUNG TO GO ON A–
HEY! YOUR HOUSE WAS JUST ON THE SCREEN FOR A SECOND, CHEREN!

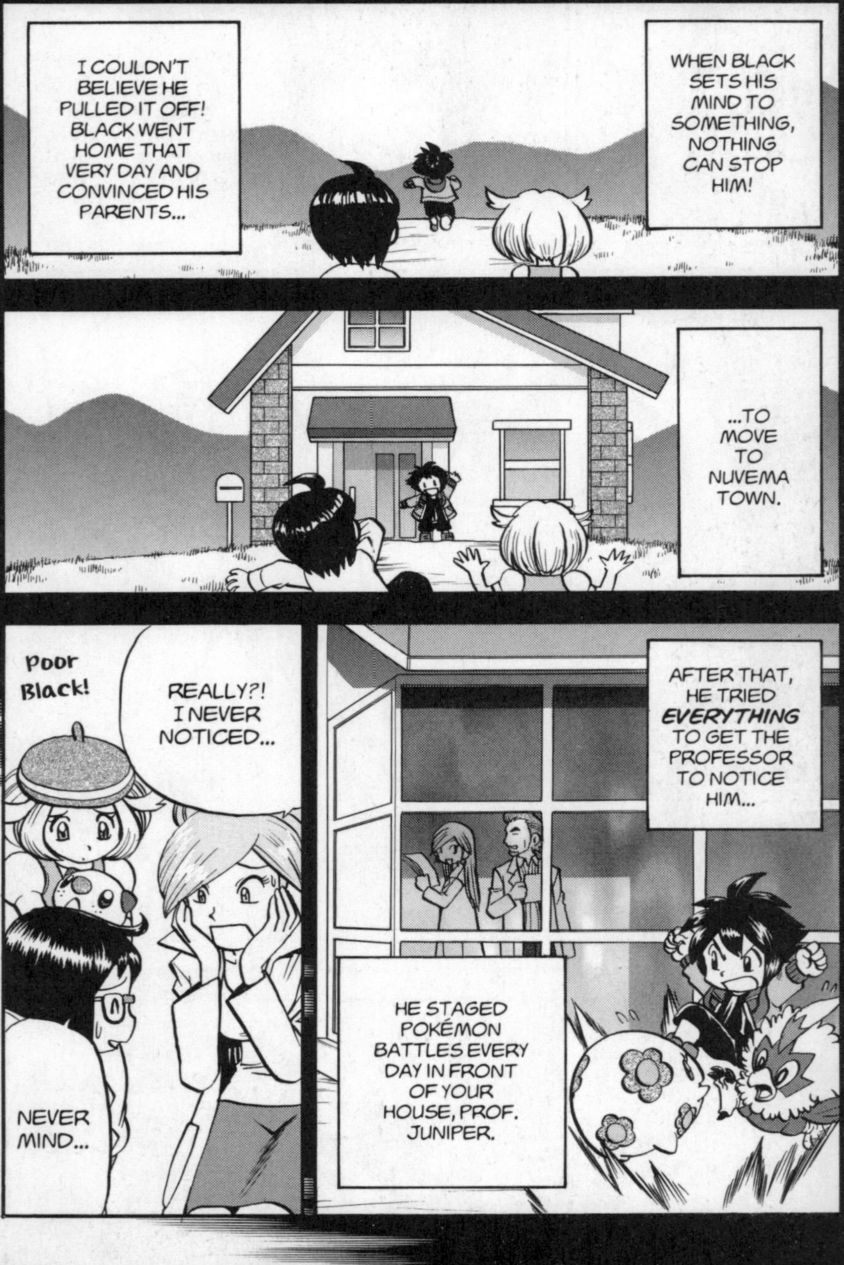
WHEN BLACK SETS HIS MIND TO SOMETHING, NOTHING CAN STOP HIM!
I COULDN'T BELIEVE HE PULLED IT OFF! BLACK WENT HOME THAT VERY DAY AND CONVINCED HIS PARENTS...
...TO MOVE TO NUVEMA TOWN.
AFTER THAT, HE TRIED *EVERYTHING* TO GET THE PROFESSOR TO NOTICE HIM...
HE STAGED POKÉMON BATTLES EVERY DAY IN FRONT OF YOUR HOUSE, PROF. JUNIPER.
REALLY?! I NEVER NOTICED...
Poor Black!
NEVER MIND...

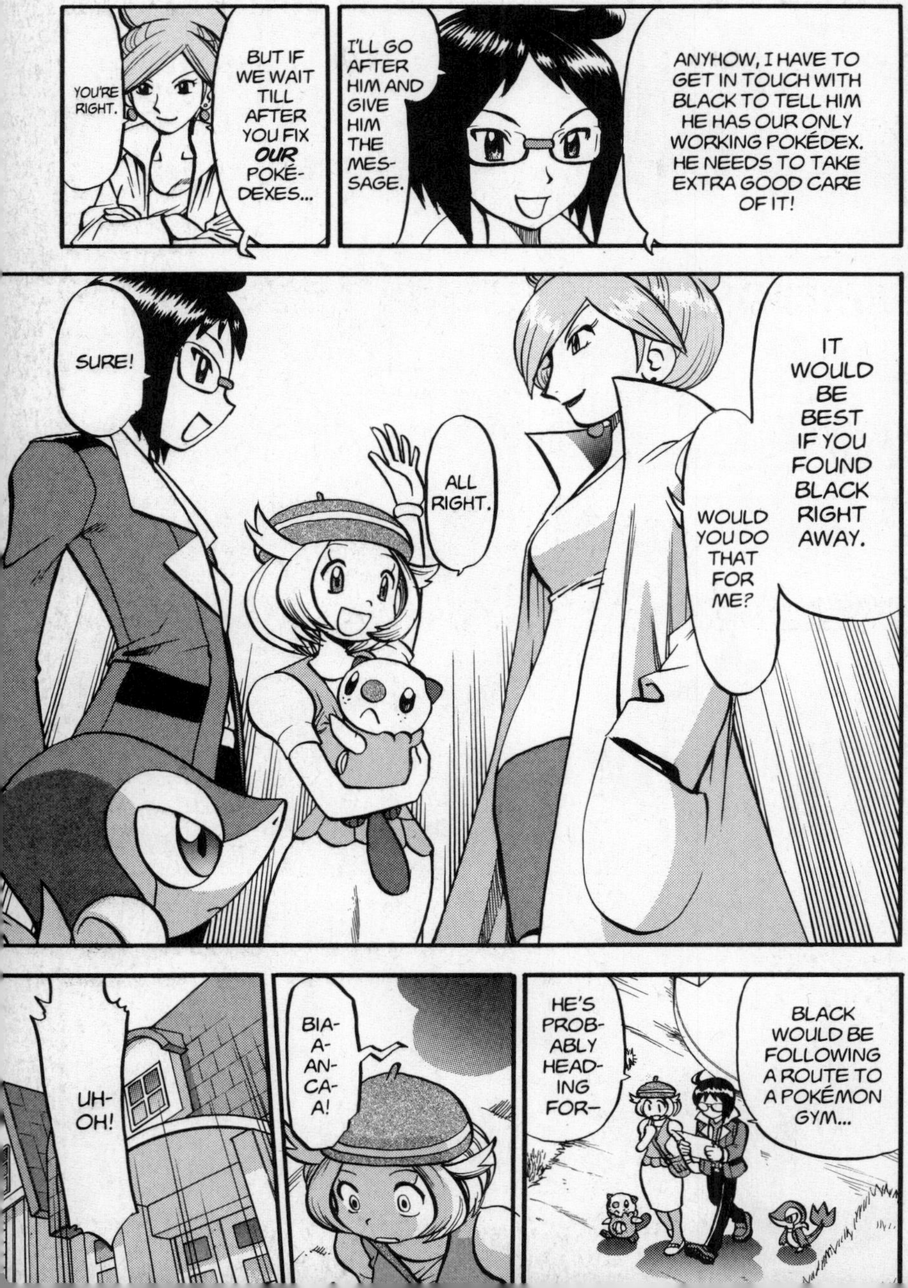
ANYHOW, I HAVE TO GET IN TOUCH WITH BLACK TO TELL HIM HE HAS OUR ONLY WORKING POKÉDEX. HE NEEDS TO TAKE EXTRA GOOD CARE OF IT!
I'LL GO AFTER HIM AND GIVE HIM THE MES-SAGE.
BUT IF WE WAIT TILL AFTER YOU FIX *OUR* POKÉ-DEXES...
YOU'RE RIGHT.
IT WOULD BE BEST IF YOU FOUND BLACK RIGHT AWAY.
WOULD YOU DO THAT FOR ME?
ALL RIGHT.
SURE!
BLACK WOULD BE FOLLOWING A ROUTE TO A POKÉMON GYM...
HE'S PROB-ABLY HEAD-ING FOR–
BIA-A-AN-CA-A!
UH-OH!

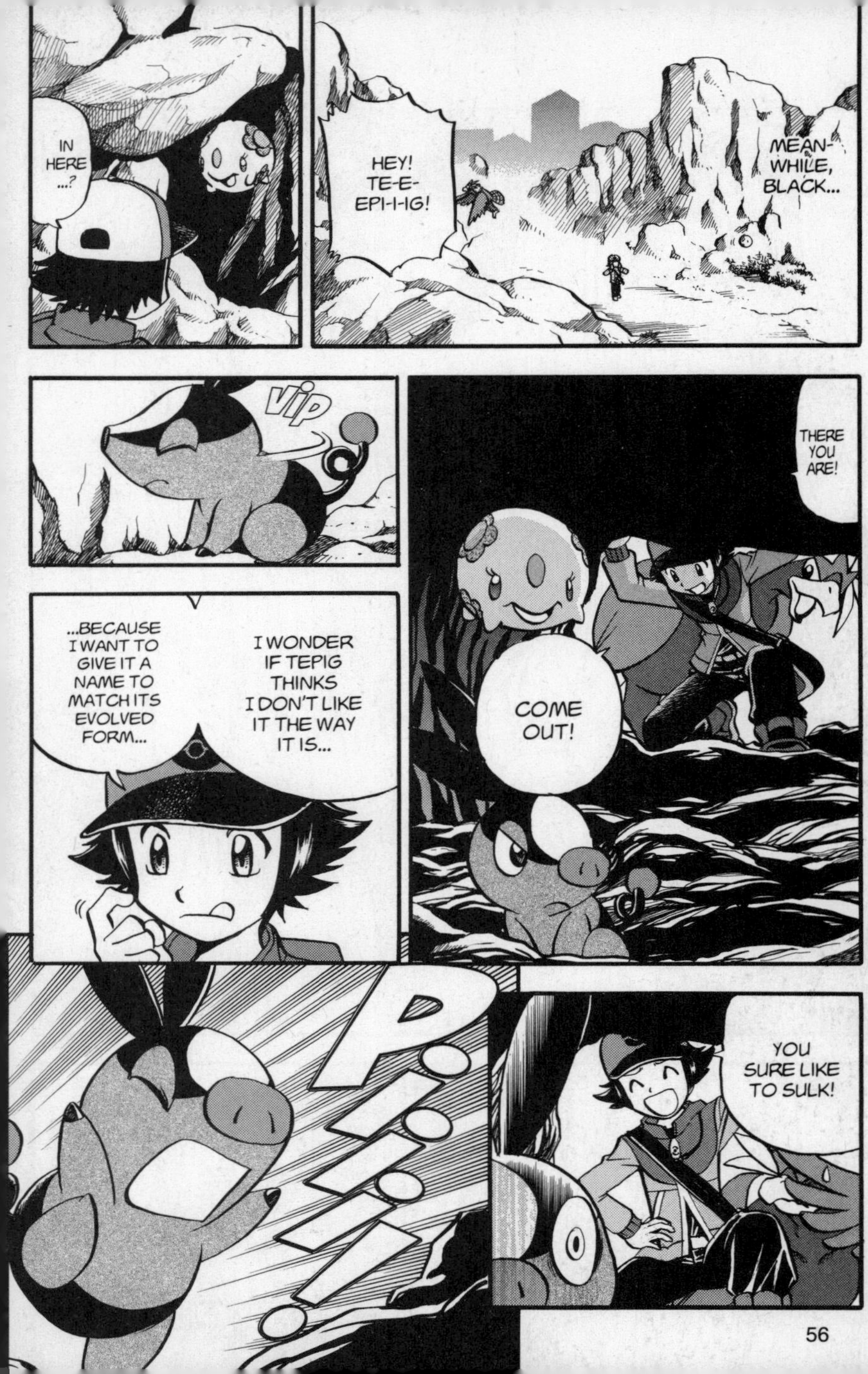
MEAN-WHILE, BLACK...
HEY! TE-E-EPI-I-IG!
IN HERE ...?
THERE YOU ARE!
COME OUT!
VIP
I WONDER IF TEPIG THINKS I DON'T LIKE IT THE WAY IT IS...
...BECAUSE I WANT TO GIVE IT A NAME TO MATCH ITS EVOLVED FORM...
YOU SURE LIKE TO SULK!

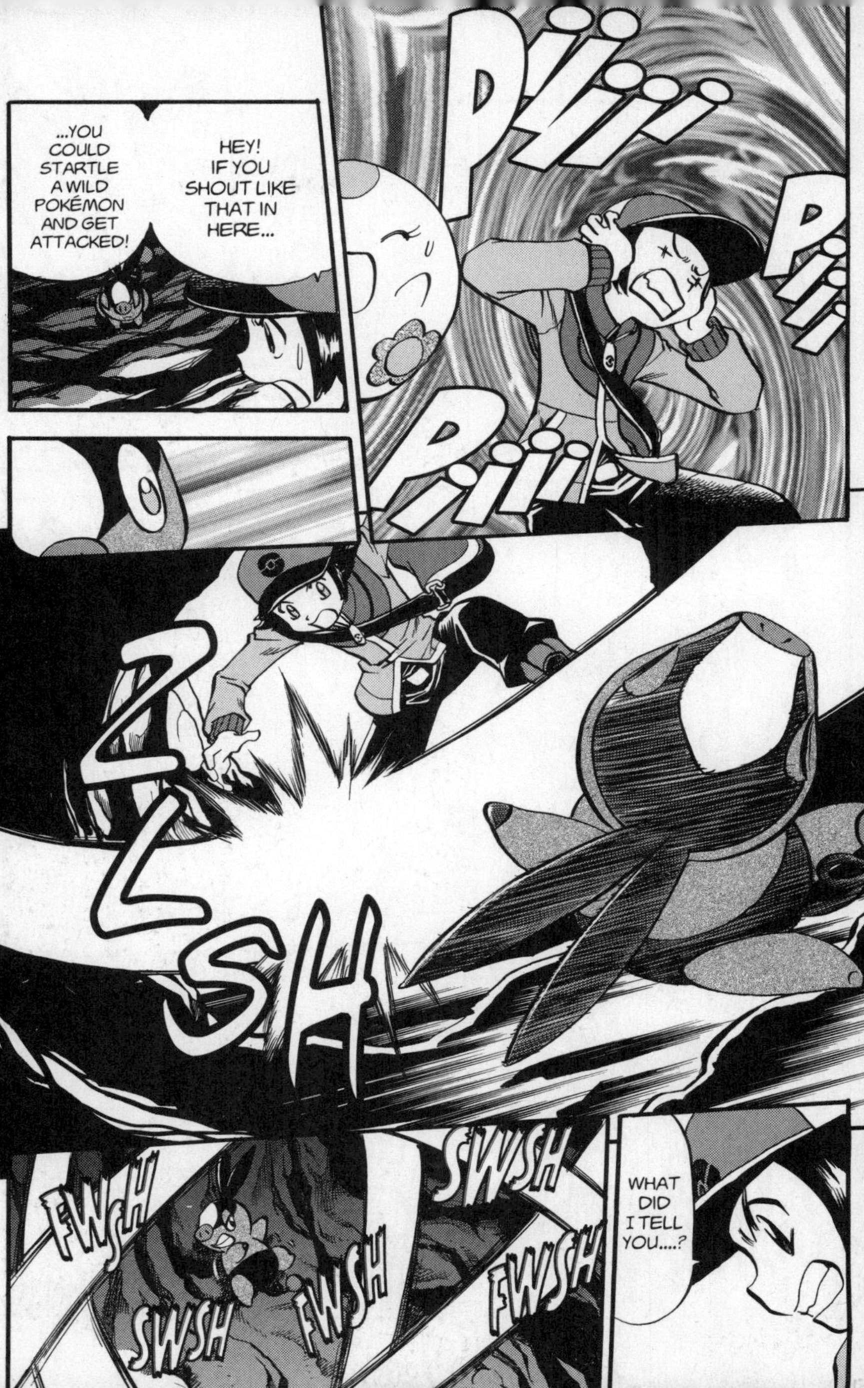
PIIII...
PIIII
PIIII
HEY! IF YOU SHOUT LIKE THAT IN HERE...
...YOU COULD STARTLE A WILD POKÉMON AND GET ATTACKED!
ZZSH
WHAT DID I TELL YOU....?
SWSH
FWSH
FWSH
FWSH
SWSH

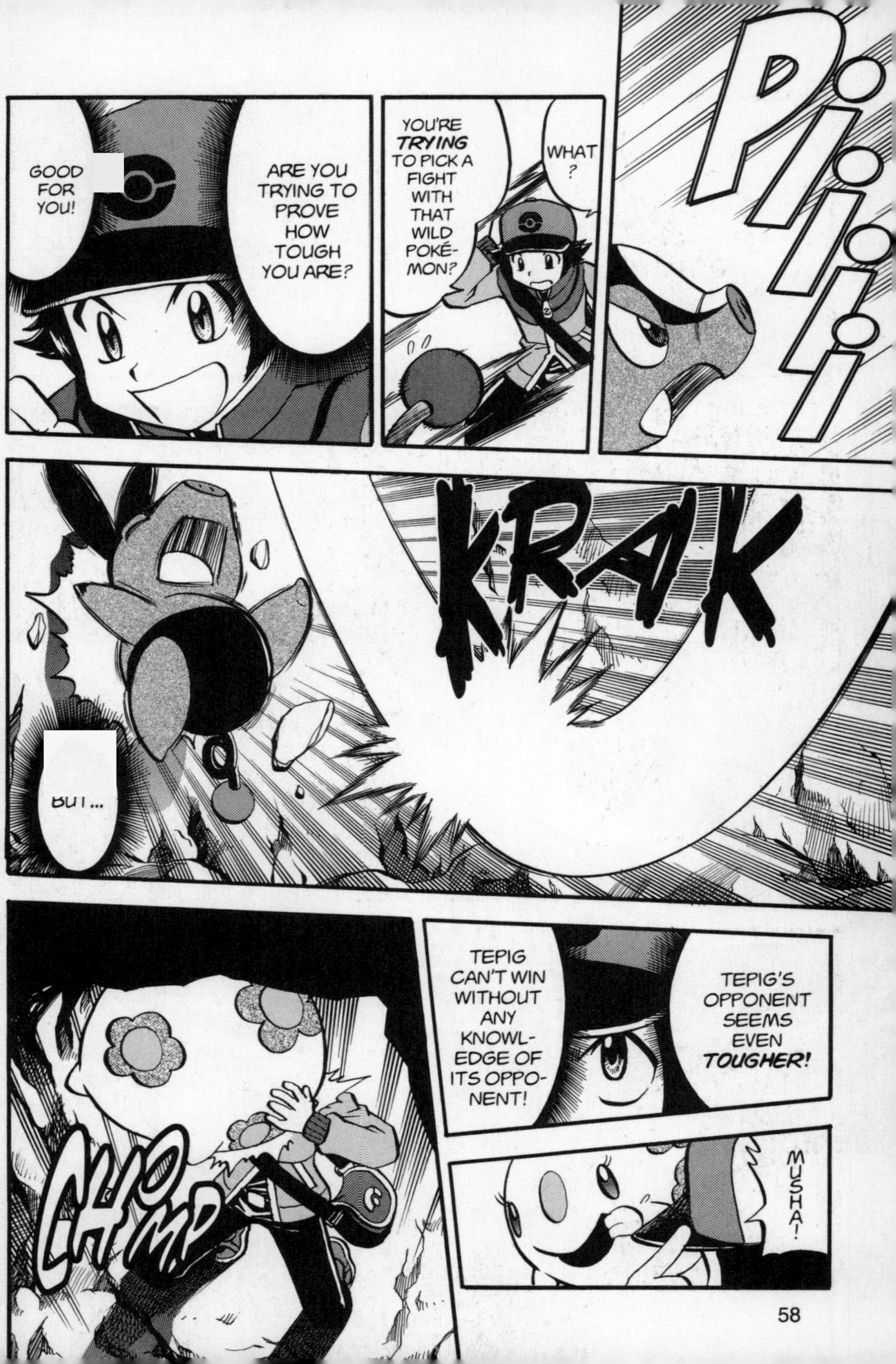
PIIIII
WHAT?
YOU'RE TRYING TO PICK A FIGHT WITH THAT WILD POKÉMON?
ARE YOU TRYING TO PROVE HOW TOUGH YOU ARE?
GOOD FOR YOU!
KRAK
BUT...
TEPIG'S OPPONENT SEEMS EVEN TOUGHER!
TEPIG CAN'T WIN WITHOUT ANY KNOWLEDGE OF ITS OPPONENT!
MUSHA!
CHOMP

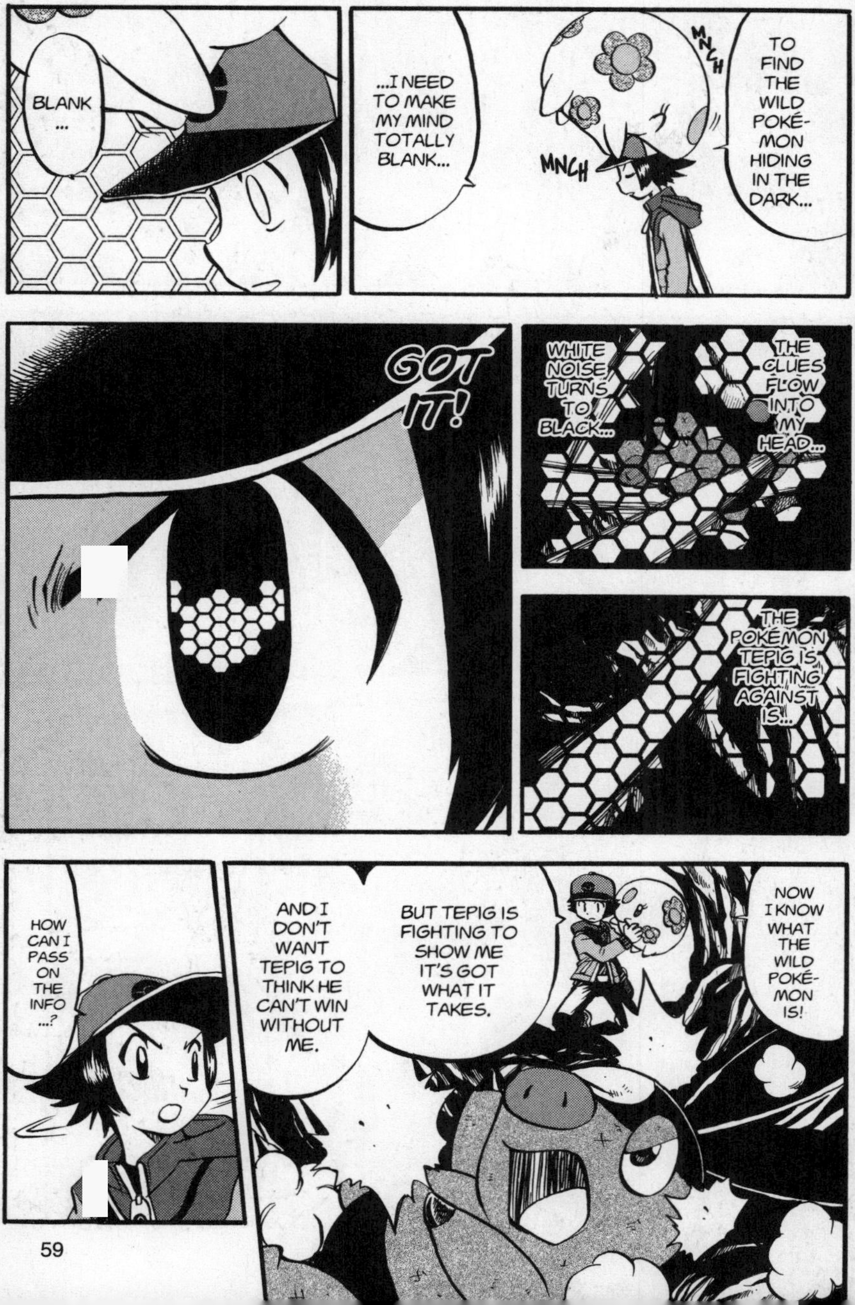
TO FIND THE WILD POKÉMON HIDING IN THE DARK...
MNCH
MNCH
...I NEED TO MAKE MY MIND TOTALLY BLANK...
BLANK ...
THE CLUES FLOW INTO MY HEAD...
WHITE NOISE TURNS TO BLACK...
THE POKÉMON TEPIG IS FIGHTING AGAINST IS...
GOT IT!
NOW I KNOW WHAT THE WILD POKÉMON IS!
BUT TEPIG IS FIGHTING TO SHOW ME IT'S GOT WHAT IT TAKES.
AND I DON'T WANT TEPIG TO THINK HE CAN'T WIN WITHOUT ME.
HOW CAN I PASS ON THE INFO ...?

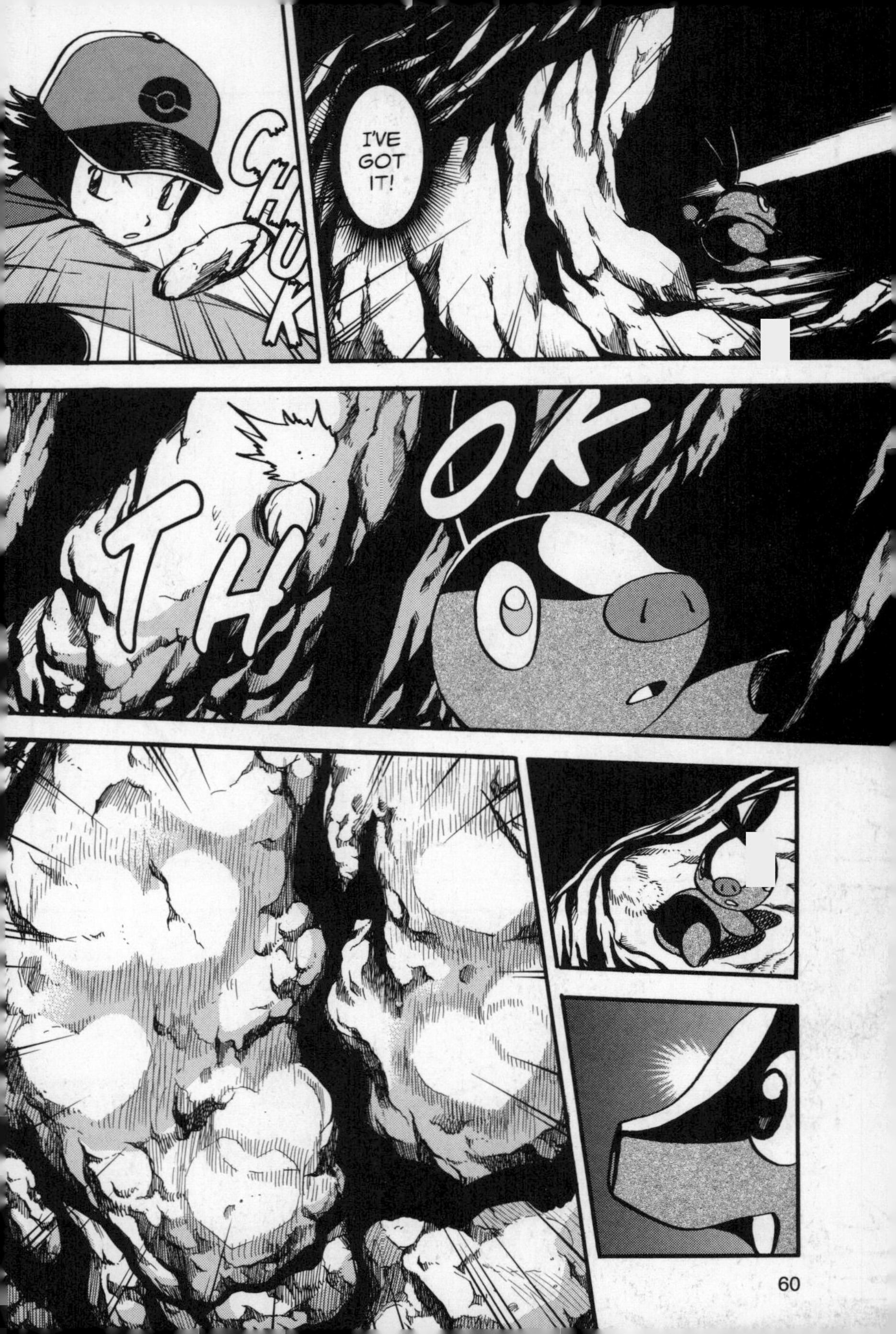
I'VE GOT IT!
CHUK
THOK

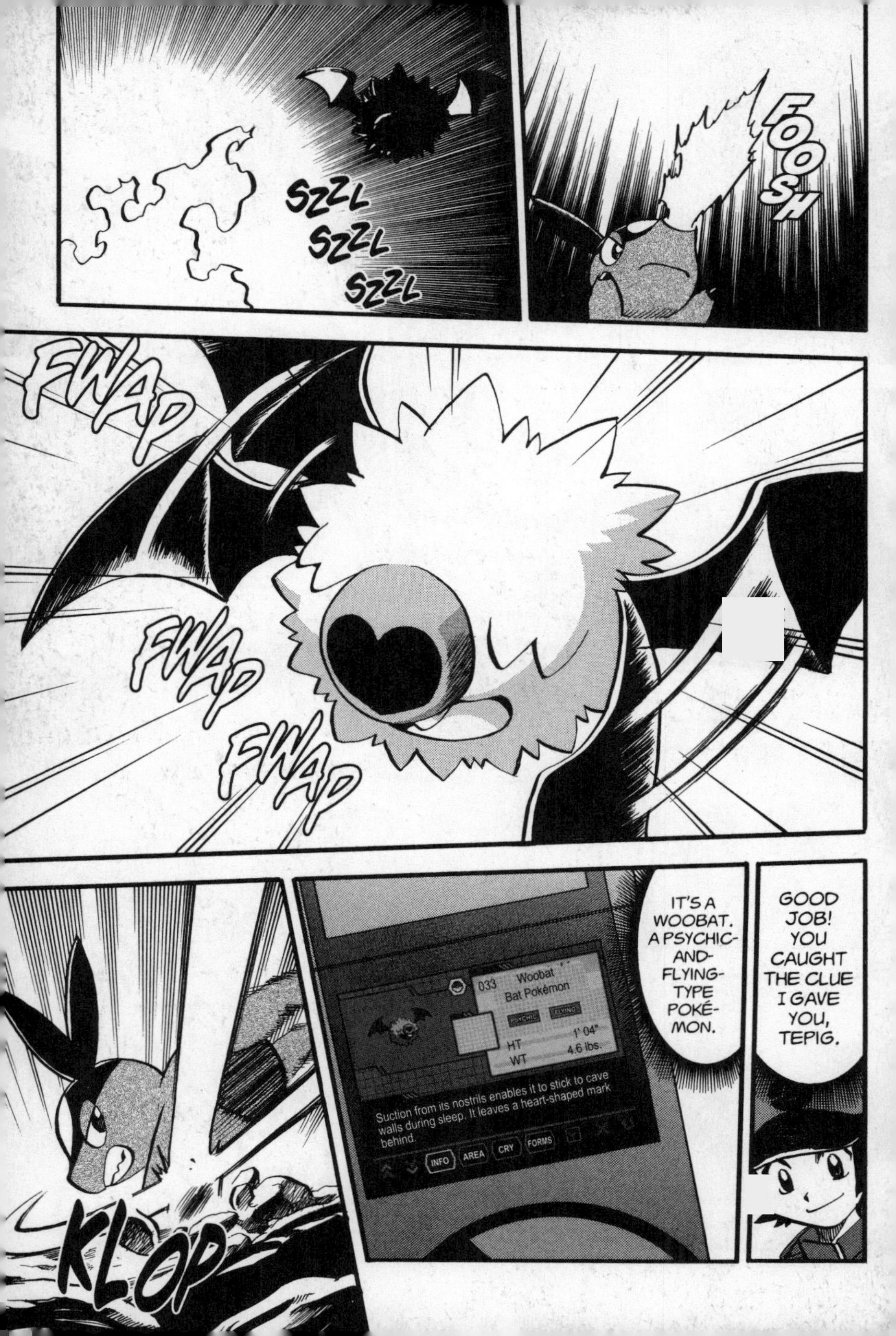
FOOSH
SZZL SZZL SZZL
FWAP FWAP FWAP
GOOD JOB! YOU CAUGHT THE CLUE I GAVE YOU, TEPIG.
IT'S A WOOBAT. A PSYCHIC-AND-FLYING-TYPE POKÉMON.
033 Woobat
Bat Pokémon
PSYCHIC FLYING
HT 1' 04"
WT 4.6 lbs.
Suction from its nostrils enables it to stick to cave walls during sleep. It leaves a heart-shaped mark behind.
INFO AREA CRY FORMS
KLOP

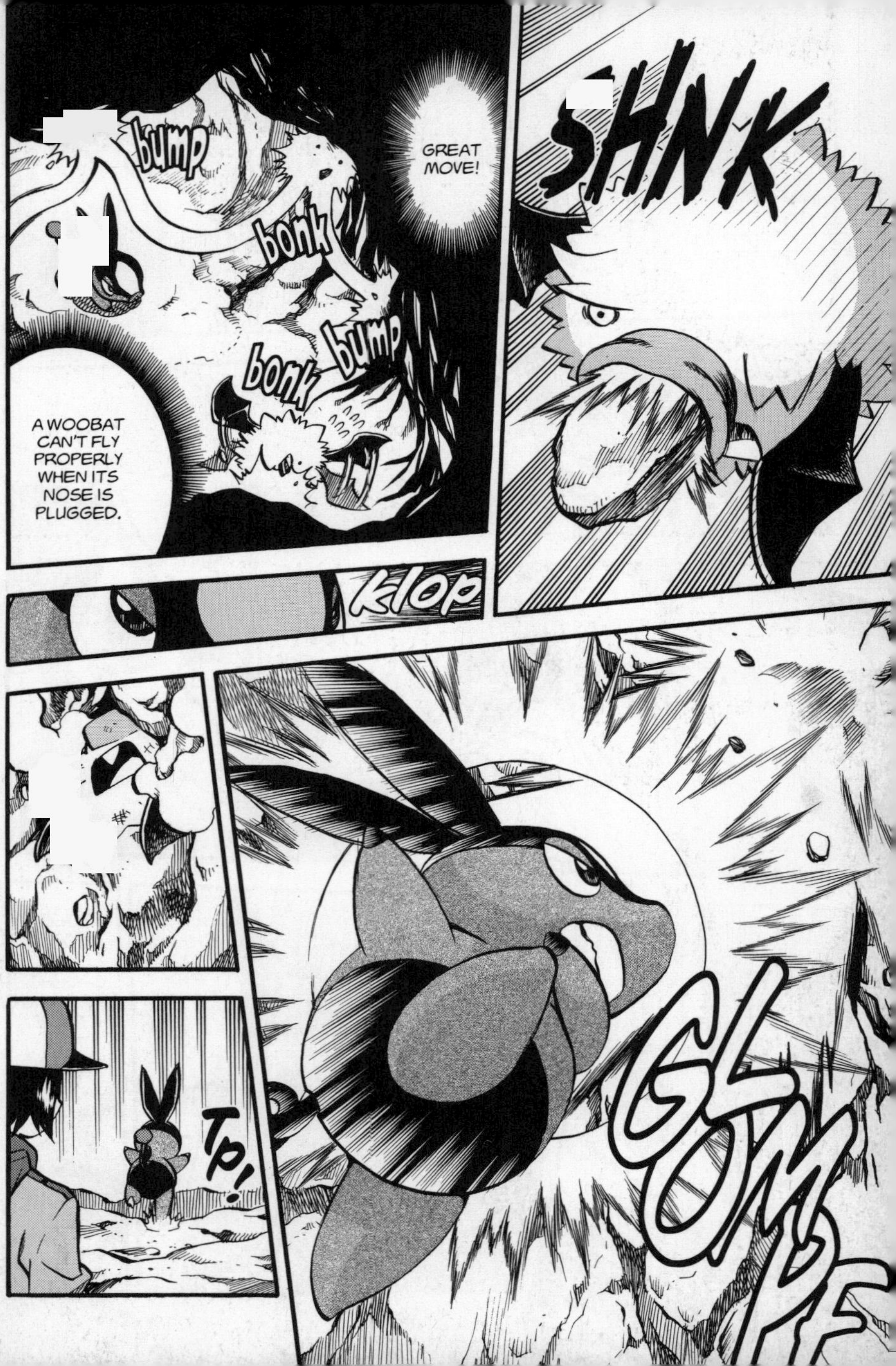
SHNK
GREAT MOVE!
bump
bonk
bump
bonk
A WOOBAT CAN'T FLY PROPERLY WHEN ITS NOSE IS PLUGGED.
klop
GLOMPF
Tp!

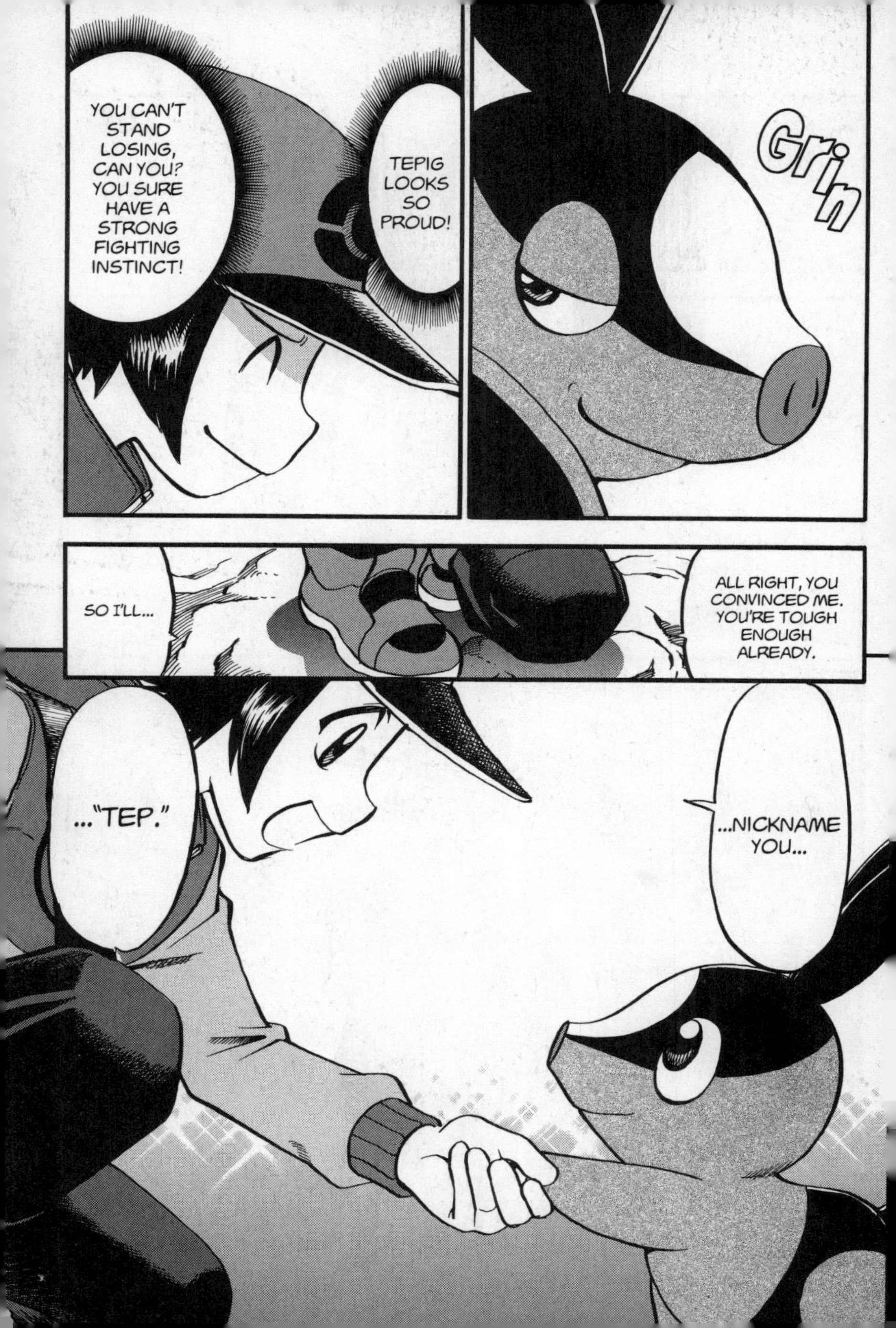
Grin
TEPIG LOOKS SO PROUD!
YOU CAN'T STAND LOSING, CAN YOU? YOU SURE HAVE A STRONG FIGHTING INSTINCT!
ALL RIGHT, YOU CONVINCED ME. YOU'RE TOUGH ENOUGH ALREADY.
SO I'LL...
...NICKNAME YOU...
..."TEP."

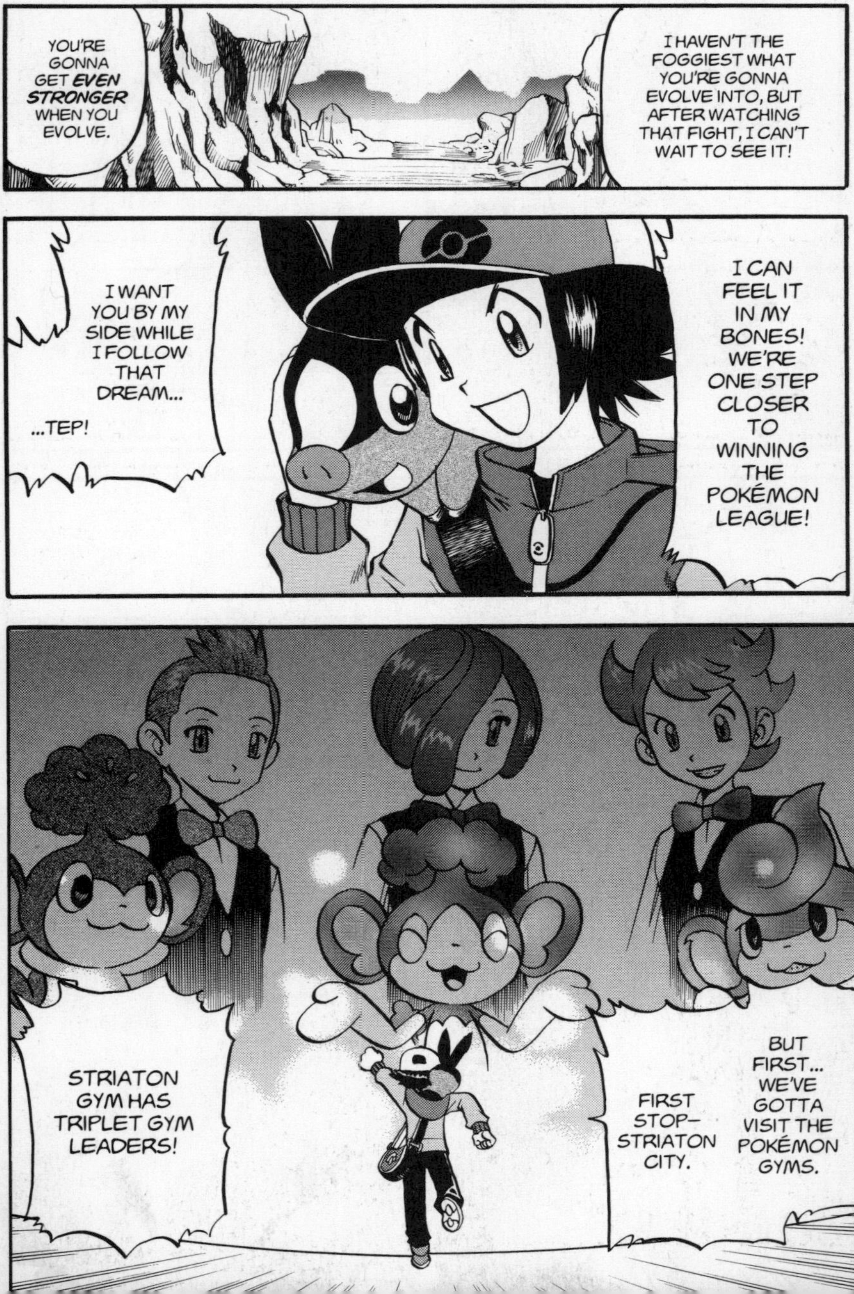
I HAVEN'T THE FOGGIEST WHAT YOU'RE GONNA EVOLVE INTO, BUT AFTER WATCHING THAT FIGHT, I CAN'T WAIT TO SEE IT!
YOU'RE GONNA GET **EVEN STRONGER** WHEN YOU EVOLVE.
I CAN FEEL IT IN MY BONES! WE'RE ONE STEP CLOSER TO WINNING THE POKÉMON LEAGUE!
I WANT YOU BY MY SIDE WHILE I FOLLOW THAT DREAM...
...TEP!
BUT FIRST... WE'VE GOTTA VISIT THE POKÉMON GYMS.
FIRST STOP—STRIATON CITY.
STRIATON GYM HAS TRIPLET GYM LEADERS!

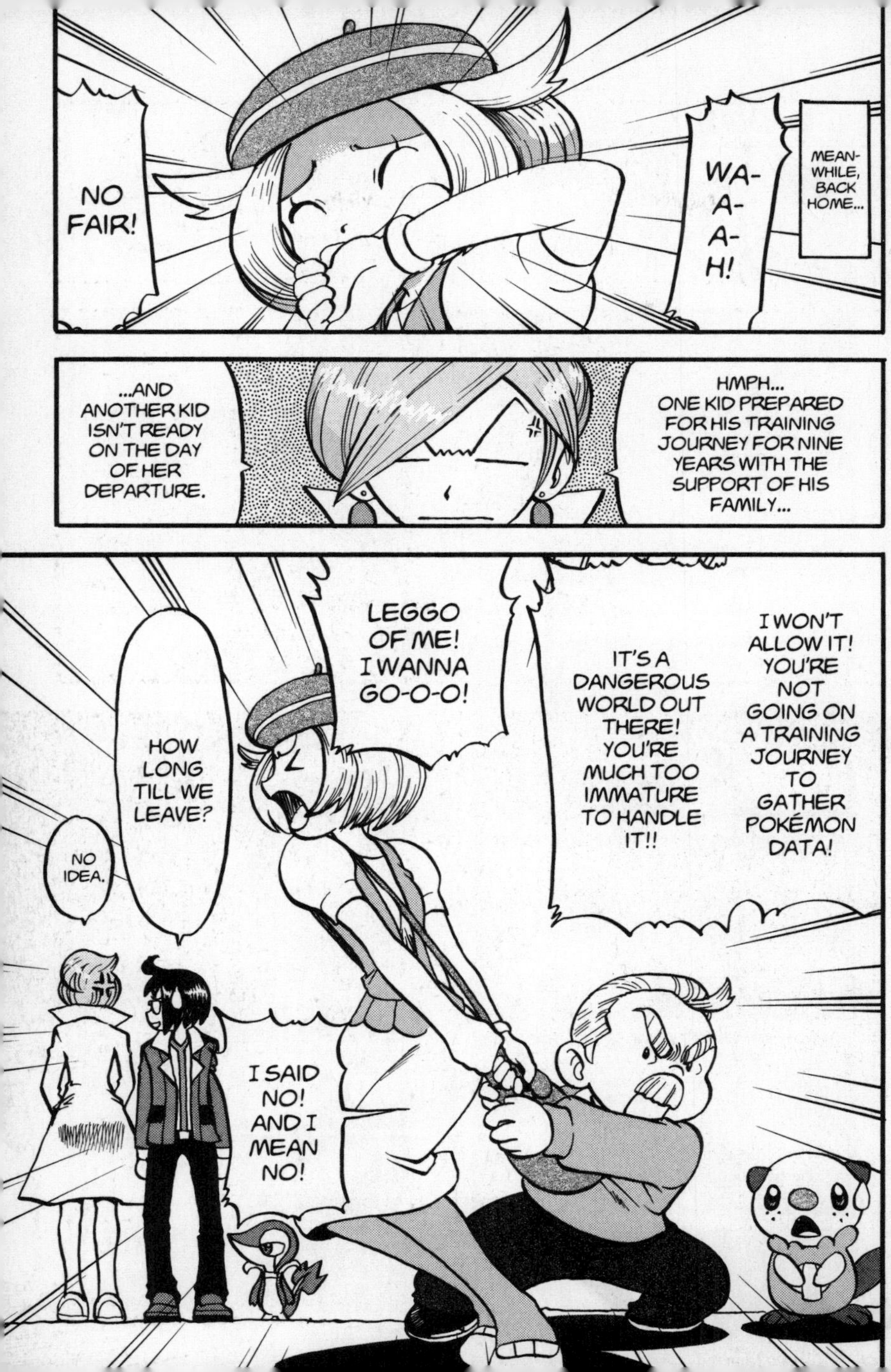
MEAN-WHILE, BACK HOME...
WA-A-A-H!
NO FAIR!
HMPH... ONE KID PREPARED FOR HIS TRAINING JOURNEY FOR NINE YEARS WITH THE SUPPORT OF HIS FAMILY...
...AND ANOTHER KID ISN'T READY ON THE DAY OF HER DEPARTURE.
I WON'T ALLOW IT! YOU'RE NOT GOING ON A TRAINING JOURNEY TO GATHER POKÉMON DATA!
IT'S A DANGEROUS WORLD OUT THERE! YOU'RE MUCH TOO IMMATURE TO HANDLE IT!!
LEGGO OF ME! I WANNA GO-O-O!
HOW LONG TILL WE LEAVE?
NO IDEA.
I SAID NO! AND I MEAN NO!

ADVENTURE MAP

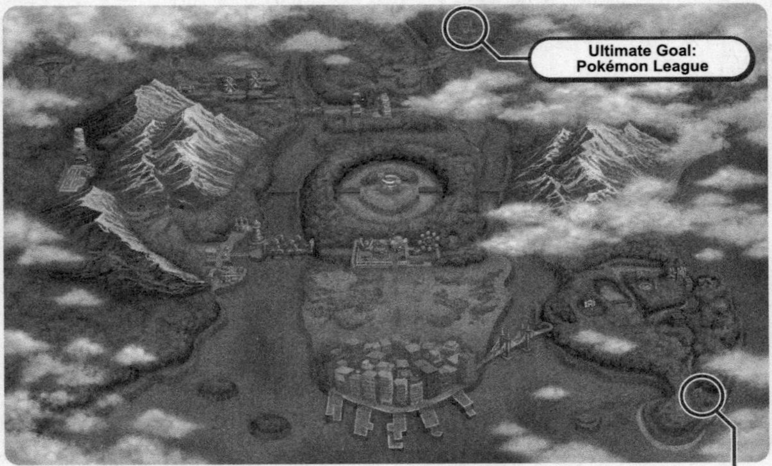
Ultimate Goal:
Pokémon League
Current Location: Route 1

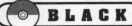

BLACK

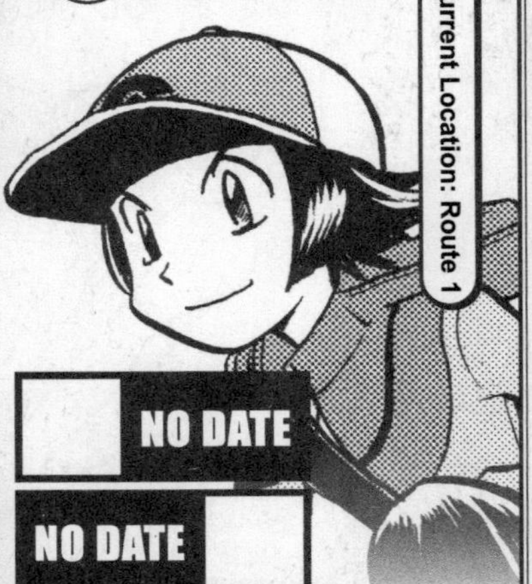

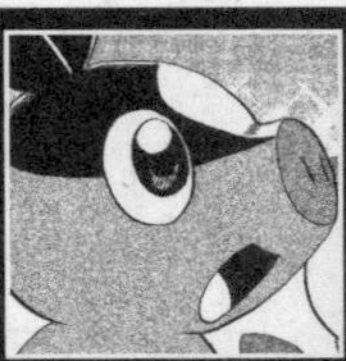

Level 15

Tep

Tepig ♂

Fire Pig Pokémon

Level 31

Musha

Munna ♂

Dream Eater Pokémon

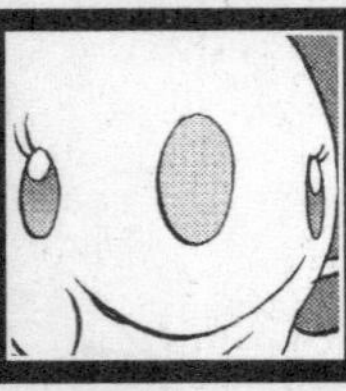

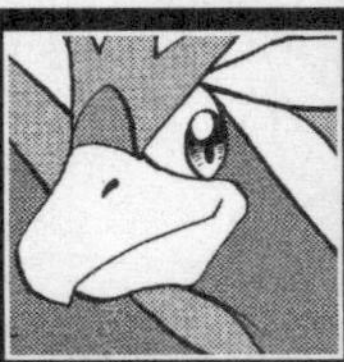

Level 54

Brav

Braviary ♂

Valiant Pokémon

NO DATE

NO DATE

NO DATE

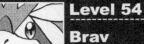

Pokémon™ Adventures Black & White

Adventure 4
Black's First Trainer Battle

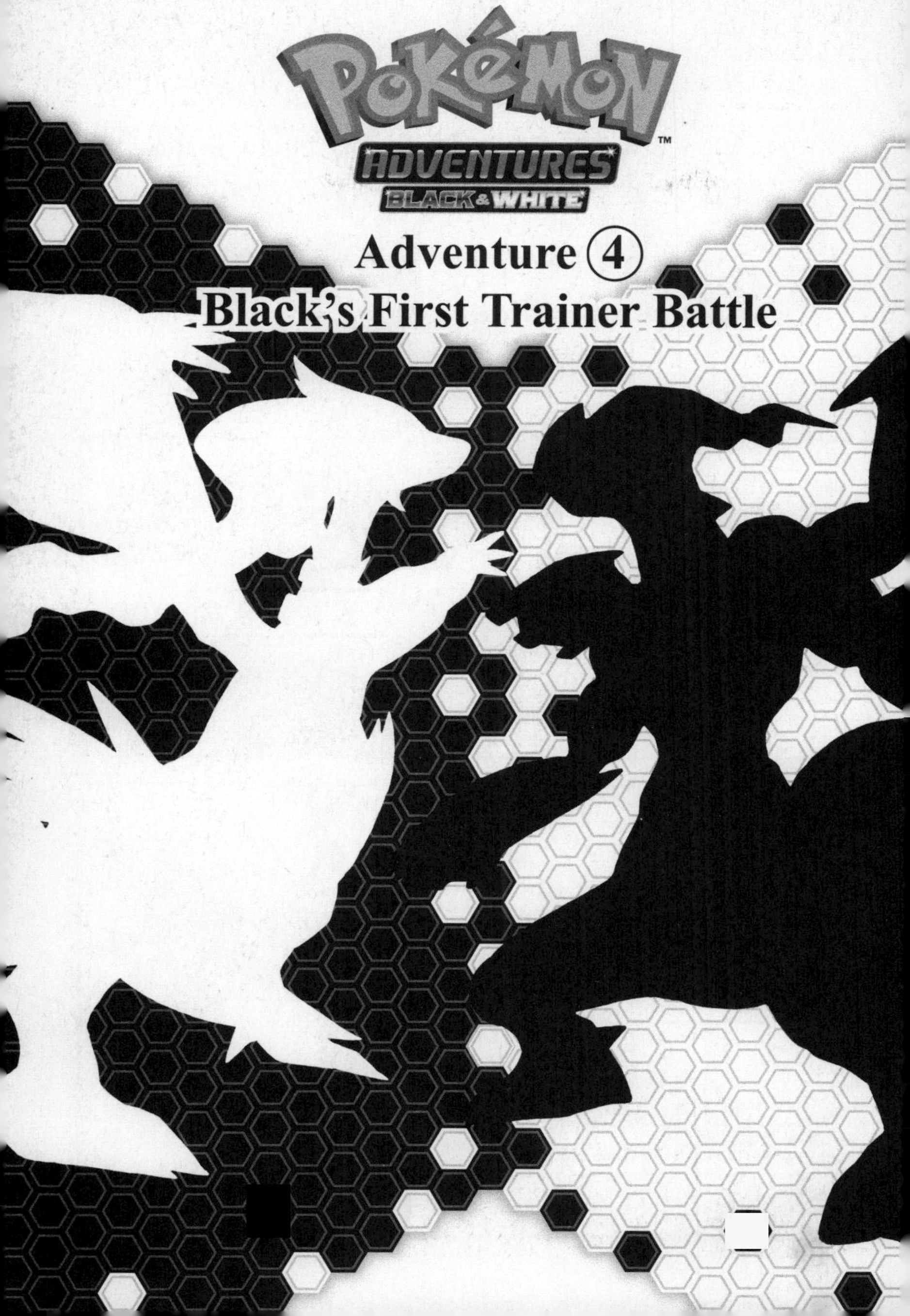

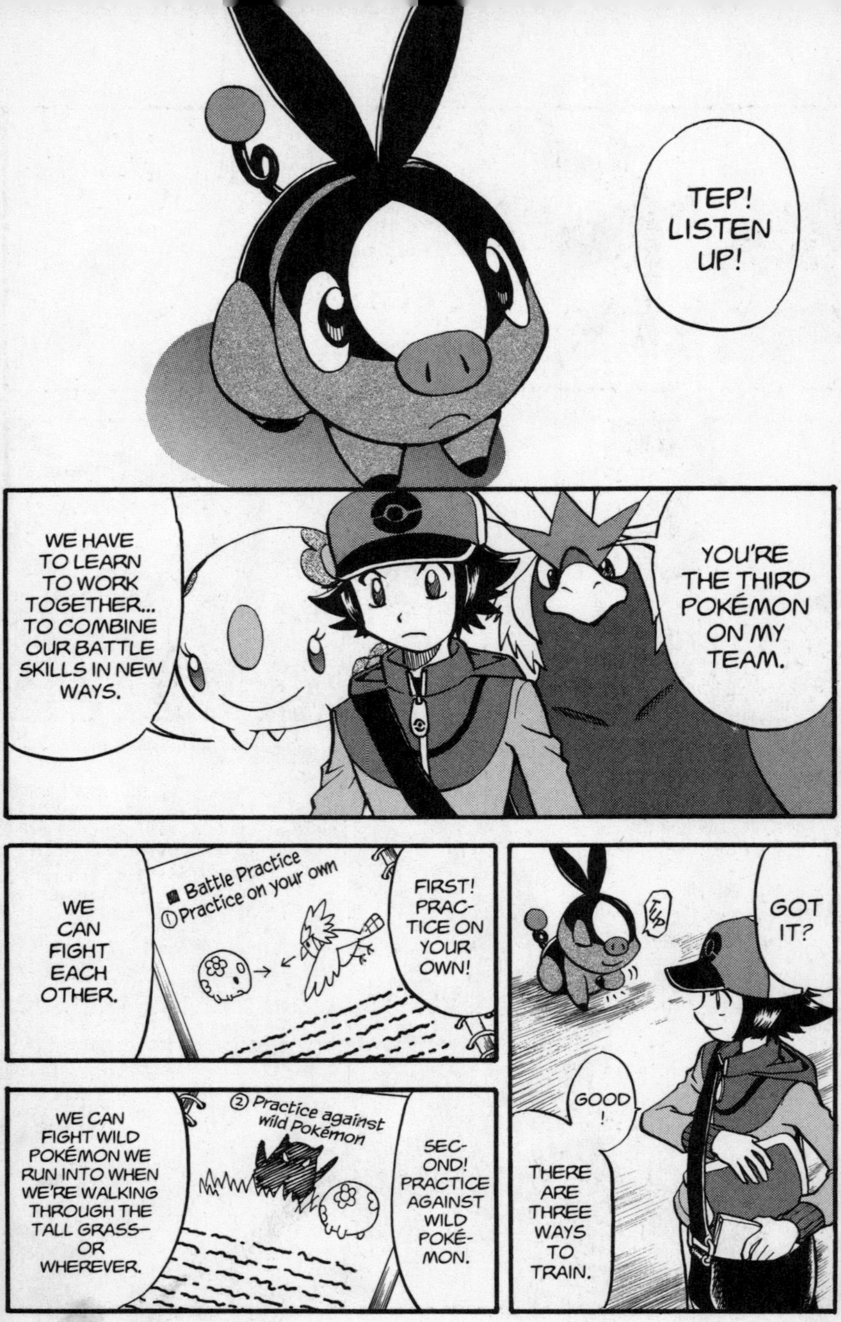

TEP! LISTEN UP!
YOU'RE THE THIRD POKÉMON ON MY TEAM.
WE HAVE TO LEARN TO WORK TOGETHER... TO COMBINE OUR BATTLE SKILLS IN NEW WAYS.
GOT IT?
TEP
GOOD!
THERE ARE THREE WAYS TO TRAIN.
FIRST! PRACTICE ON YOUR OWN!
Battle Practice
① Practice on your own
WE CAN FIGHT EACH OTHER.
SECOND! PRACTICE AGAINST WILD POKÉMON.
② Practice against wild Pokémon
WE CAN FIGHT WILD POKÉMON WE RUN INTO WHEN WE'RE WALKING THROUGH THE TALL GRASS—OR WHEREVER.

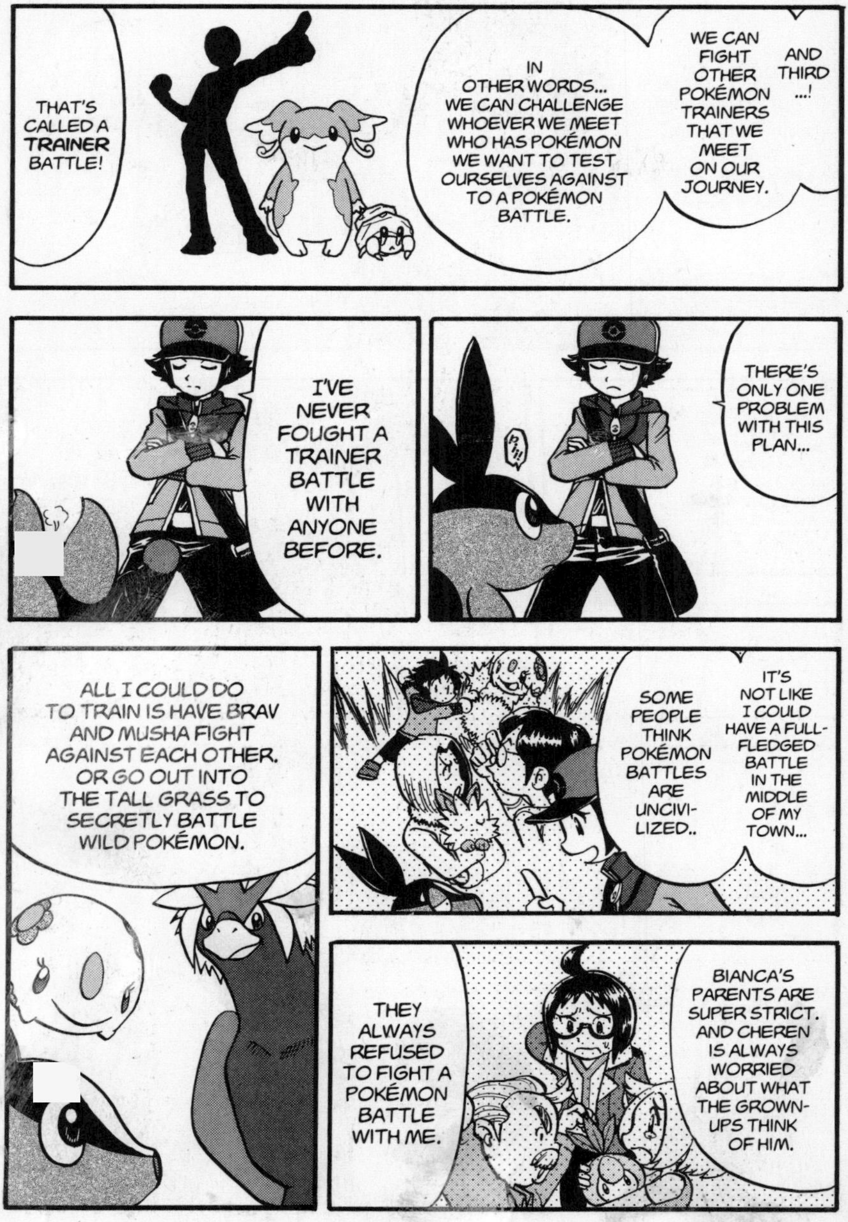
AND THIRD ...!
WE CAN FIGHT OTHER POKÉMON TRAINERS THAT WE MEET ON OUR JOURNEY.
IN OTHER WORDS... WE CAN CHALLENGE WHOEVER WE MEET WHO HAS POKÉMON WE WANT TO TEST OURSELVES AGAINST TO A POKÉMON BATTLE.
THAT'S CALLED A **TRAINER** BATTLE!
THERE'S ONLY ONE PROBLEM WITH THIS PLAN...
I'VE NEVER FOUGHT A TRAINER BATTLE WITH ANYONE BEFORE.
IT'S NOT LIKE I COULD HAVE A FULL-FLEDGED BATTLE IN THE MIDDLE OF MY TOWN...
SOME PEOPLE THINK POKÉMON BATTLES ARE UNCIVILIZED..
BIANCA'S PARENTS ARE SUPER STRICT. AND CHEREN IS ALWAYS WORRIED ABOUT WHAT THE GROWN-UPS THINK OF HIM.
THEY ALWAYS REFUSED TO FIGHT A POKÉMON BATTLE WITH ME.
ALL I COULD DO TO TRAIN IS HAVE BRAV AND MUSHA FIGHT AGAINST EACH OTHER. OR GO OUT INTO THE TALL GRASS TO SECRETLY BATTLE WILD POKÉMON.

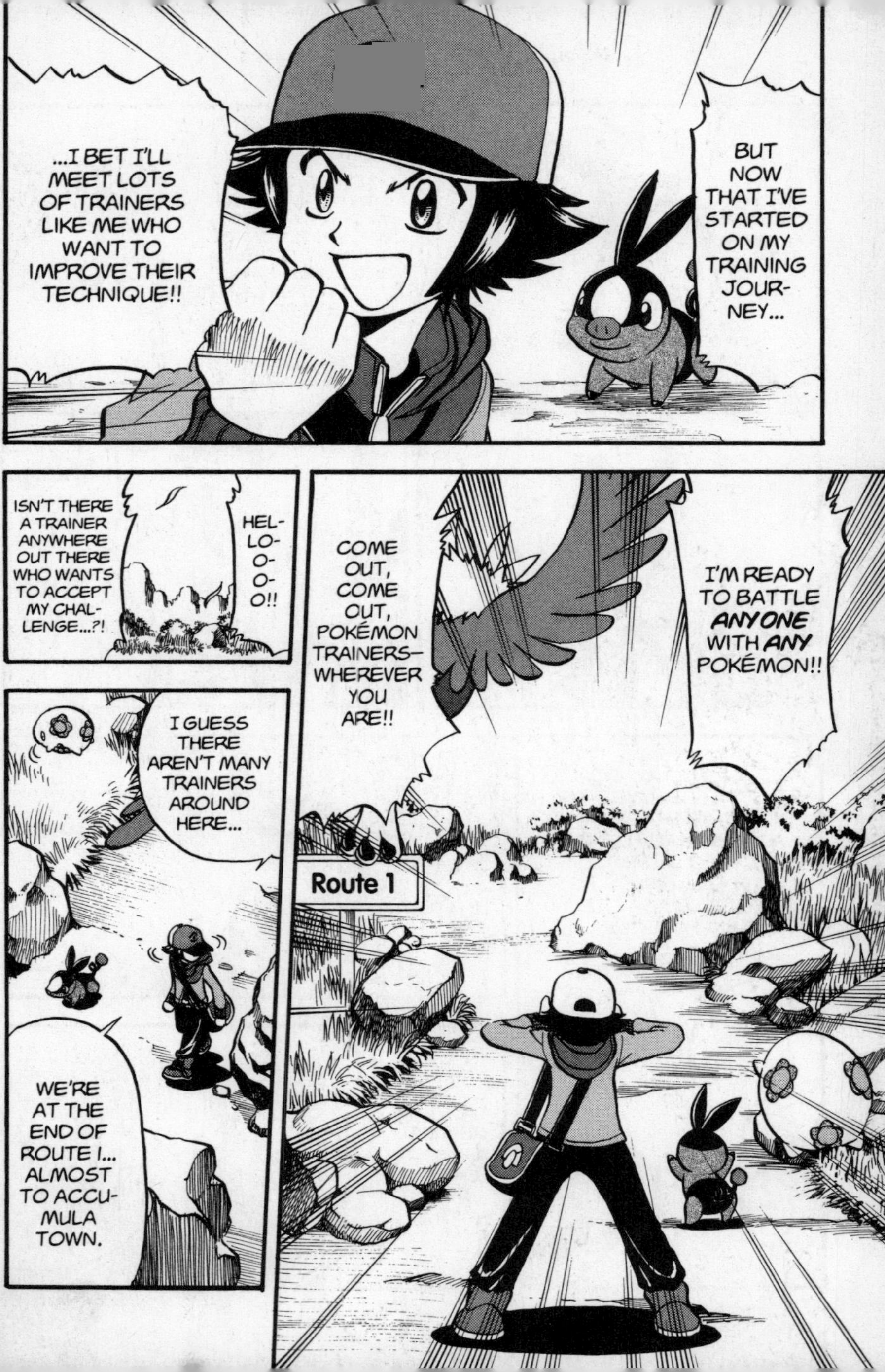
BUT NOW THAT I'VE STARTED ON MY TRAINING JOURNEY...
...I BET I'LL MEET LOTS OF TRAINERS LIKE ME WHO WANT TO IMPROVE THEIR TECHNIQUE!!
I'M READY TO BATTLE ANYONE WITH ANY POKÉMON!!
COME OUT, COME OUT, POKÉMON TRAINERS—WHEREVER YOU ARE!!
Route 1
HEL-LO-O-O-O!!
ISN'T THERE A TRAINER ANYWHERE OUT THERE WHO WANTS TO ACCEPT MY CHALLENGE...?!
I GUESS THERE AREN'T MANY TRAINERS AROUND HERE...
WE'RE AT THE END OF ROUTE 1... ALMOST TO ACCUMULA TOWN.

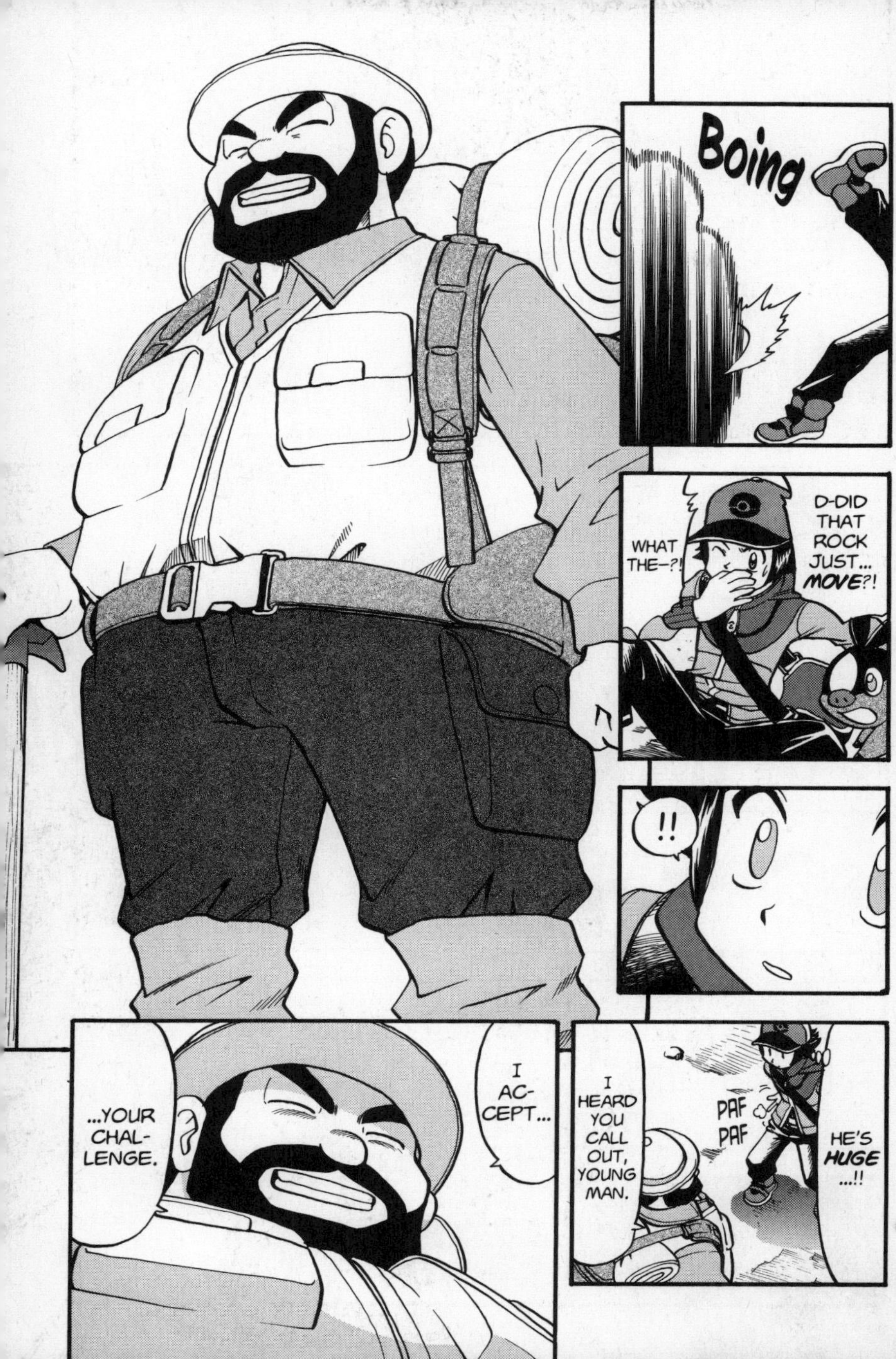
Boing
D-DID THAT ROCK JUST... MOVE?!
WHAT THE-?!
!!
HE'S HUGE ...!!
PAF PAF
I HEARD YOU CALL OUT, YOUNG MAN.
I AC-CEPT...
...YOUR CHAL-LENGE.

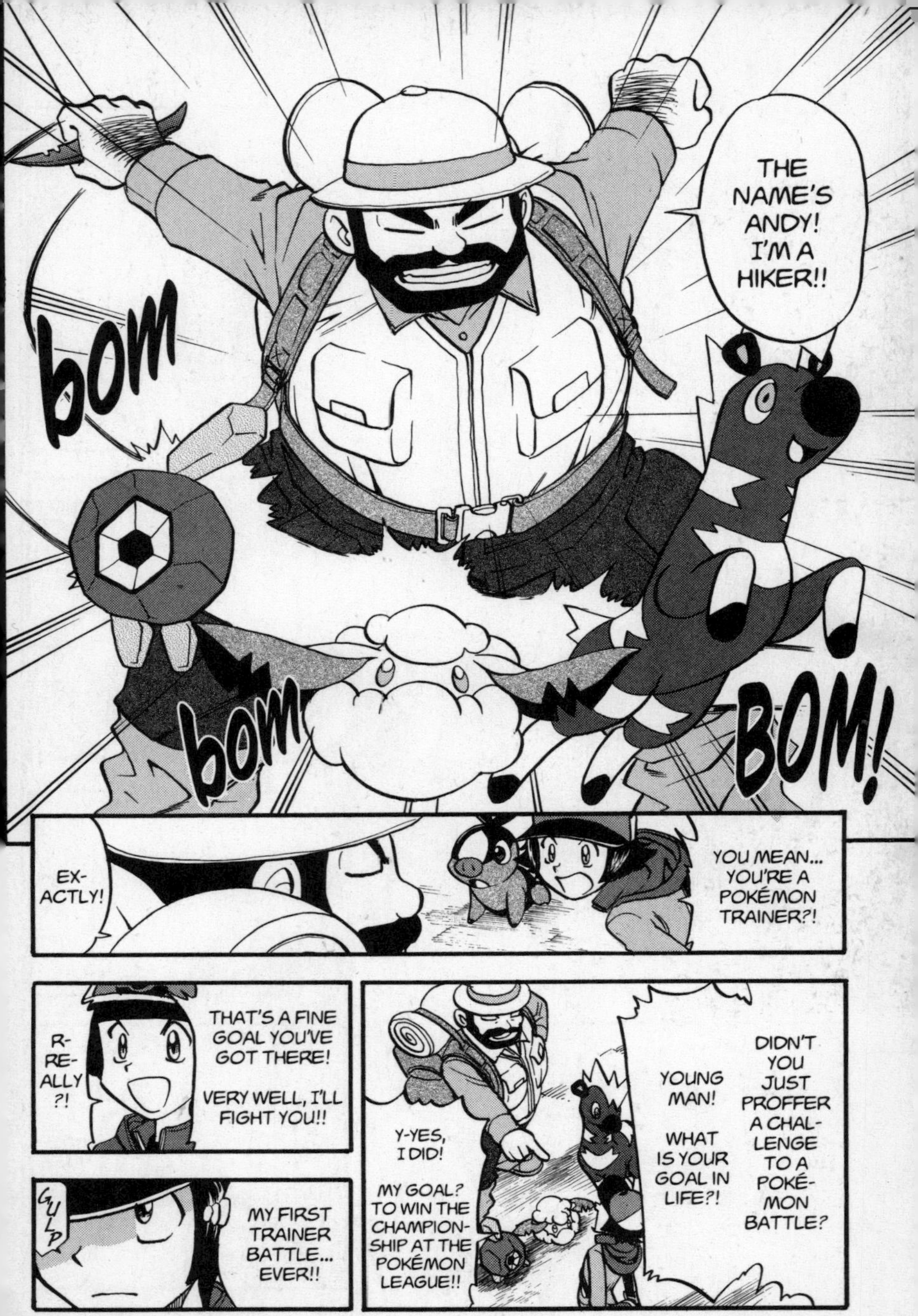
THE NAME'S ANDY! I'M A HIKER!!
BOM!
bom
bom
YOU MEAN... YOU'RE A POKÉMON TRAINER?!
EX-ACTLY!
DIDN'T YOU JUST PROFFER A CHAL-LENGE TO A POKÉ-MON BATTLE?
YOUNG MAN!
WHAT IS YOUR GOAL IN LIFE?!
Y-YES, I DID!
MY GOAL? TO WIN THE CHAMPION-SHIP AT THE POKÉMON LEAGUE!!
THAT'S A FINE GOAL YOU'VE GOT THERE!
VERY WELL, I'LL FIGHT YOU!!
R-RE-ALLY?!
MY FIRST TRAINER BATTLE... EVER!!
GULP

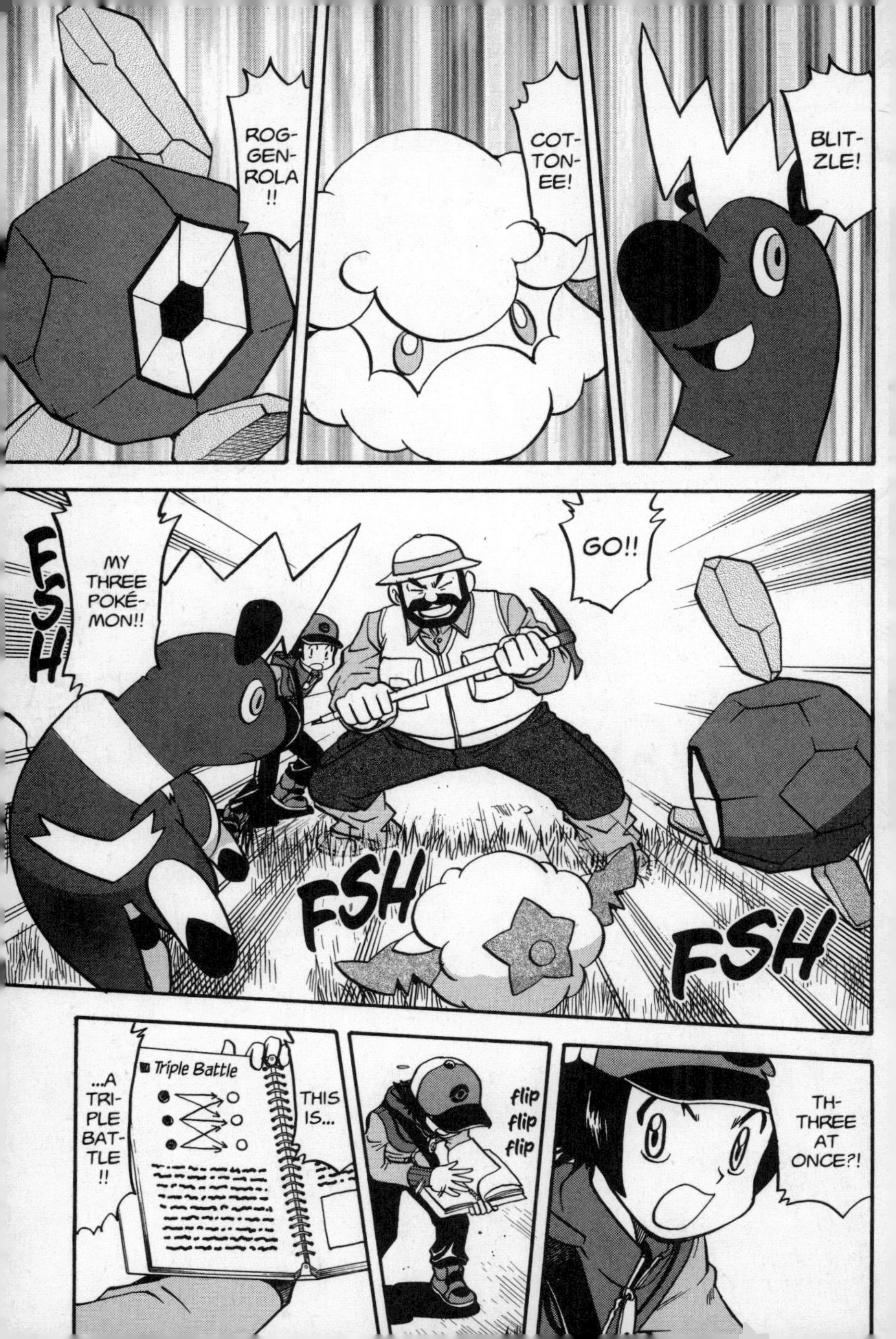
BLIT-ZLE!
COT-TON-EE!
ROG-GEN-ROLA!!
GO!!
MY THREE POKÉ-MON!!
FSH
FSH
FSH
TH-THREE AT ONCE?!
flip flip flip
THIS IS...
Triple Battle
...A TRI-PLE BAT-TLE!!

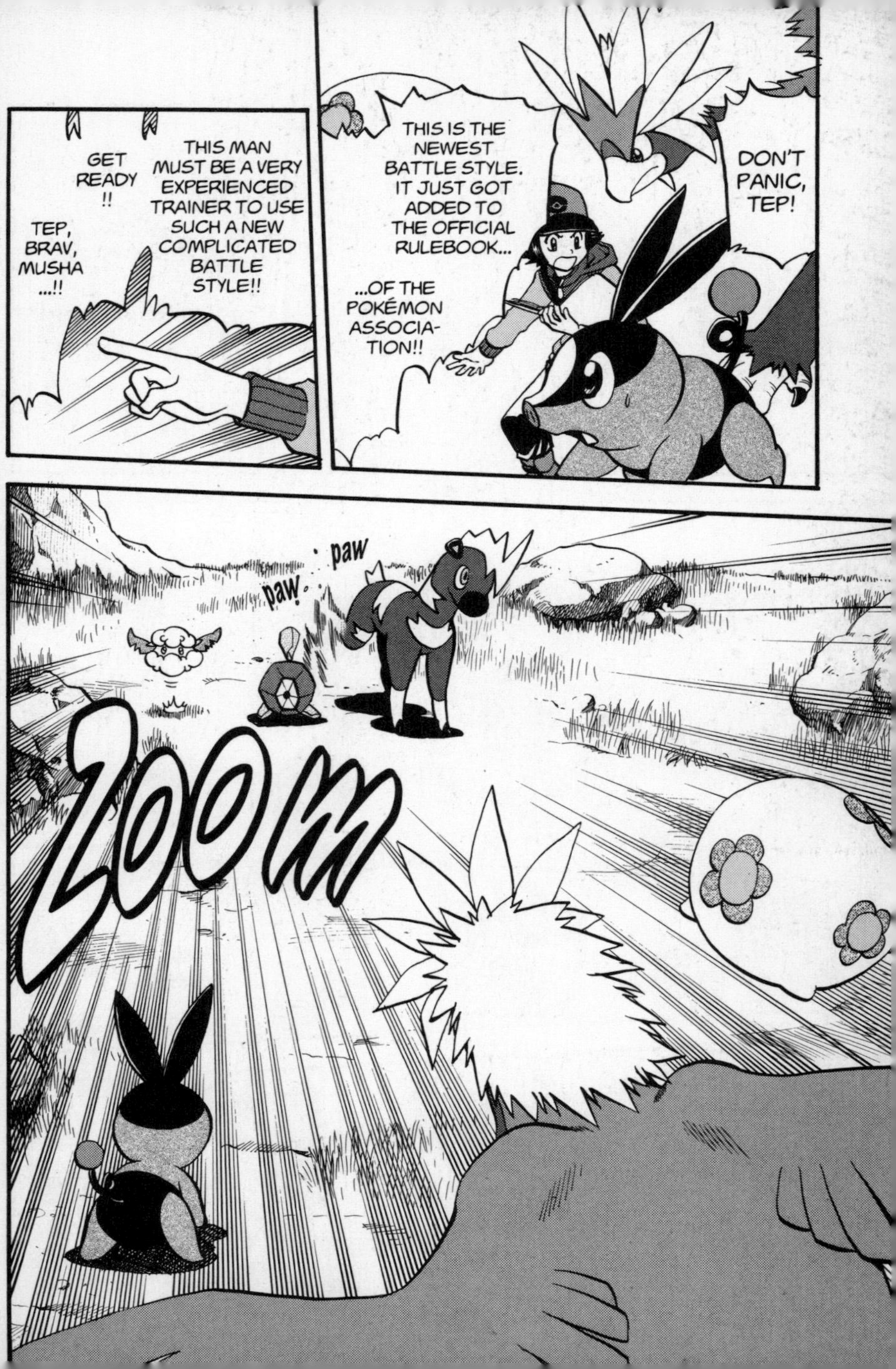
DON'T PANIC, TEP!
THIS IS THE NEWEST BATTLE STYLE. IT JUST GOT ADDED TO THE OFFICIAL RULEBOOK...
...OF THE POKÉMON ASSOCIATION!!
THIS MAN MUST BE A VERY EXPERIENCED TRAINER TO USE SUCH A NEW COMPLICATED BATTLE STYLE!!
GET READY !!
TEP, BRAV, MUSHA ...!!
paw
paw
ZOOM

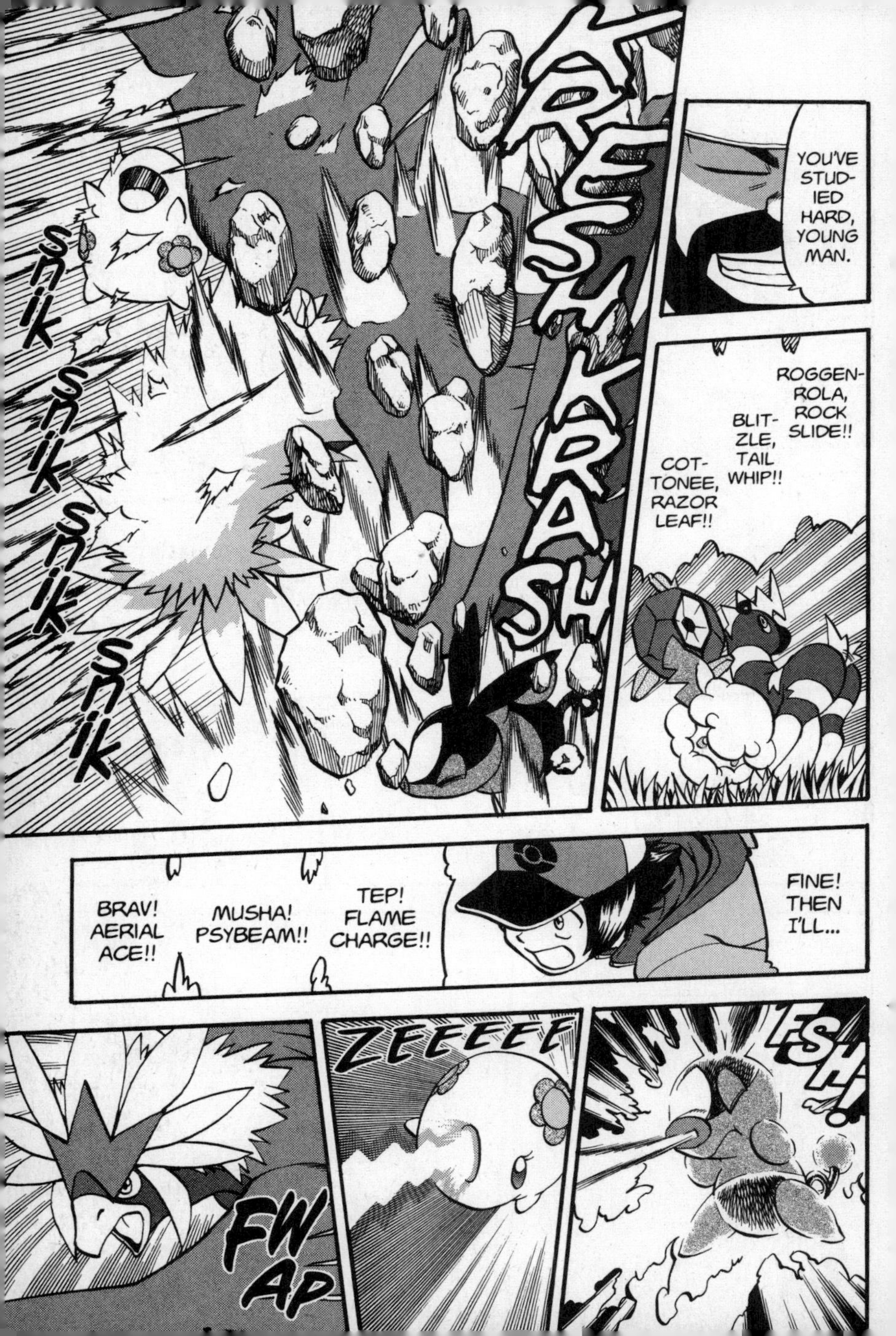
YOU'VE STUDIED HARD, YOUNG MAN.
ROGGENROLA, ROCK SLIDE!!
BLITZLE, TAIL WHIP!!
COTTONEE, RAZOR LEAF!!
KRESHKRASH
SNIK SNIK SNIK SNIK SNIK
FINE! THEN I'LL...
TEP! FLAME CHARGE!!
MUSHA! PSYBEAM!!
BRAV! AERIAL ACE!!
FSH!
ZEEEEEE
FWAP

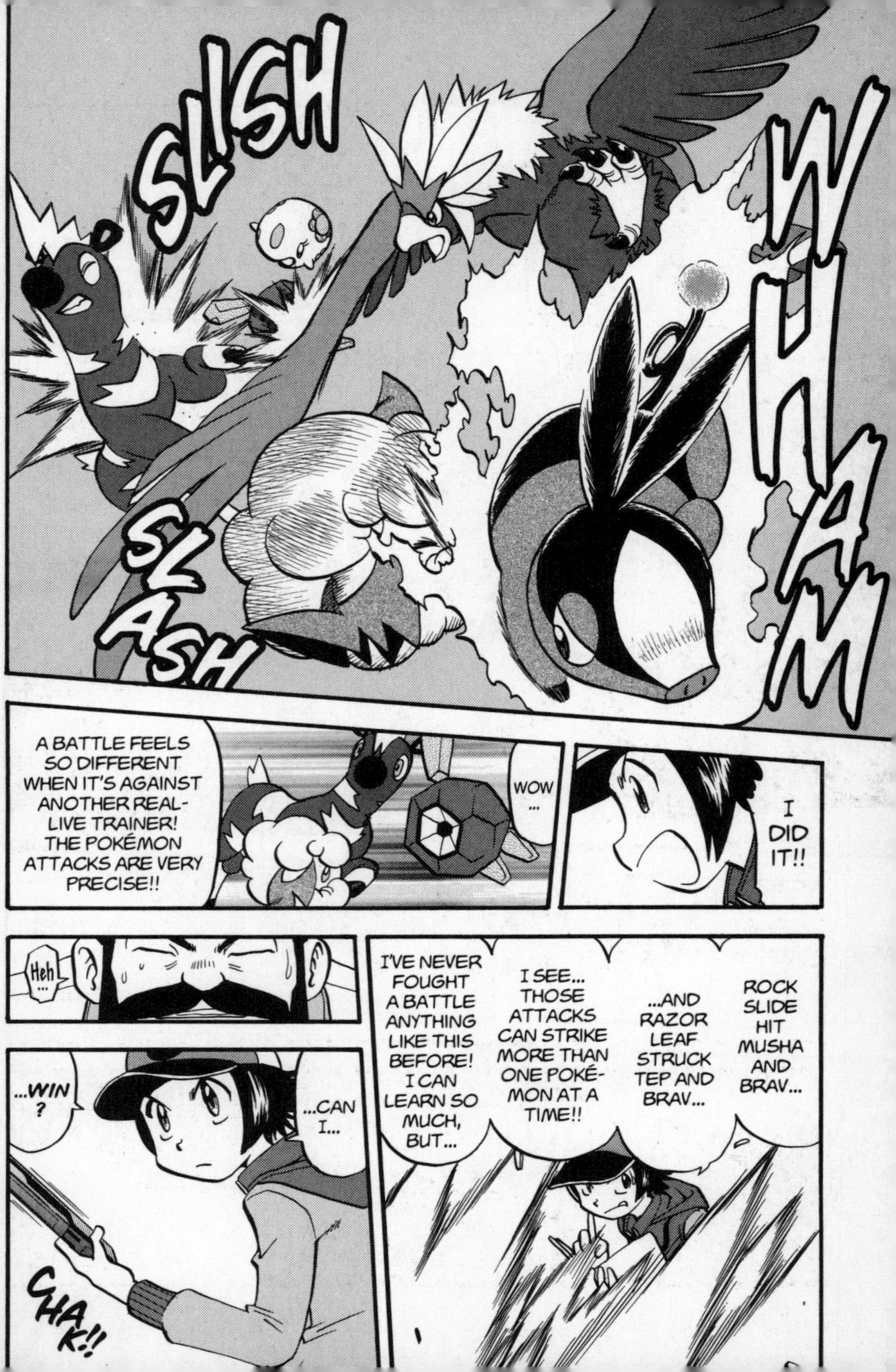
WHAM
SLISH
SLASH
I DID IT!!
WOW ...
A BATTLE FEELS SO DIFFERENT WHEN IT'S AGAINST ANOTHER REAL-LIVE TRAINER! THE POKÉMON ATTACKS ARE VERY PRECISE!!
ROCK SLIDE HIT MUSHA AND BRAV...
...AND RAZOR LEAF STRUCK TEP AND BRAV...
I SEE... THOSE ATTACKS CAN STRIKE MORE THAN ONE POKÉ-MON AT A TIME!!
I'VE NEVER FOUGHT A BATTLE ANYTHING LIKE THIS BEFORE! I CAN LEARN SO MUCH, BUT...
Heh ...
...CAN I...
...WIN ?
CHAK!!

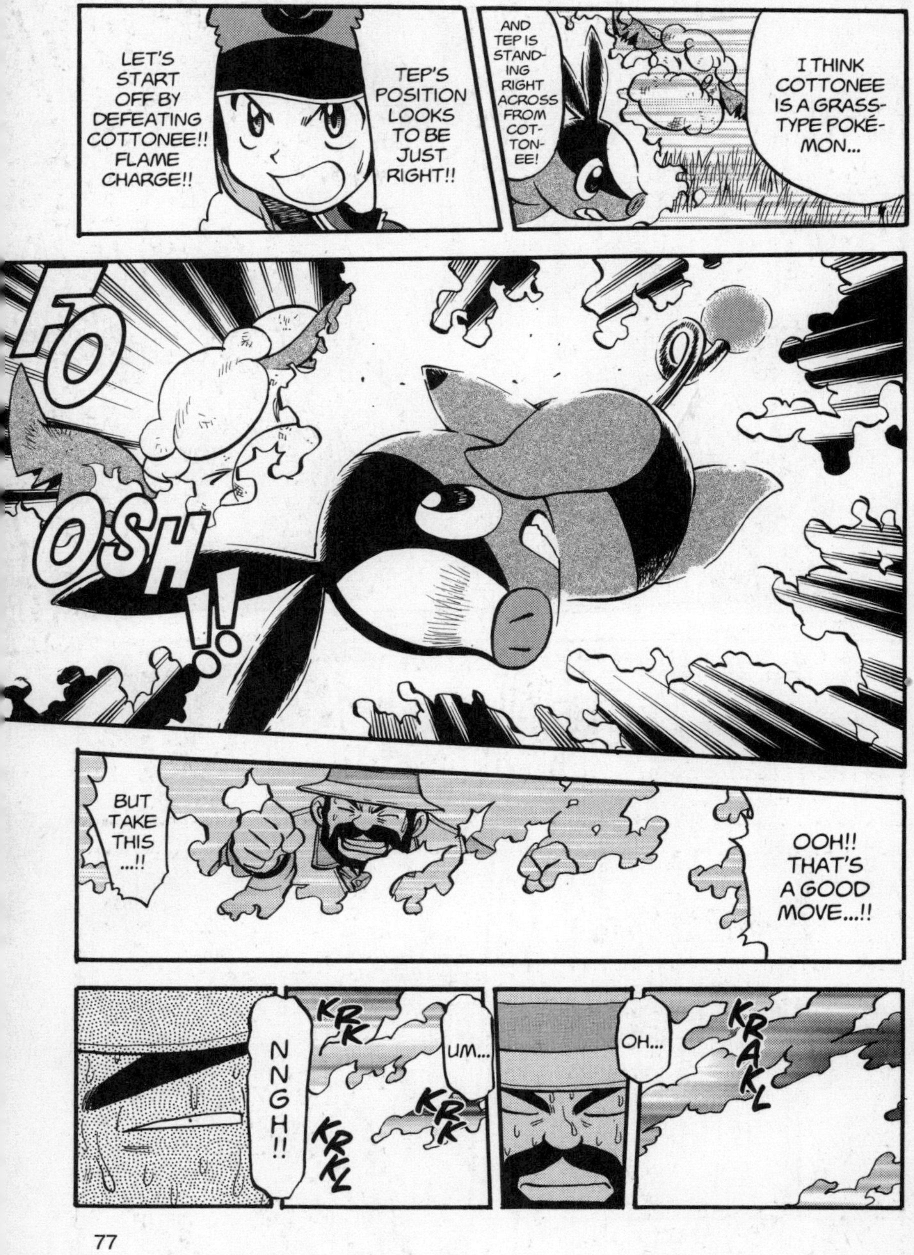
I THINK COTTONEE IS A GRASS-TYPE POKÉMON...
AND TEP IS STANDING RIGHT ACROSS FROM COTTONEE!
TEP'S POSITION LOOKS TO BE JUST RIGHT!!
LET'S START OFF BY DEFEATING COTTONEE!! FLAME CHARGE!!
FOOSH!!
OOH!! THAT'S A GOOD MOVE...!!
BUT TAKE THIS ...!!
KRAKL
OH...
UM...
KRK
KRK
NNGH!!
KRKL

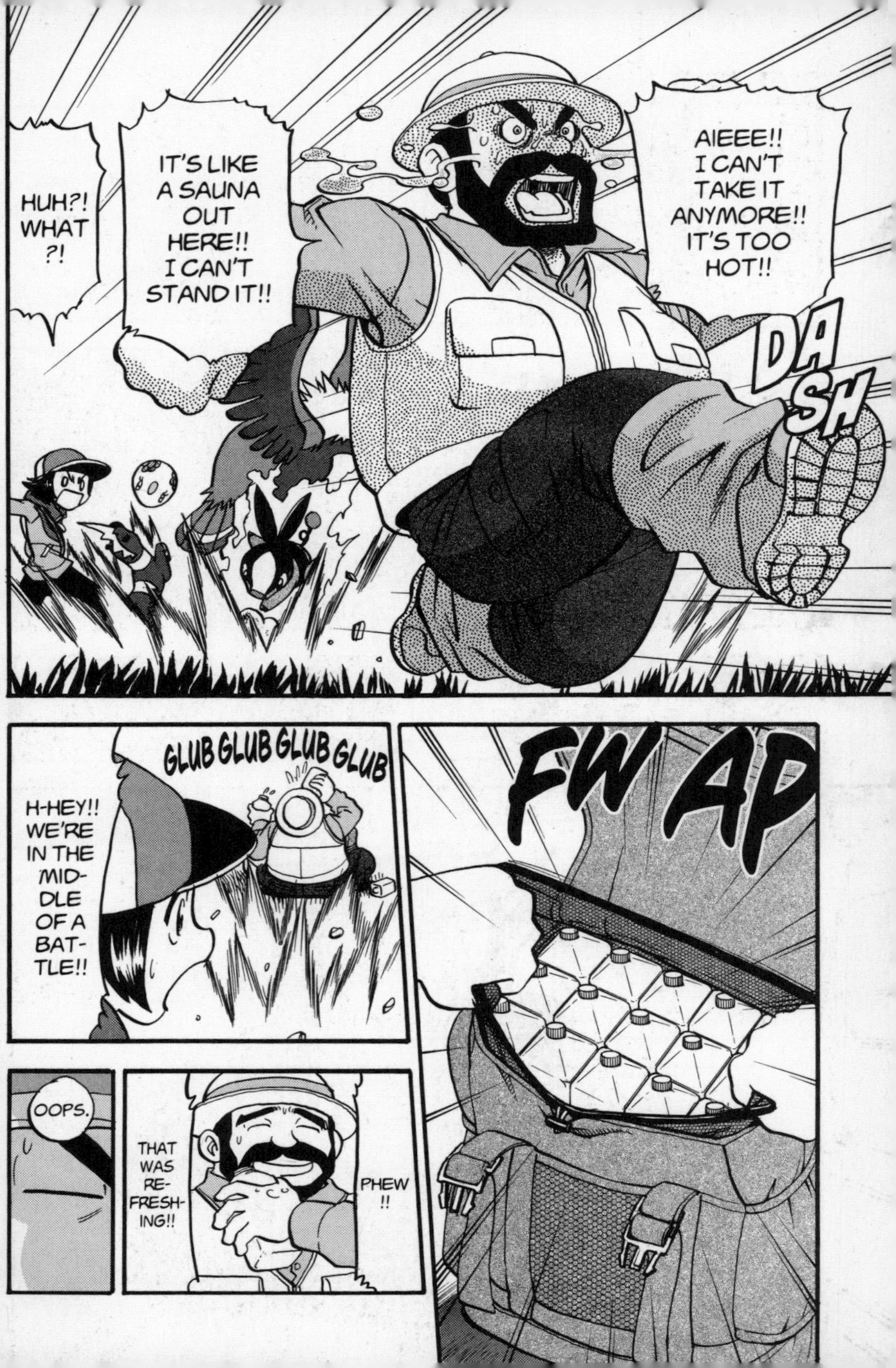
AIEEE!! I CAN'T TAKE IT ANYMORE!! IT'S TOO HOT!!
DASH
IT'S LIKE A SAUNA OUT HERE!! I CAN'T STAND IT!!
HUH?! WHAT ?!
FWAP
GLUB GLUB GLUB GLUB
H-HEY!! WE'RE IN THE MID-DLE OF A BAT-TLE!!
PHEW !!
THAT WAS RE-FRESH-ING!!
OOPS.

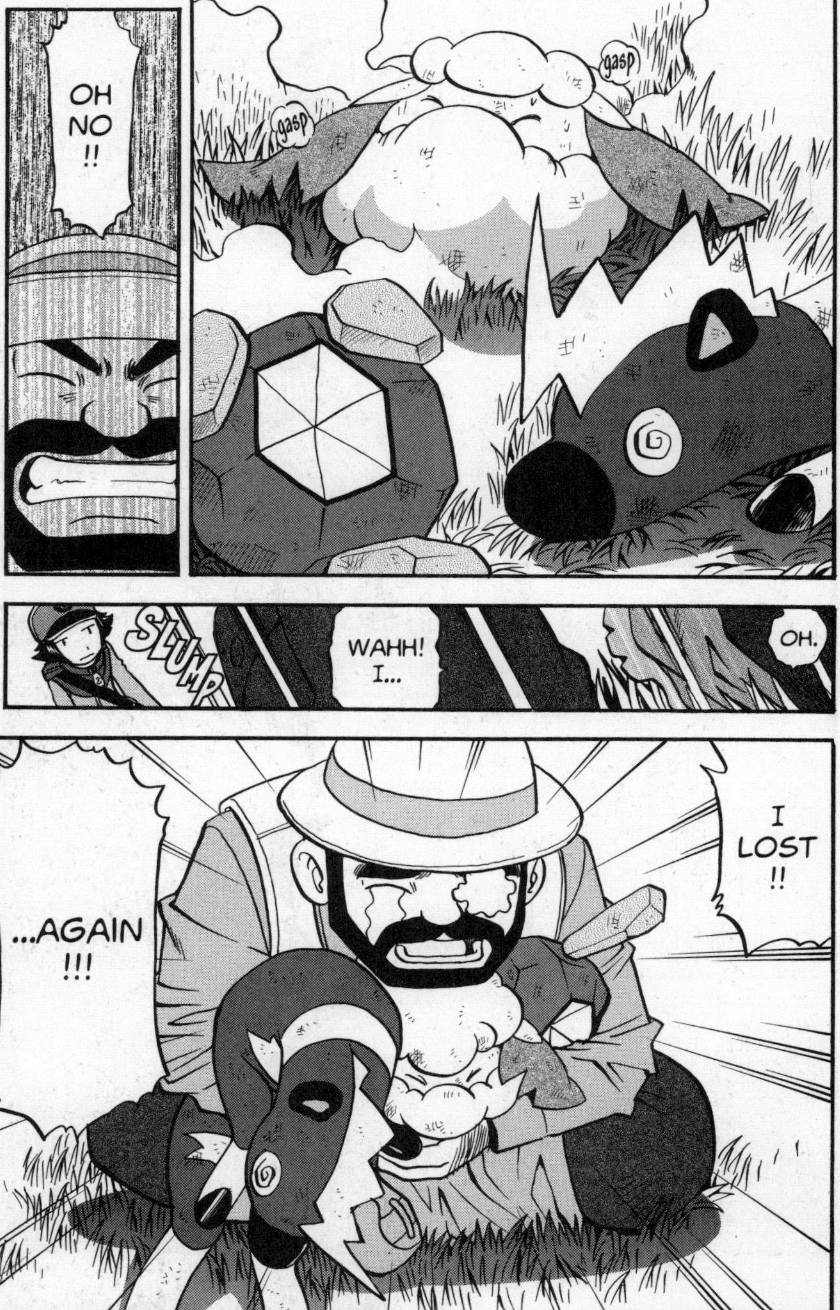
gasp
gasp
OH NO !!
OH.
WAHH! I...
SLUMP
I LOST !!
...AGAIN !!!

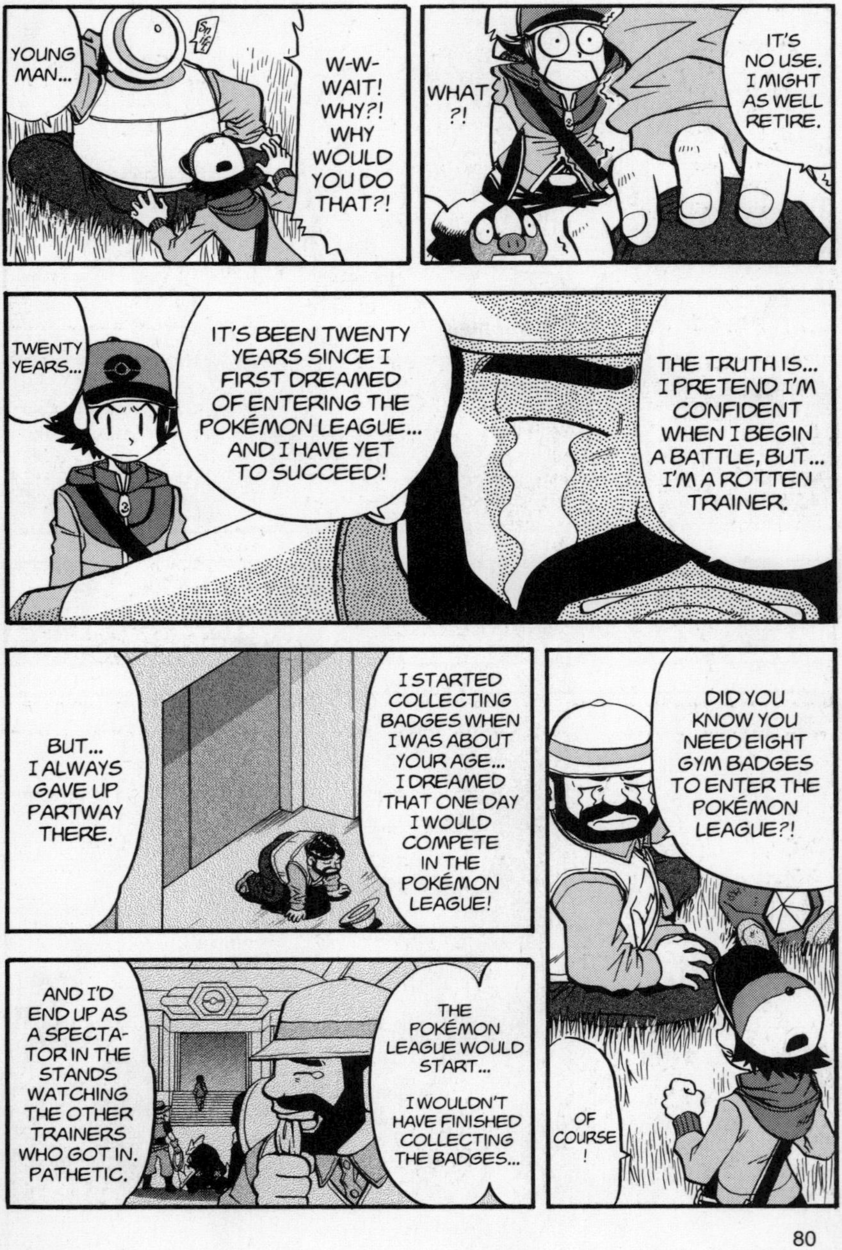
IT'S NO USE. I MIGHT AS WELL RETIRE.
WHAT?!
W-W-WAIT! WHY?! WHY WOULD YOU DO THAT?!
YOUNG MAN...
THE TRUTH IS... I PRETEND I'M CONFIDENT WHEN I BEGIN A BATTLE, BUT... I'M A ROTTEN TRAINER.
IT'S BEEN TWENTY YEARS SINCE I FIRST DREAMED OF ENTERING THE POKÉMON LEAGUE... AND I HAVE YET TO SUCCEED!
TWENTY YEARS...
DID YOU KNOW YOU NEED EIGHT GYM BADGES TO ENTER THE POKÉMON LEAGUE?!
OF COURSE!
I STARTED COLLECTING BADGES WHEN I WAS ABOUT YOUR AGE... I DREAMED THAT ONE DAY I WOULD COMPETE IN THE POKÉMON LEAGUE!
BUT... I ALWAYS GAVE UP PARTWAY THERE.
THE POKÉMON LEAGUE WOULD START...
I WOULDN'T HAVE FINISHED COLLECTING THE BADGES...
AND I'D END UP AS A SPECTATOR IN THE STANDS WATCHING THE OTHER TRAINERS WHO GOT IN. PATHETIC.

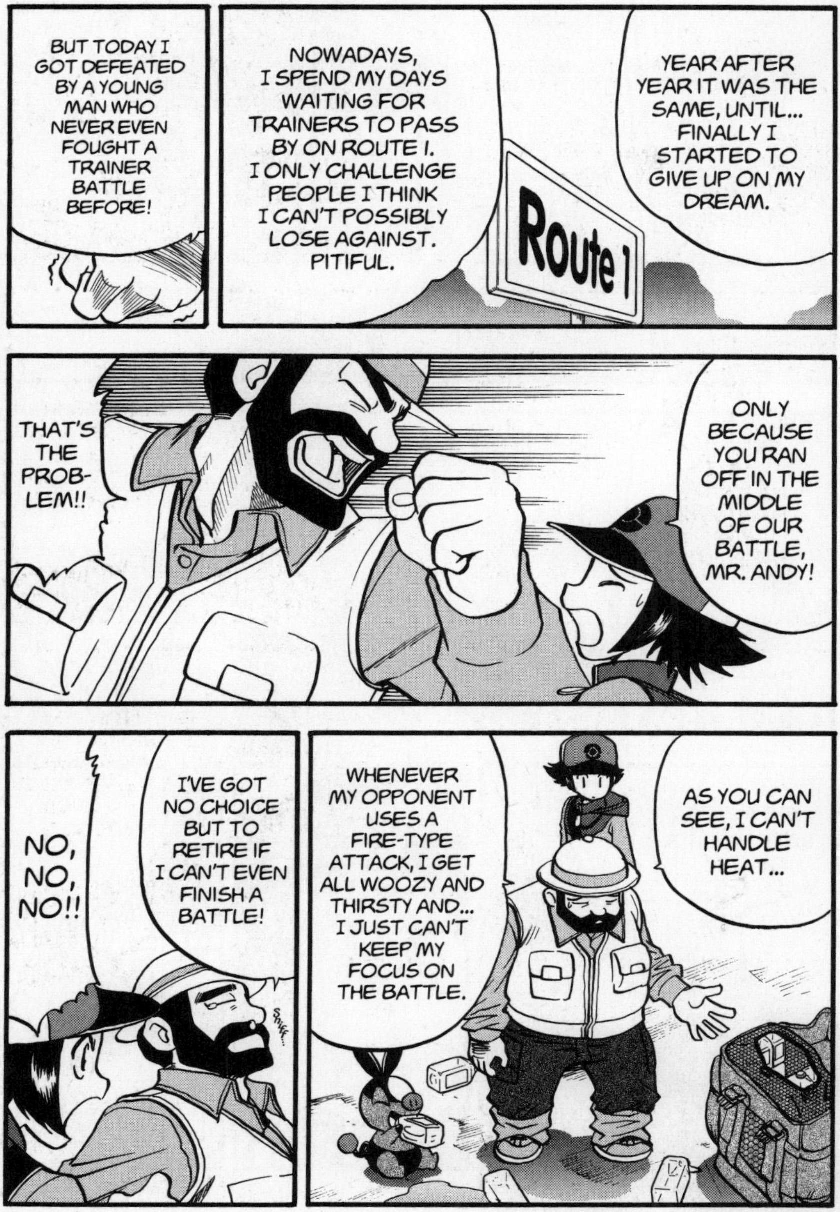
YEAR AFTER YEAR IT WAS THE SAME, UNTIL... FINALLY I STARTED TO GIVE UP ON MY DREAM.
Route 1
NOWADAYS, I SPEND MY DAYS WAITING FOR TRAINERS TO PASS BY ON ROUTE 1. I ONLY CHALLENGE PEOPLE I THINK I CAN'T POSSIBLY LOSE AGAINST. PITIFUL.
BUT TODAY I GOT DEFEATED BY A YOUNG MAN WHO NEVER EVEN FOUGHT A TRAINER BATTLE BEFORE!
ONLY BECAUSE YOU RAN OFF IN THE MIDDLE OF OUR BATTLE, MR. ANDY!
THAT'S THE PROB-LEM!!
AS YOU CAN SEE, I CAN'T HANDLE HEAT...
WHENEVER MY OPPONENT USES A FIRE-TYPE ATTACK, I GET ALL WOOZY AND THIRSTY AND... I JUST CAN'T KEEP MY FOCUS ON THE BATTLE.
I'VE GOT NO CHOICE BUT TO RETIRE IF I CAN'T EVEN FINISH A BATTLE!
NO, NO, NO!!
SNIFF...

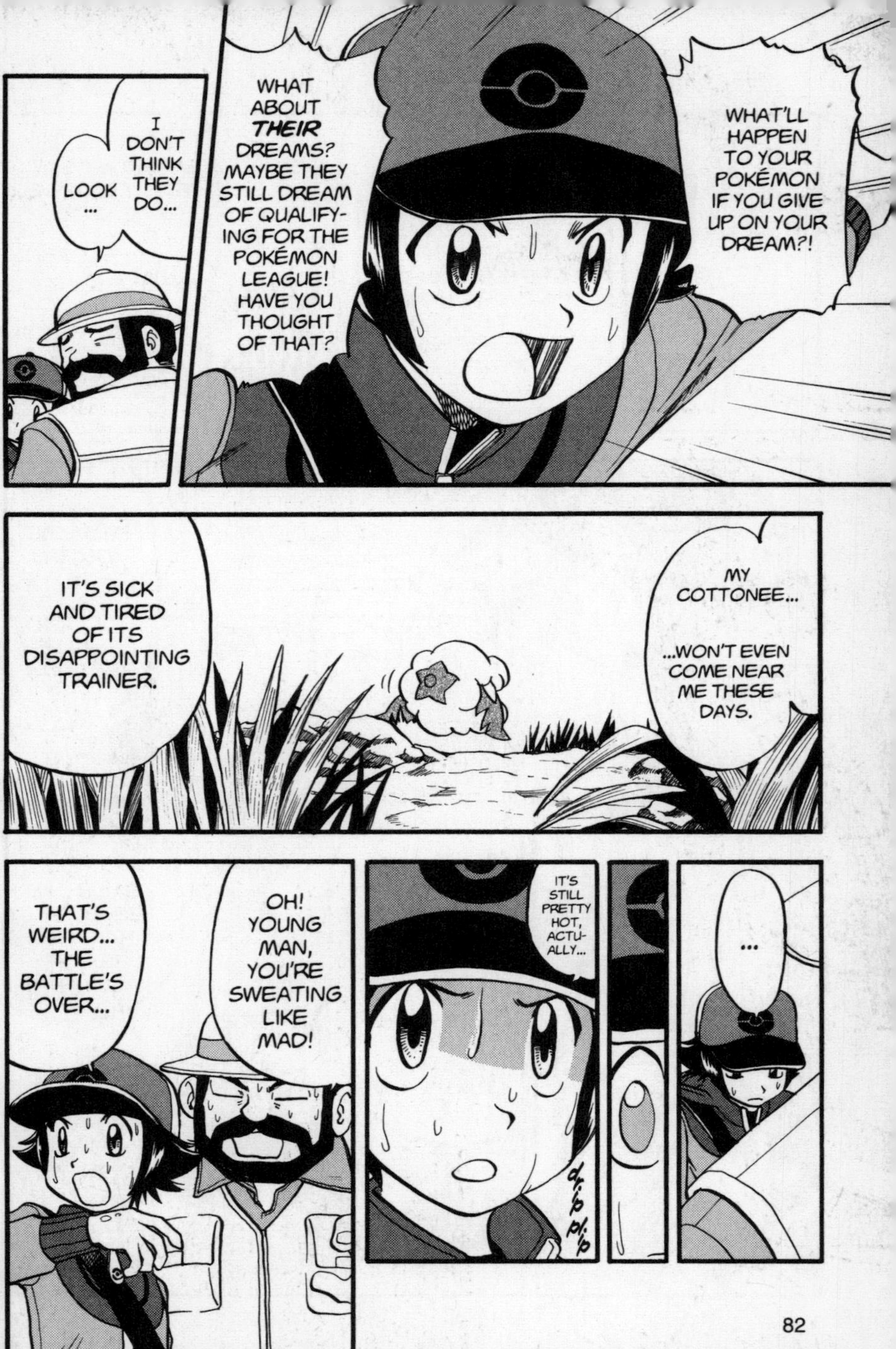
WHAT'LL HAPPEN TO YOUR POKÉMON IF YOU GIVE UP ON YOUR DREAM?!
WHAT ABOUT THEIR DREAMS? MAYBE THEY STILL DREAM OF QUALIFYING FOR THE POKÉMON LEAGUE! HAVE YOU THOUGHT OF THAT?
I DON'T THINK THEY DO...
LOOK...
MY COTTONEE...
...WON'T EVEN COME NEAR ME THESE DAYS.
IT'S SICK AND TIRED OF ITS DISAPPOINTING TRAINER.
...
IT'S STILL PRETTY HOT, ACTUALLY...
drip plip
OH! YOUNG MAN, YOU'RE SWEATING LIKE MAD!
THAT'S WEIRD... THE BATTLE'S OVER...

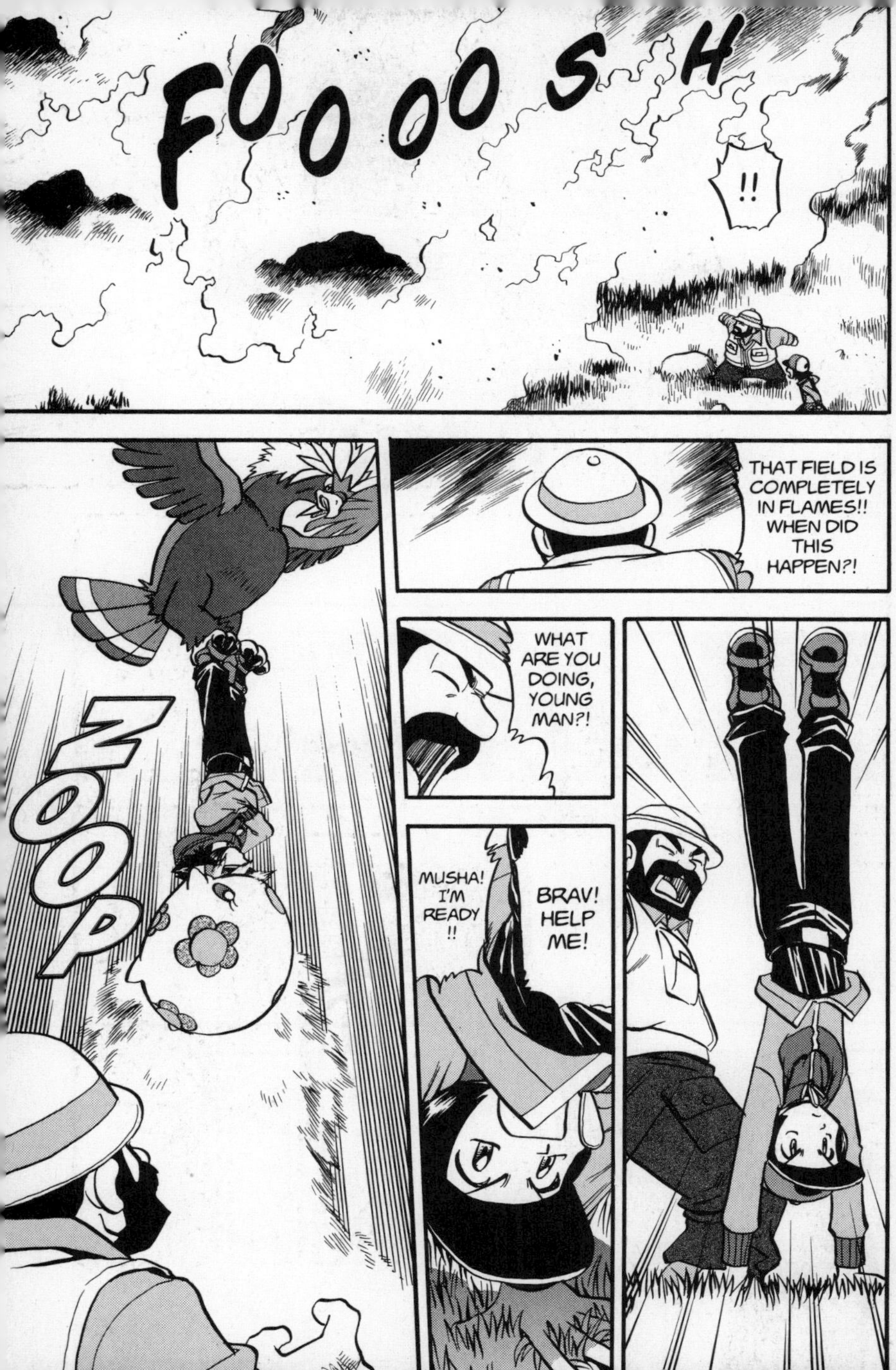
FOOOOSH
!!
THAT FIELD IS COMPLETELY IN FLAMES!! WHEN DID THIS HAPPEN?!
WHAT ARE YOU DOING, YOUNG MAN?!
BRAV! HELP ME!
MUSHA! I'M READY !!
ZOOOP

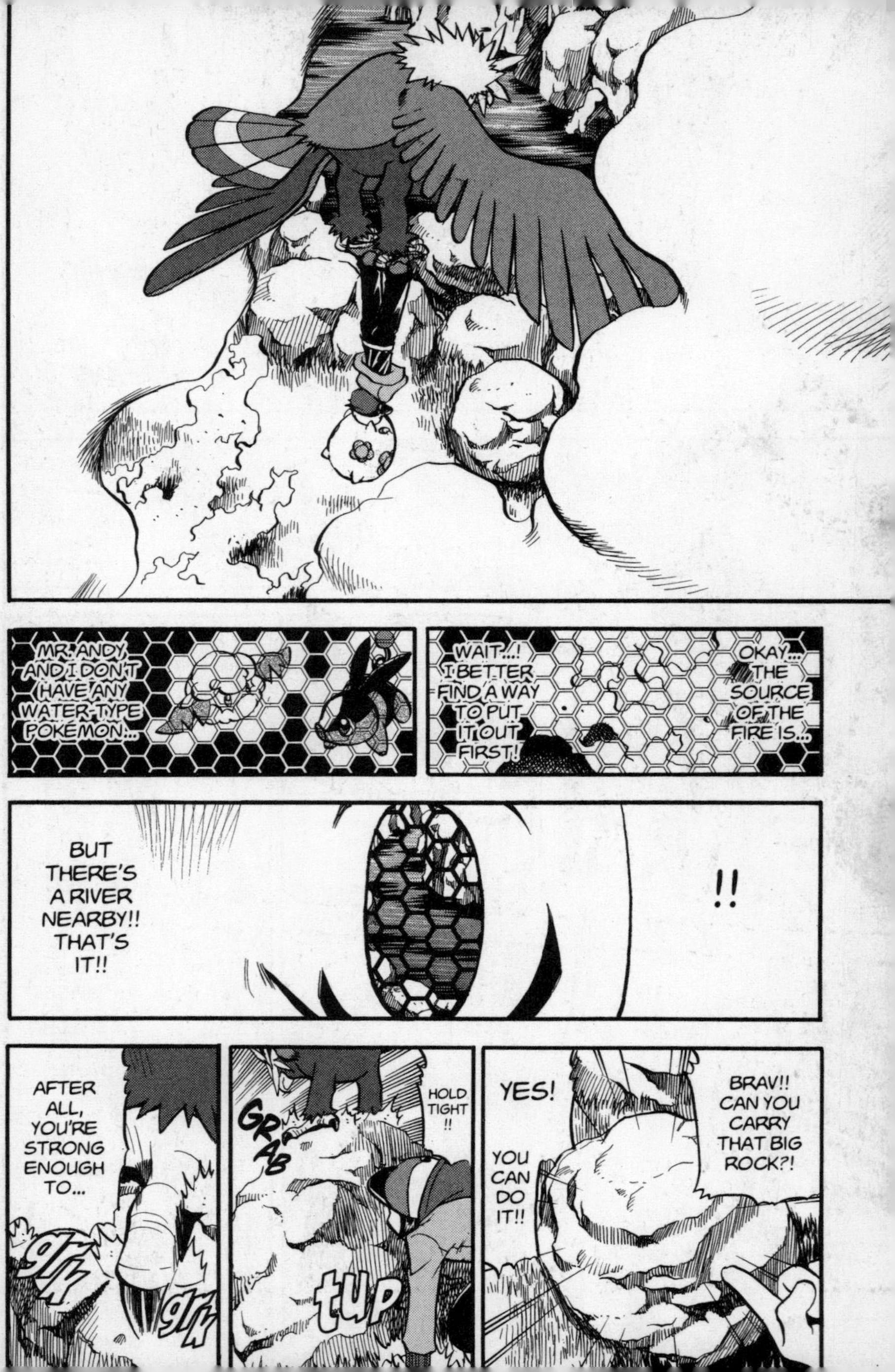
OKAY... THE SOURCE OF THE FIRE IS...
WAIT...! I BETTER FIND A WAY TO PUT IT OUT FIRST!
MR. ANDY AND I DON'T HAVE ANY WATER-TYPE POKÉMON...
!!
BUT THERE'S A RIVER NEARBY!! THAT'S IT!!
BRAV!! CAN YOU CARRY THAT BIG ROCK?!
YES!
YOU CAN DO IT!!
HOLD TIGHT!!
GRAB
TUP
AFTER ALL, YOU'RE STRONG ENOUGH TO...
grk
grk

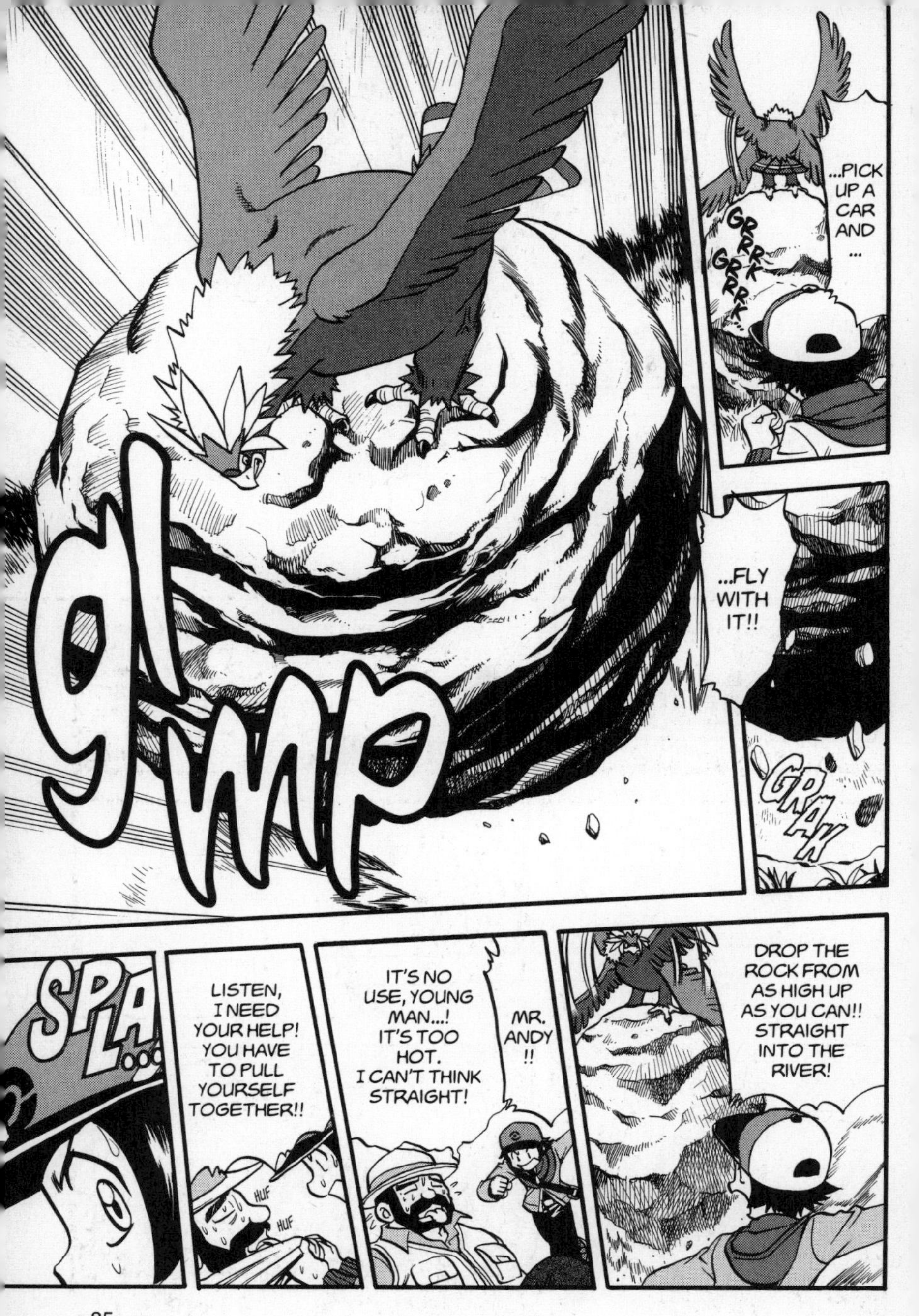
...PICK UP A CAR AND ...
GRRRK GRRRK
...FLY WITH IT!!
GRAK
GLMP
DROP THE ROCK FROM AS HIGH UP AS YOU CAN!! STRAIGHT INTO THE RIVER!
MR. ANDY !!
IT'S NO USE, YOUNG MAN...! IT'S TOO HOT. I CAN'T THINK STRAIGHT!
LISTEN, I NEED YOUR HELP! YOU HAVE TO PULL YOURSELF TOGETHER!!
HUF
HUF
SPLA...

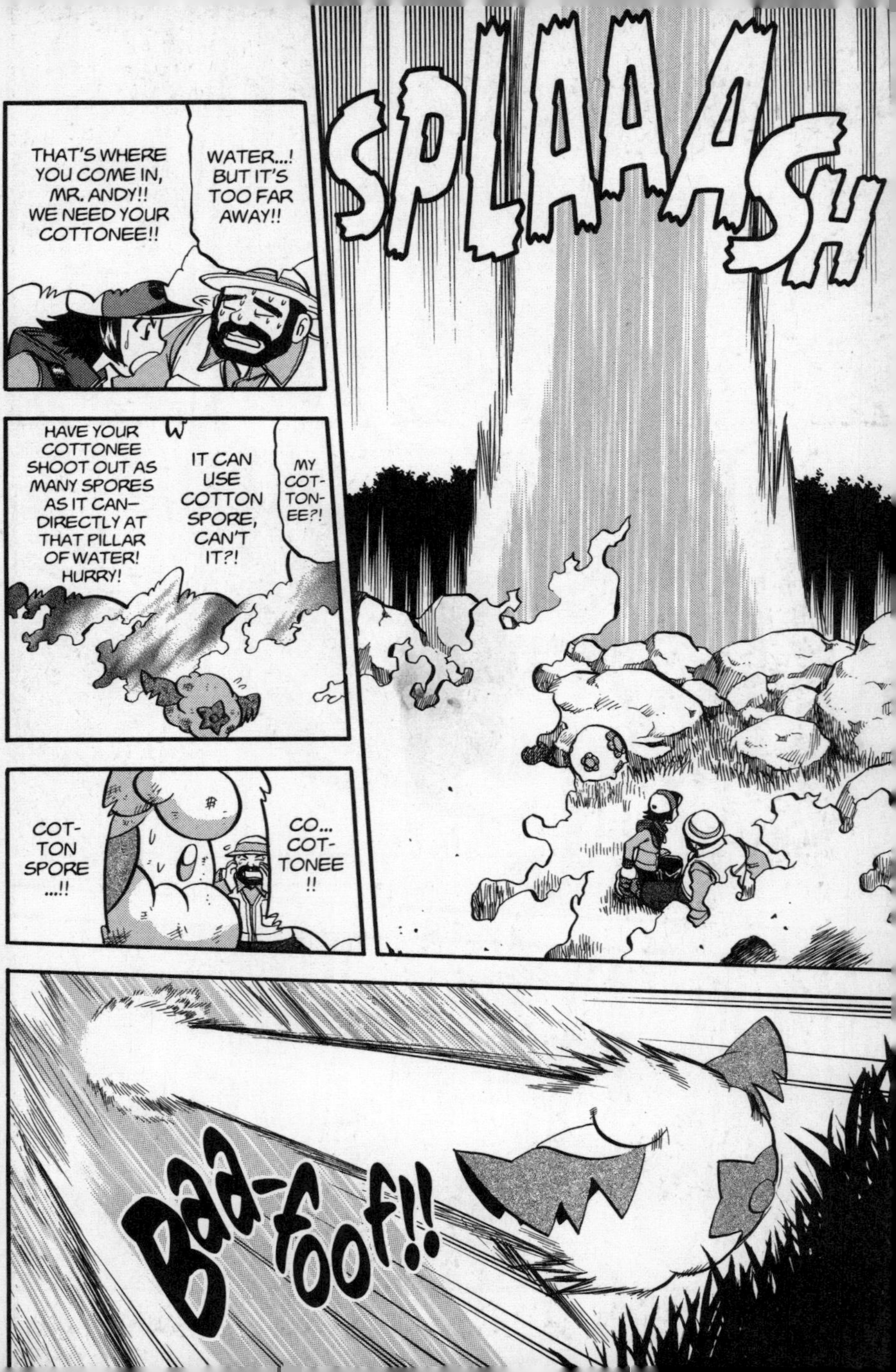
SPLAAASH
WATER...! BUT IT'S TOO FAR AWAY!!
THAT'S WHERE YOU COME IN, MR. ANDY!! WE NEED YOUR COTTONEE!!
MY COT-TON-EE?!
IT CAN USE COTTON SPORE, CAN'T IT?!
HAVE YOUR COTTONEE SHOOT OUT AS MANY SPORES AS IT CAN—DIRECTLY AT THAT PILLAR OF WATER! HURRY!
CO... COT-TONEE !!
COT-TON SPORE ...!!
Baa-foof!!

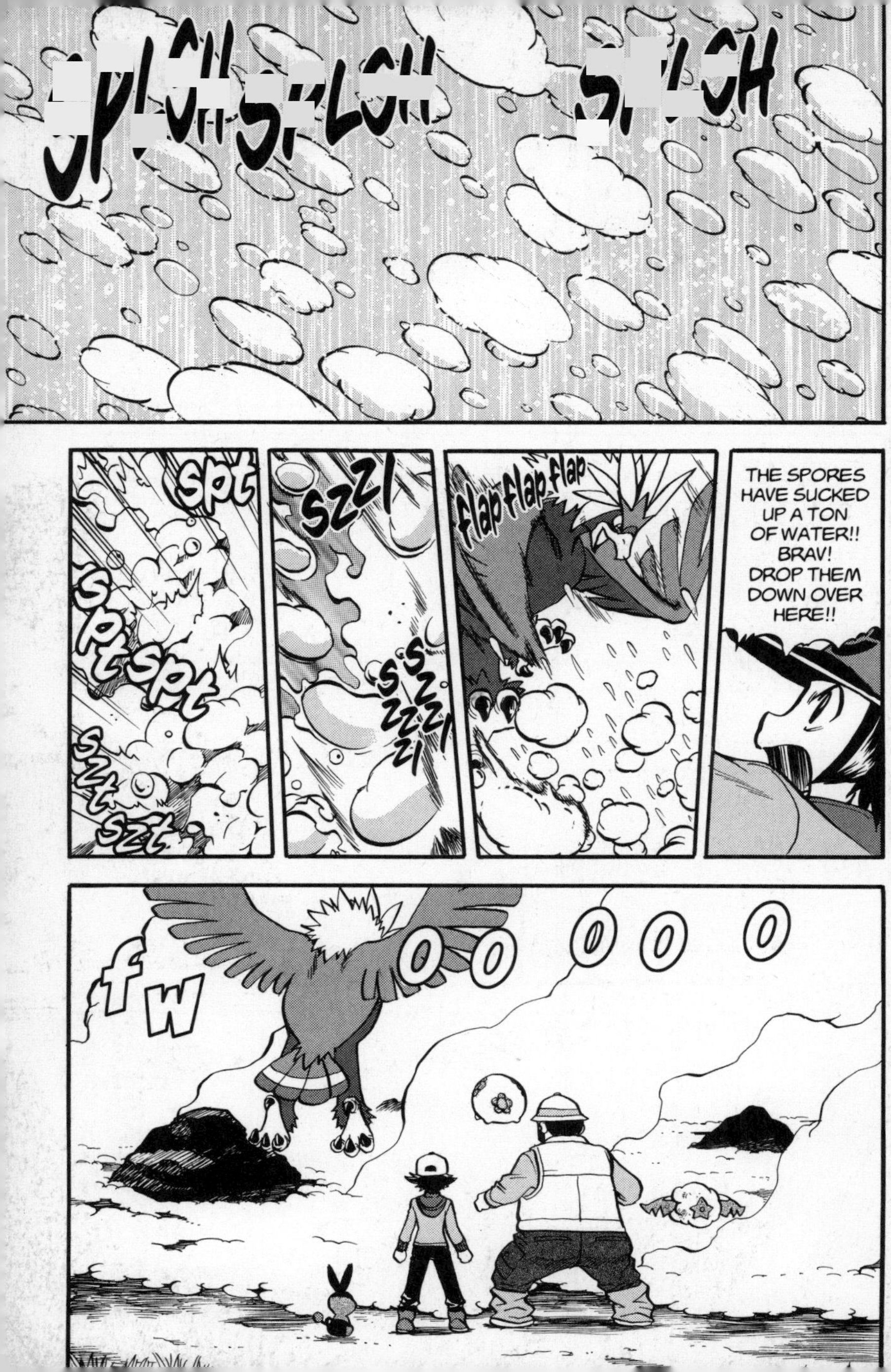
THE SPORES HAVE SUCKED UP A TON OF WATER!! BRAV! DROP THEM DOWN OVER HERE!!
flap flap flap
szzl
spt
spt spt
szt szt
fw

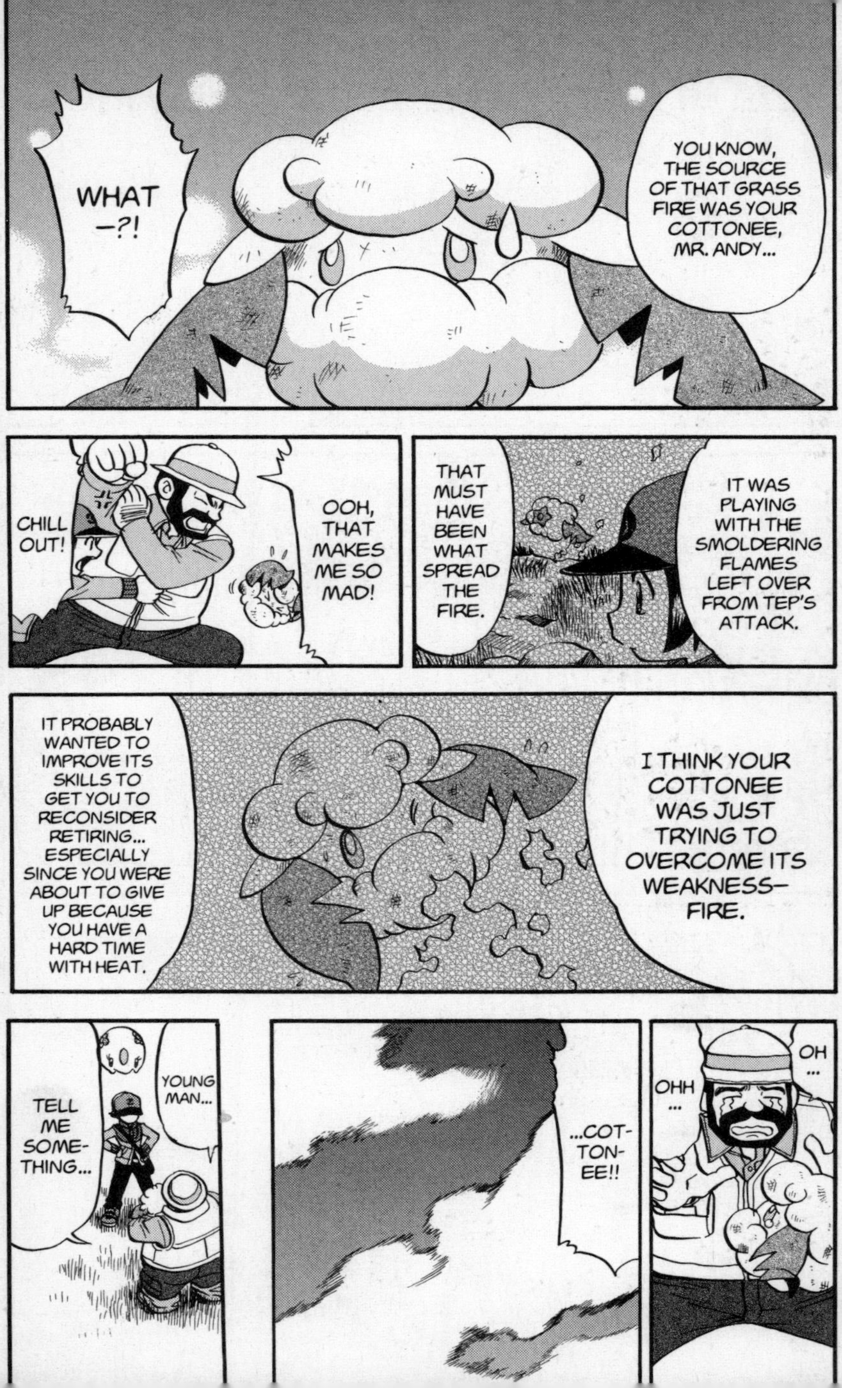
YOU KNOW, THE SOURCE OF THAT GRASS FIRE WAS YOUR COTTONEE, MR. ANDY...
WHAT —?!
IT WAS PLAYING WITH THE SMOLDERING FLAMES LEFT OVER FROM TEP'S ATTACK.
THAT MUST HAVE BEEN WHAT SPREAD THE FIRE.
OOH, THAT MAKES ME SO MAD!
CHILL OUT!
I THINK YOUR COTTONEE WAS JUST TRYING TO OVERCOME ITS WEAKNESS— FIRE.
IT PROBABLY WANTED TO IMPROVE ITS SKILLS TO GET YOU TO RECONSIDER RETIRING... ESPECIALLY SINCE YOU WERE ABOUT TO GIVE UP BECAUSE YOU HAVE A HARD TIME WITH HEAT.
OH ...
OHH ...
...COT-TON-EE!!
YOUNG MAN...
TELL ME SOME-THING...

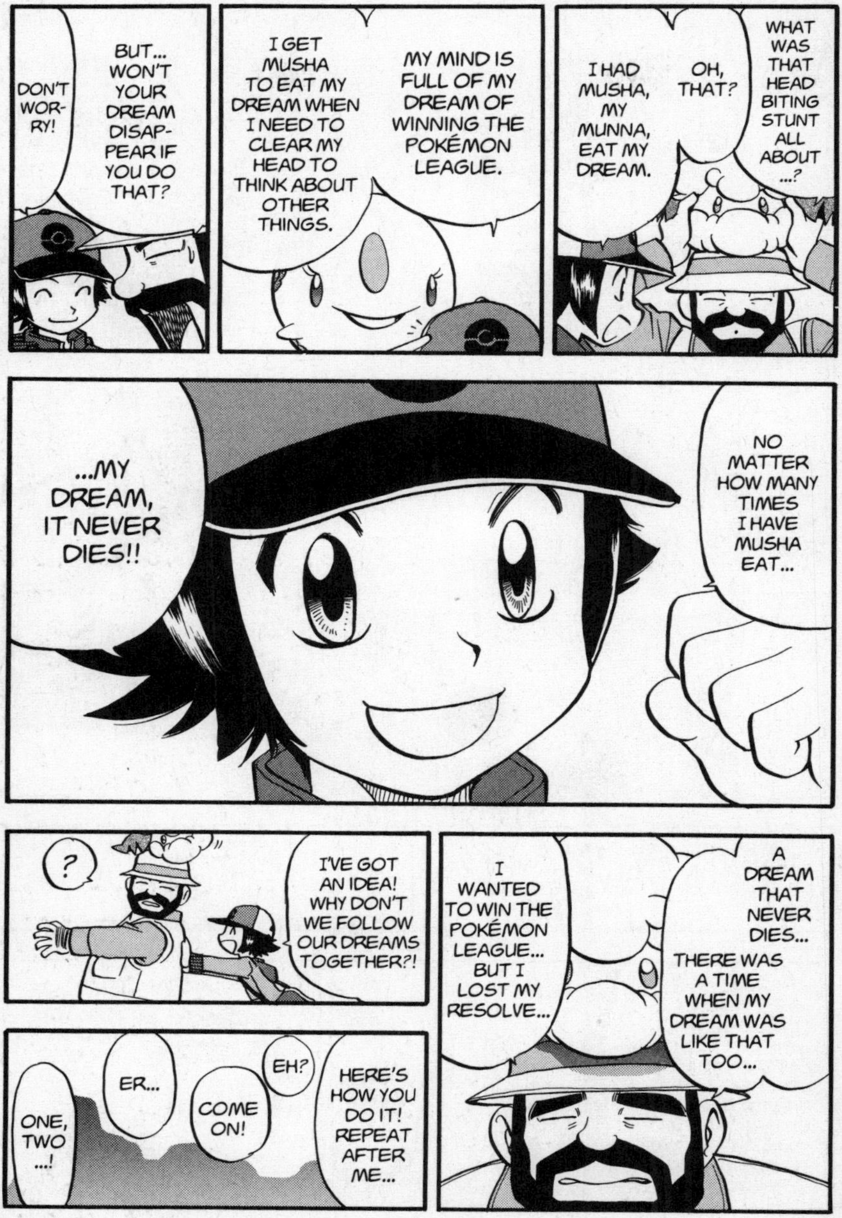
WHAT WAS THAT HEAD BITING STUNT ALL ABOUT ...?
OH, THAT?
I HAD MUSHA, MY MUNNA, EAT MY DREAM.
MY MIND IS FULL OF MY DREAM OF WINNING THE POKÉMON LEAGUE.
I GET MUSHA TO EAT MY DREAM WHEN I NEED TO CLEAR MY HEAD TO THINK ABOUT OTHER THINGS.
BUT... WON'T YOUR DREAM DISAPPEAR IF YOU DO THAT?
DON'T WORRY!
NO MATTER HOW MANY TIMES I HAVE MUSHA EAT...
...MY DREAM, IT NEVER DIES!!
A DREAM THAT NEVER DIES...
THERE WAS A TIME WHEN MY DREAM WAS LIKE THAT TOO...
I WANTED TO WIN THE POKÉMON LEAGUE... BUT I LOST MY RESOLVE...
I'VE GOT AN IDEA! WHY DON'T WE FOLLOW OUR DREAMS TOGETHER?!
?
HERE'S HOW YOU DO IT! REPEAT AFTER ME...
EH?
COME ON!
ER...
ONE, TWO ...!

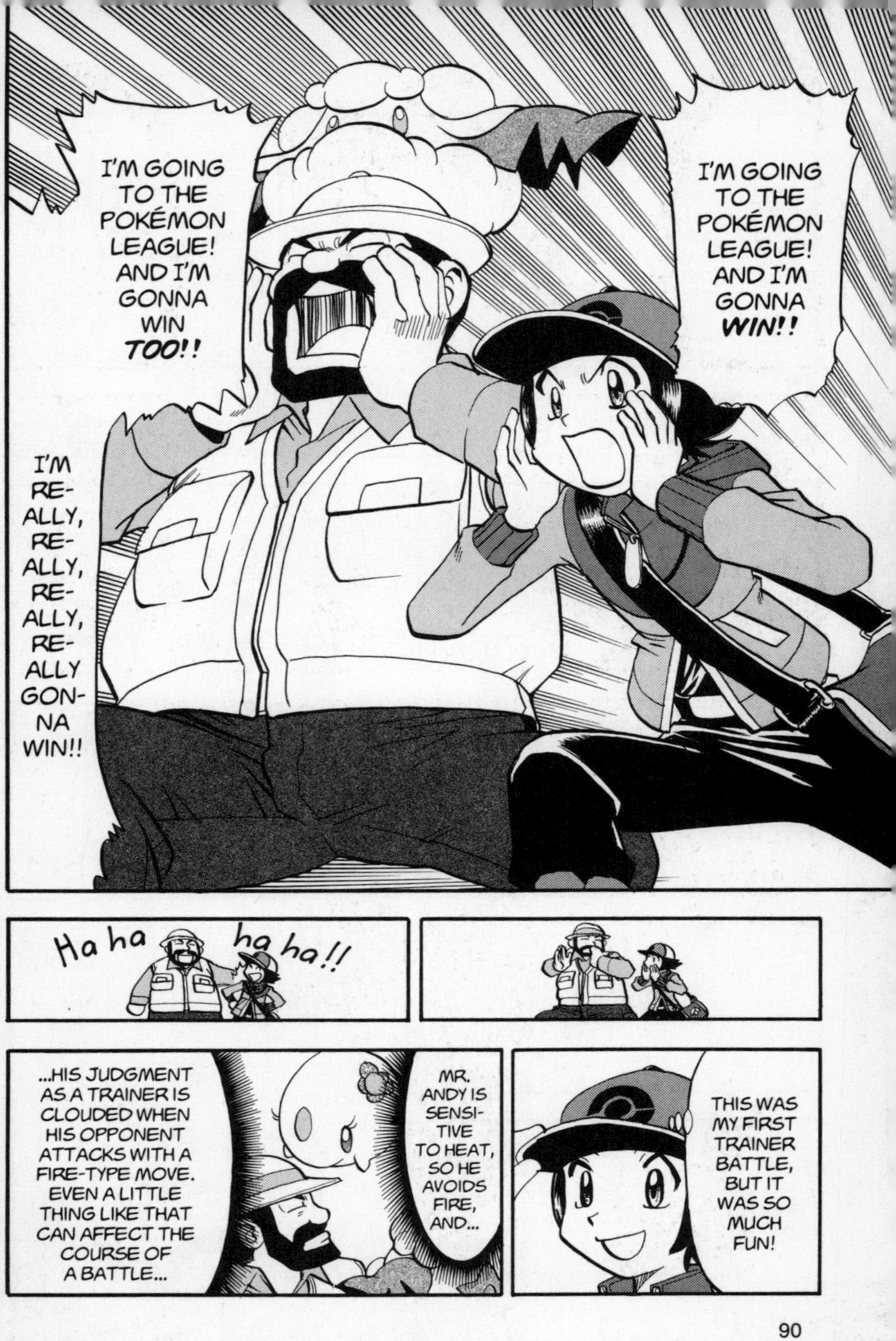
I'M GOING TO THE POKÉMON LEAGUE! AND I'M GONNA WIN!!
I'M GOING TO THE POKÉMON LEAGUE! AND I'M GONNA WIN TOO!!
I'M RE-ALLY, RE-ALLY, RE-ALLY, RE-ALLY GON-NA WIN!!
Ha ha ha ha!!
THIS WAS MY FIRST TRAINER BATTLE, BUT IT WAS SO MUCH FUN!
MR. ANDY IS SENSI-TIVE TO HEAT, SO HE AVOIDS FIRE, AND...
...HIS JUDGMENT AS A TRAINER IS CLOUDED WHEN HIS OPPONENT ATTACKS WITH A FIRE-TYPE MOVE. EVEN A LITTLE THING LIKE THAT CAN AFFECT THE COURSE OF A BATTLE...

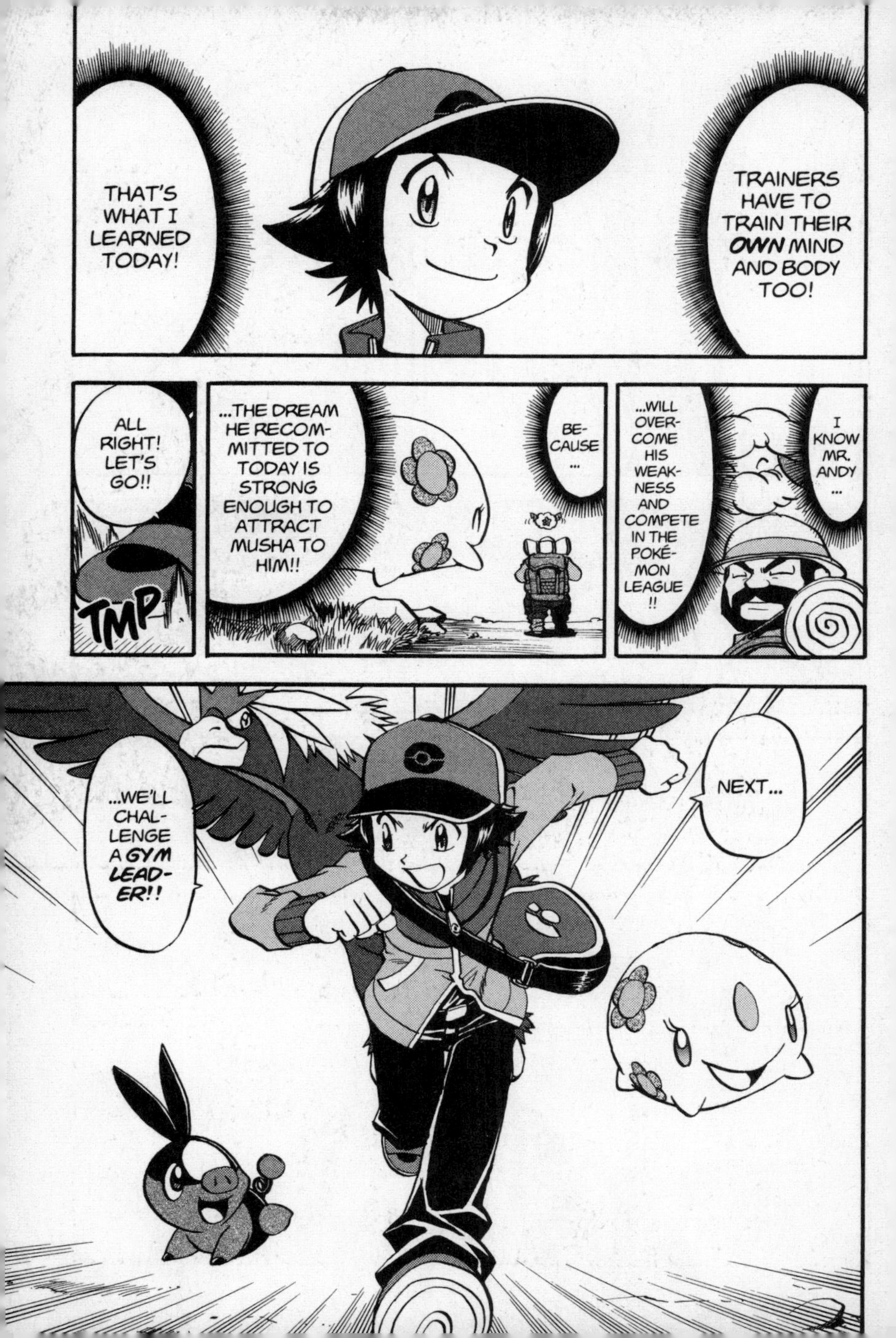
TRAINERS HAVE TO TRAIN THEIR **OWN** MIND AND BODY TOO!
THAT'S WHAT I LEARNED TODAY!
I KNOW MR. ANDY ...
...WILL OVER-COME HIS WEAK-NESS AND COMPETE IN THE POKÉ-MON LEAGUE !!
BE-CAUSE ...
...THE DREAM HE RECOM-MITTED TO TODAY IS STRONG ENOUGH TO ATTRACT MUSHA TO HIM!!
ALL RIGHT! LET'S GO!!
TMP
NEXT...
...WE'LL CHAL-LENGE A ***GYM LEAD-ER!!***

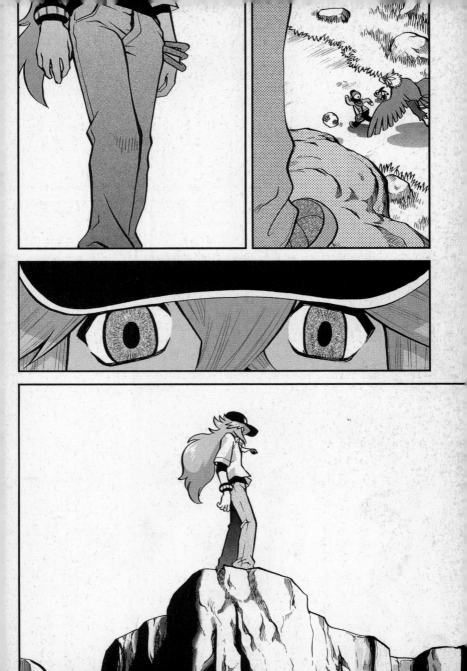

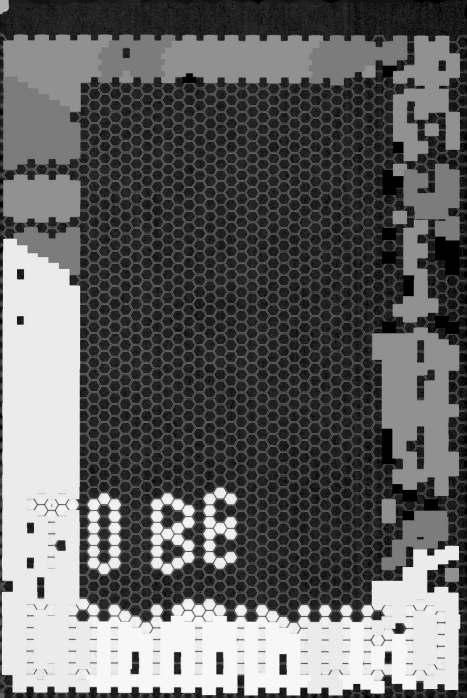

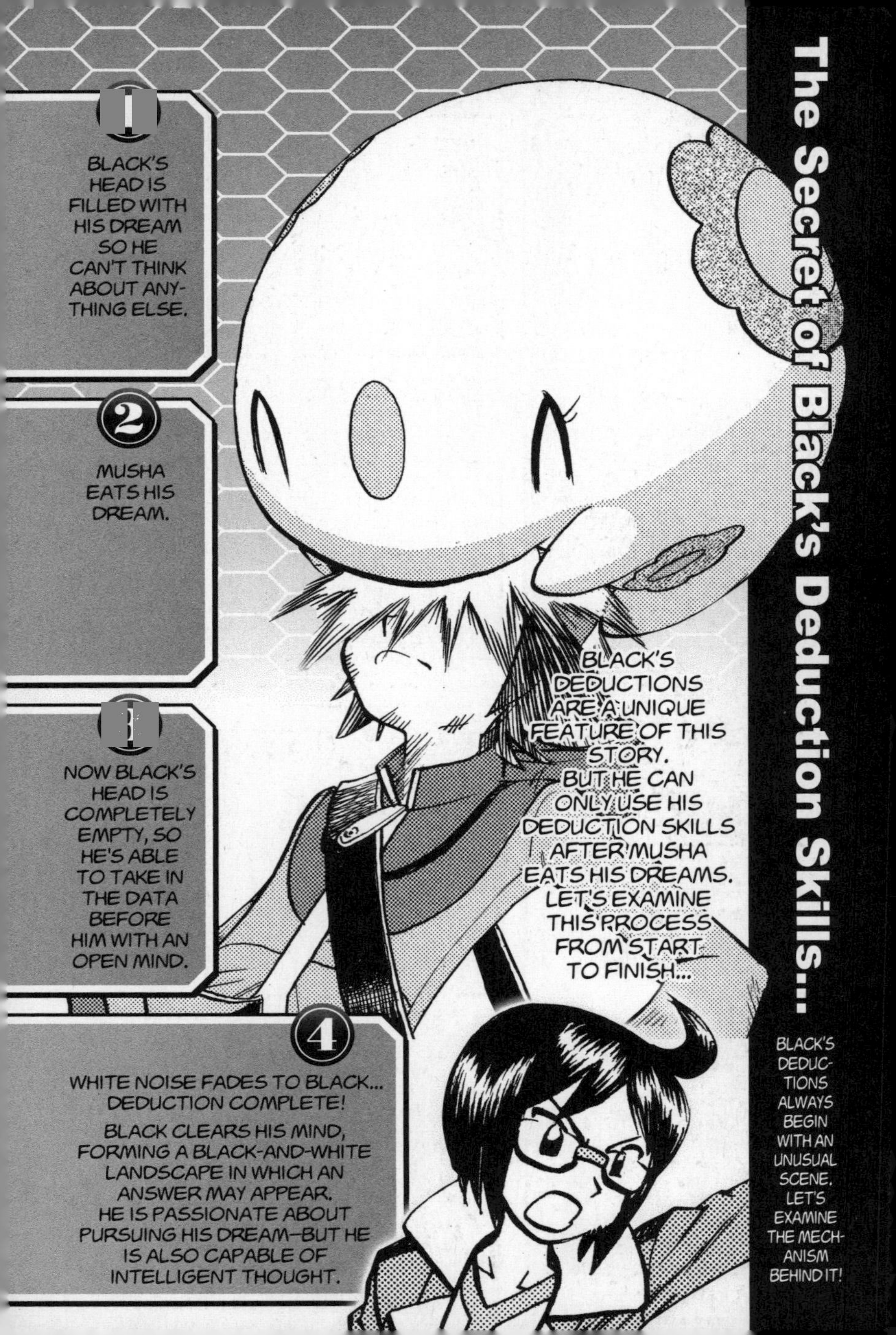
The Secret of Black's Deduction Skills...
BLACK'S DEDUCTIONS ALWAYS BEGIN WITH AN UNUSUAL SCENE. LET'S EXAMINE THE MECHANISM BEHIND IT!
BLACK'S DEDUCTIONS ARE A UNIQUE FEATURE OF THIS STORY. BUT HE CAN ONLY USE HIS DEDUCTION SKILLS AFTER MUSHA EATS HIS DREAMS. LET'S EXAMINE THIS PROCESS FROM START TO FINISH...
1
BLACK'S HEAD IS FILLED WITH HIS DREAM SO HE CAN'T THINK ABOUT ANYTHING ELSE.
2
MUSHA EATS HIS DREAM.
3
NOW BLACK'S HEAD IS COMPLETELY EMPTY, SO HE'S ABLE TO TAKE IN THE DATA BEFORE HIM WITH AN OPEN MIND.
4
WHITE NOISE FADES TO BLACK... DEDUCTION COMPLETE!
BLACK CLEARS HIS MIND, FORMING A BLACK-AND-WHITE LANDSCAPE IN WHICH AN ANSWER MAY APPEAR. HE IS PASSIONATE ABOUT PURSUING HIS DREAM—BUT HE IS ALSO CAPABLE OF INTELLIGENT THOUGHT.

What is Munna?

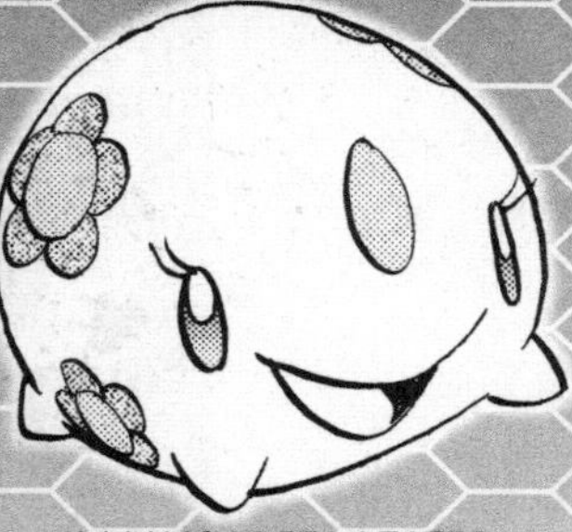

MUNNA IS A DREAM EATER POKÉMON. AS YOU MIGHT SUSPECT FROM ITS CATEGORY NAME, IT EATS THE DREAMS OF PEOPLE AND POKÉMON. BLACK'S DEDUCTION SKILLS DEPEND ON MUNNA EATING UP HIS DREAM. SINCE HIS DREAM ALWAYS IMMEDIATELY RE-ENTERS HIS HEAD, BLACK DOESN'T MIND.

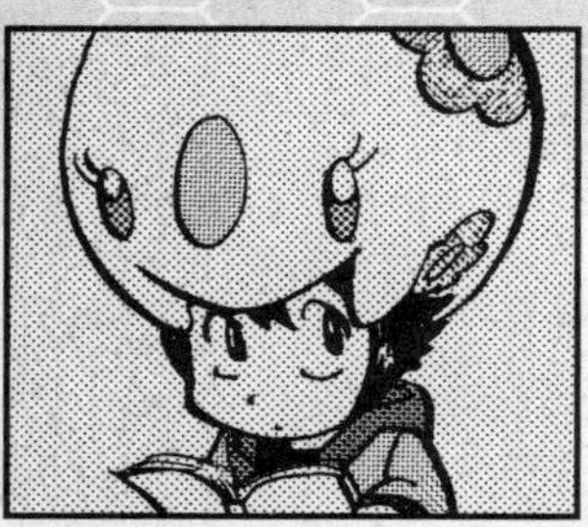

▲THIS MUSHA HAS KNOWN BLACK SINCE HE WAS A SMALL CHILD. MUSHA ARE DRAWN TO PEOPLE WITH BIG DREAMS.

By the way...

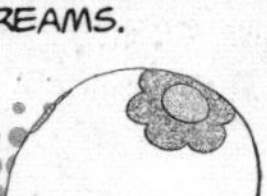

WHAT HAPPENS WHEN BLACK TRIES TO THINK HARD WITHOUT FIRST GETTING MUSHA TO EAT HIS DREAM...?

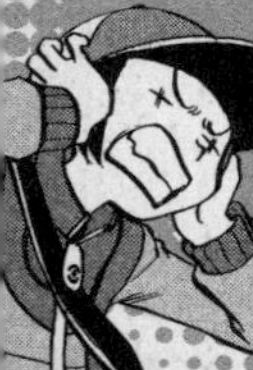

BLACK'S HEAD CAN'T HANDLE ALL THOSE THOUGHTS AND HIS BRAIN SHORT-CIRCUITS!

How awful!!

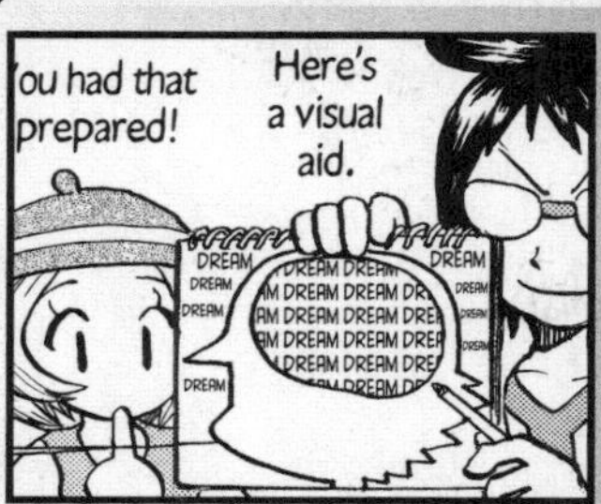
Here's a visual aid.
ou had that prepared!

BLACK'S HEAD IS FILLED WITH HIS DREAM OF WINNING THE POKÉMON LEAGUE. THAT'S ALL HE THINKS ABOUT, SO HE DOESN'T HAVE ANY ROOM LEFT OVER FOR OTHER THINGS...

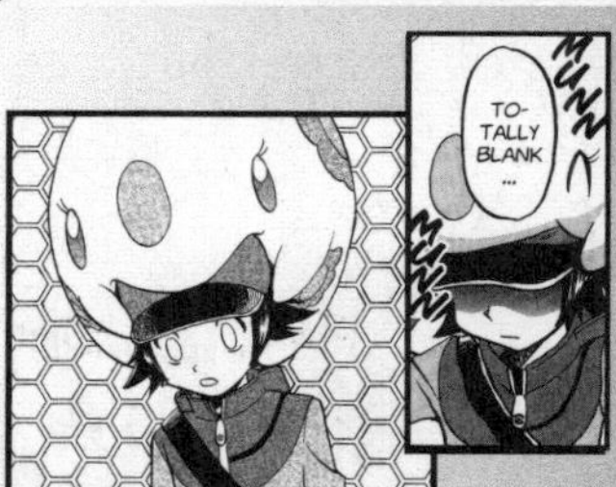
TO-TALLY BLANK ...

BLACK EMPTIES HIS MIND BY HAVING MUSHA EAT HIS DREAM. ONCE HIS MIND IS EMPTY AND WIPED CLEAN, HE CAN START TO THINK DEDUCTIVELY AND INDUCTIVELY.

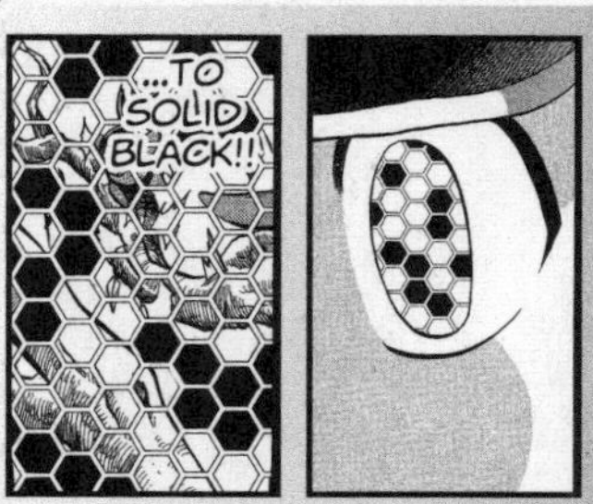
...TO SOLID BLACK!!

BLACK'S CLEARED MIND GRADUALLY REFILLS WITH THE DATA HE HAS GATHERED. THEN HE SHINES THE LIGHT OF REASON ON THESE FACTS... AND REVEALS HIDDEN TRUTHS!

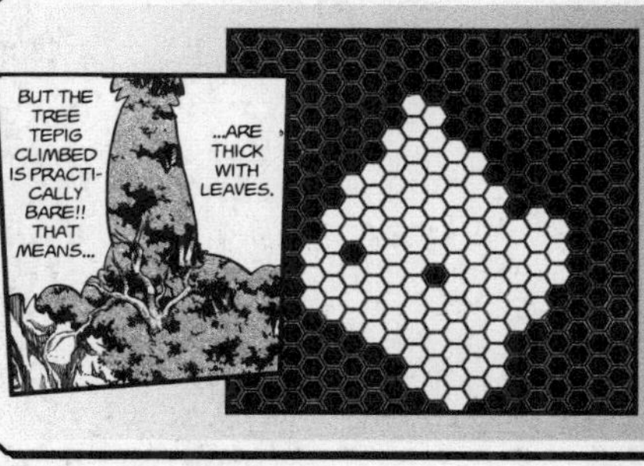
BUT THE TREE TEPIG CLIMBED IS PRACTI-CALLY BARE!! THAT MEANS...
...ARE THICK WITH LEAVES.

BLACK IS BOTH EMOTIONAL AND RATIONAL!

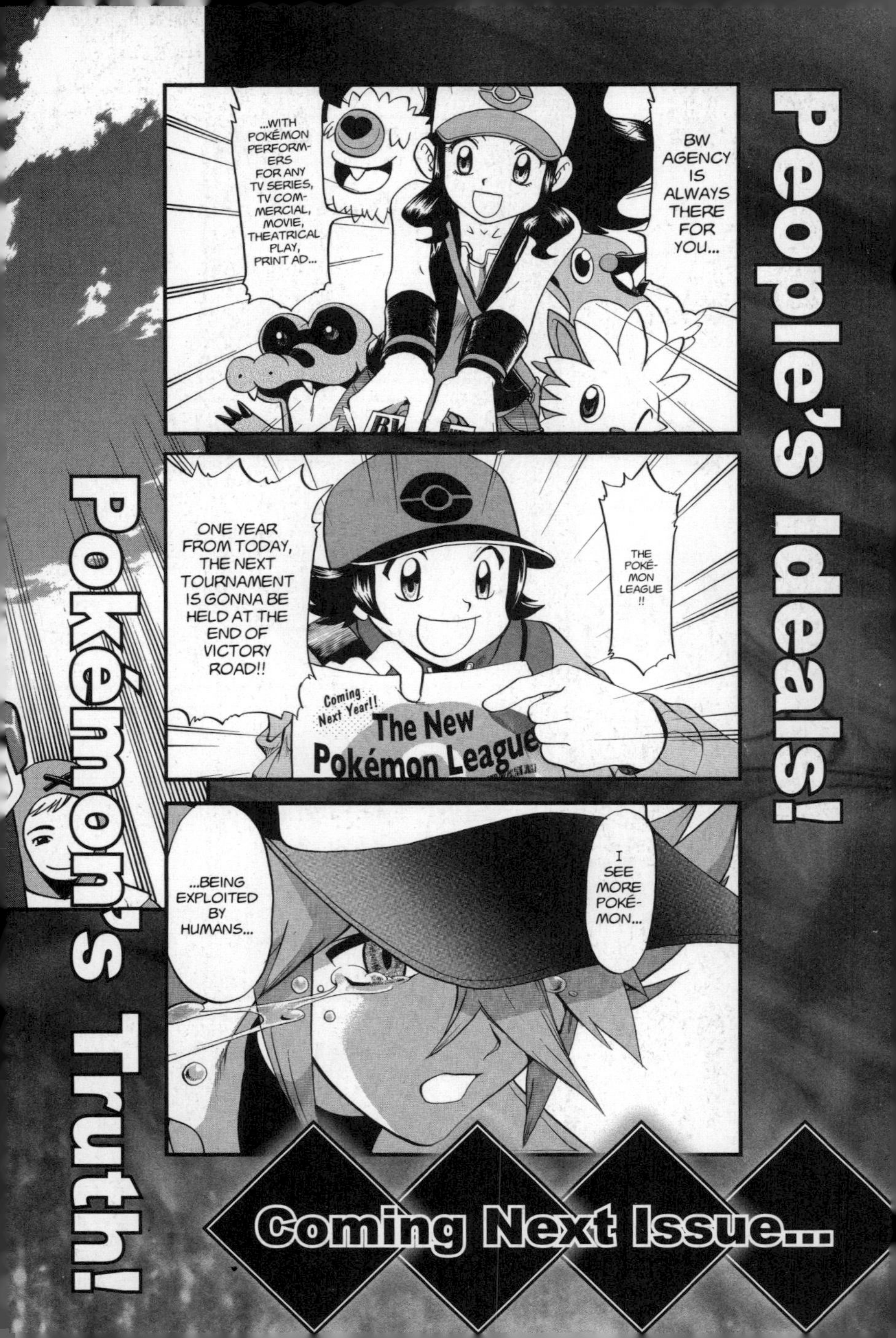
People's Ideals!
BW AGENCY IS ALWAYS THERE FOR YOU...
...WITH POKÉMON PERFORMERS FOR ANY TV SERIES, TV COMMERCIAL, MOVIE, THEATRICAL PLAY, PRINT AD...
THE POKÉMON LEAGUE!!
ONE YEAR FROM TODAY, THE NEXT TOURNAMENT IS GONNA BE HELD AT THE END OF VICTORY ROAD!!
Coming Next Year!!
The New Pokémon League
I SEE MORE POKÉMON...
...BEING EXPLOITED BY HUMANS...
Pokémon's Truth!
Coming Next Issue...

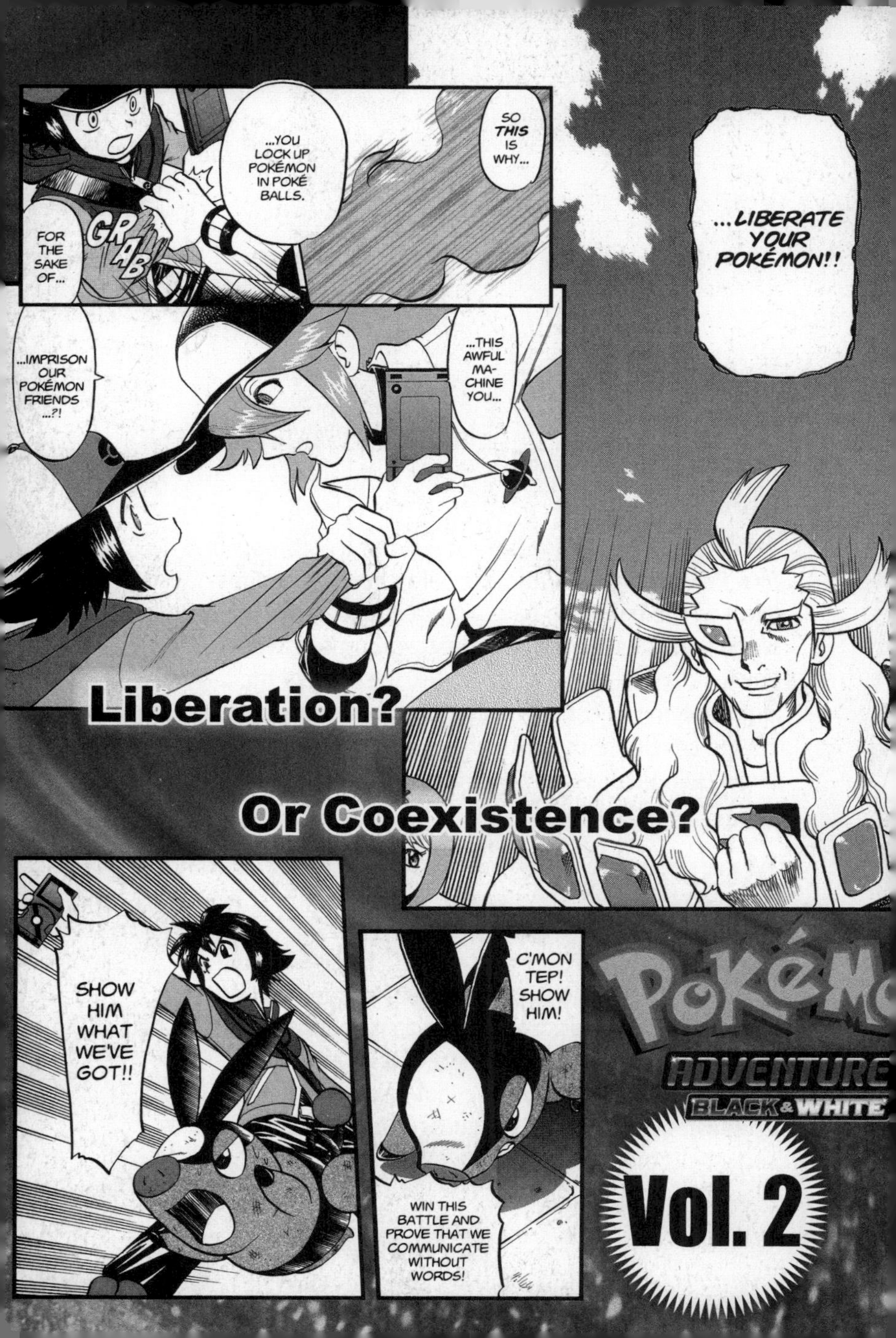
...LIBERATE YOUR POKÉMON!!
SO THIS IS WHY...
...YOU LOCK UP POKÉMON IN POKÉ BALLS.
FOR THE SAKE OF...
GRAB
...THIS AWFUL MA-CHINE YOU...
...IMPRISON OUR POKÉMON FRIENDS ...?!
Liberation?
Or Coexistence?
BLACK & WHITE
Vol. 2
C'MON TEP! SHOW HIM!
WIN THIS BATTLE AND PROVE THAT WE COMMUNICATE WITHOUT WORDS!
SHOW HIM WHAT WE'VE GOT!!

Message from
Hidenori Kusaka

Pokémon Black and White is one of the few completely new Pokémon games to come out in quite some time. Since all the Pokémon have acquired new attributes, working on this story is rejuvenating for me as well! I'm so happy that this new chapter, the story of the Unova region, is coming to English-speaking readers. Let the adventure of our new heroes, Black and White, begin! Join them as they take off on their journey...!

Message from
Satoshi Yamamoto

"I want to win the Pokémon League!" That's what one hero of this manga declares. I've only created quirky characters in the past, so drawing a straightforward one like Black is refreshing. Since this is *Pokémon Adventures*, it's not surprising that he's a real fireball, is it? And come to think of it, I guess he does throw a few curve balls too... (LOL)

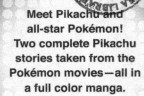

mameshiba On the LOOSE!

stories by **james turner**
art by **jorge monlongo**
"Mameshiba Shorts" by **gemma correll**

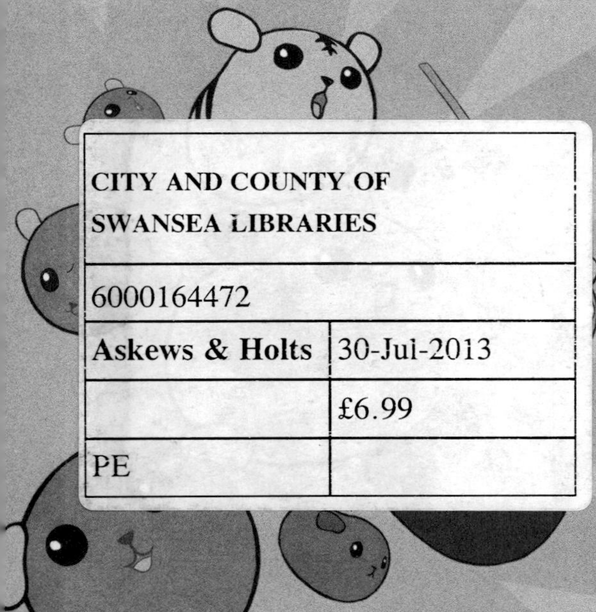

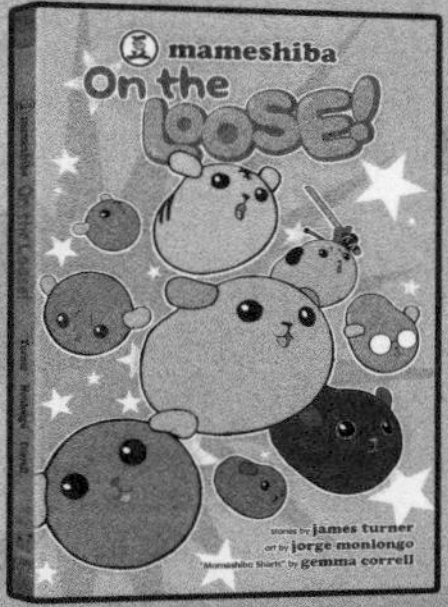

mameshiba
On the
LOOSE!
stories by james turner
art by jorge monlongo
"Mameshiba Shorts" by gemma correll

PRICE: $6.99 USA $7.99 CAN
ISBN: 9781421538808
Available NOW! in your local bookstore or comic shop

It's a BEAN! It's a DOG! It's...*BOTH*?!

Meet **Mameshiba**, the cute little bean dogs with bite! Starring in their first-ever adventures, they rescue friends, explore outer space and offer interesting bits of trivia when you least expect it! Hold on tight–Mameshiba are on the **LOOSE**!

RATED A FOR ALL AGES ratings.viz.com

www.viz.com **www.vizkids.com**

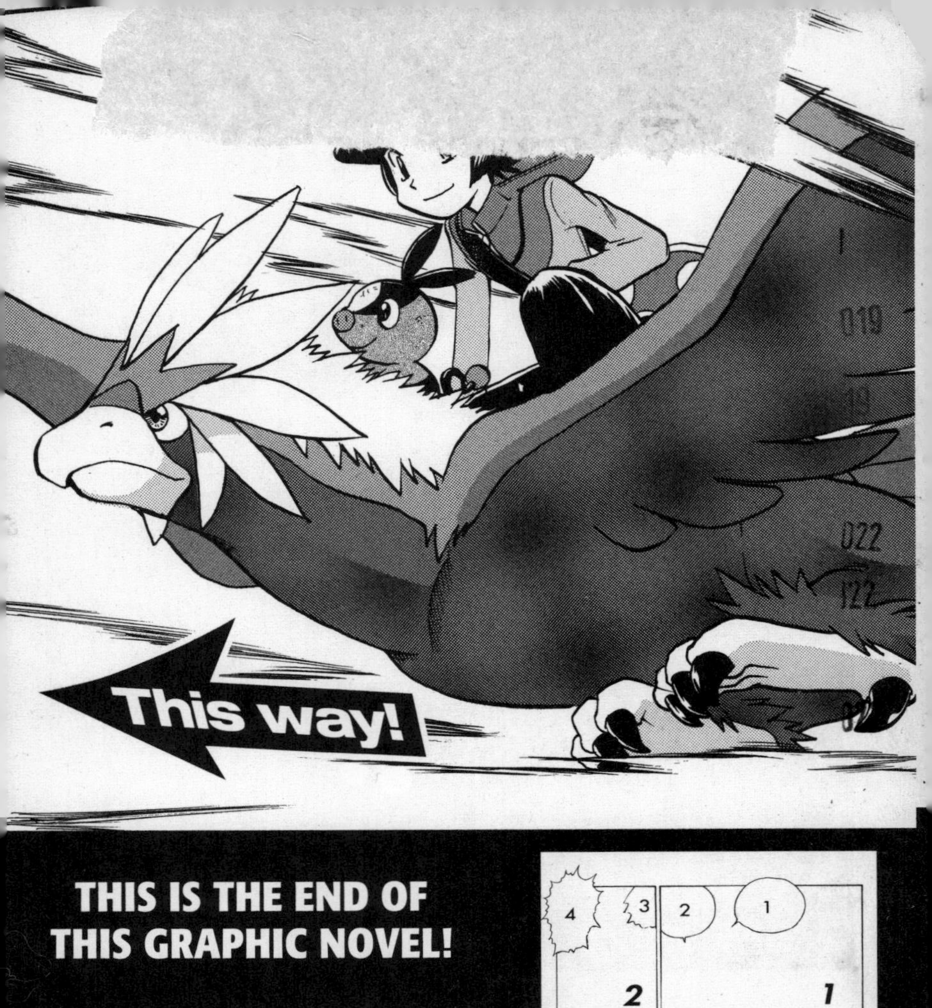
This way!

THIS IS THE END OF THIS GRAPHIC NOVEL!

To properly enjoy this VIZ Media graphic novel, please turn it around and begin reading from right to left.

This book has been printed in the original Japanese format in order to preserve

original art

Have fun w

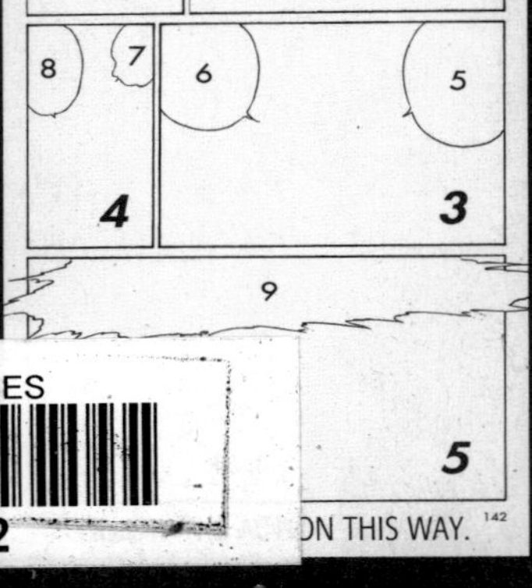
ON THIS WAY.